M000280142

FOUR
SQUARES

ALSO BY BOBBY FINGER

The Old Place

FOUR SQUARES

A Novel

BOBBY FINGER

G. P. Putnam's Sons • New York

PUTNAM
— EST. 1838 —
G. P. PUTNAM'S SONS
Publishers Since 1838
An imprint of Penguin Random House LLC
penguinrandomhouse.com

Copyright © 2024 by Robert Finger
Penguin Random House supports copyright. Copyright fuels creativity, encourages
diverse voices, promotes free speech, and creates a vibrant culture. Thank you
for buying an authorized edition of this book and for complying with copyright
laws by not reproducing, scanning, or distributing any part of it in any
form without permission. You are supporting writers and allowing
Penguin Random House to continue to publish books for every reader.

Library of Congress Cataloging-in-Publication Data

Names: Finger, Bobby, author.
Title: Four squares: a novel / Bobby Finger.
Identifiers: LCCN 2023059610 (print) | LCCN 2023059611 (ebook) |
ISBN 9780593713556 (hardcover) | ISBN 9780593713563 (epub)
Subjects: LCGFT: Gay fiction. | Novels.
Classification: LCC PS3606.I53378 F68 2024 (print) |
LCC PS3606.I53378 (ebook) |
DDC 813/.6—dc23/eng/20230109
LC record available at https://lccn.loc.gov/2023059610
LC ebook record available at https://lccn.loc.gov/2023059611

Printed in the United States of America
1st Printing

Title page art: Brownstone homes © Maaike Boot / Shutterstock
Book design by Alison Cnockaert

This is a work of fiction. Names, characters, places, and incidents either
are the product of the author's imagination or are used fictitiously, and any
resemblance to actual persons, living or dead, businesses, companies,
events, or locales is entirely coincidental.

For Tony

"It's a new generation," Troy said finally. "Our kind are old meat. They're not better or worse. Just new."

"They're freer," Killer said. "But not enough."

Sarah Schulman, Rat Bohemia

·‒·•◦●◦•·‒·

My nails are a mess
and I couldn't care less
I'm calling it love
'cause there's no other word
and it's all because of him

Jimmy Somerville, "Because of Him"

FOUR
SQUARES

1

1992

THE MAN AT the computer felt like he'd been writing different versions of the same sentence his whole life, but it had been only eight hours in the middle of his thirtieth birthday.

- Cookie Squares. They're anything but.
- These cookies aren't square. They're Squares.
- These Squares aren't square.
- Can you Square it?
- The shape of cookies to come.
- Cookie Squares.
- It's hip to eat Squares.
- The first Square meal of your day.
- Your first Square meal is anything but.
- Now you're square.
- Now it's square.

- Get square.
- Get Squares.
- Cookies: part of a square meal.
- Part of a square meal.

Artie Anderson turned away from his computer screen, squeezed the back of his aching neck, and looked at the clock above the corkboard to his left. It had just turned 4:58 p.m., according to a second hand that turned with an unnerving, stealthy smoothness. Artie believed a second hand ought to tick, that time should be delineated by an infinite parade of percussive seconds that could be drowned out but never entirely quieted, so that when you shut up, there it was, that mechanical ticking and tocking, reminding you of everything that could or couldn't be. He gave a quick massage to the muscles along his spine, the ones whose tightness seemed to radiate and made his head ache every weekday around this time, then went back to the word processor.

In the past eight hours he'd written 298 potential taglines for a new sugary breakfast cereal targeted at children precisely one-third his age. Though he didn't much enjoy the sample that Pearl Mills had FedExed to the office earlier in the month, he did feel like Cookie Squares deserved better than the nearly three hundred lines he'd written so far. "Quantity leads to quality," his boss told him his first week on the job, baring his mouthful of glistening, eerily perfect teeth. "The most reliable way to write one great tagline is to write a thousand bad ones first." Over the past two years, Artie had found the pithy advice to be more or less correct. Though a successful line could be written in mere seconds during a brainstorming session with coworkers—in fact, no fewer than ten creatives in his office still claimed credit for Video Gallery's beloved "Bring Hollywood Home Tonight" line—most of them were trees sprouted from the seeds of a dense, healthy forest. It was a forest whose perpetual creation brought him a sense of actual calm, since the more time he spent alone writing copy, filling page after page with every possible expression of a single idea, the less time he spent thinking about how profoundly uncomfortable he felt around his coworkers. Today there were no standouts on his list of four-to-ten-word phrases meant to convince petulant children to demand colorful boxes of die-cut sugar from their miserable parents, but there were enough of them that he felt as though work had been done. Artie sent the document to the printer, ripped off the perforated edges, and marched down the hall to Joe's office in the building's southeastern corner.

He knocked gently, then pushed the half-open door enough to see Joe squinting at a pile of paper on his desk and rubbing his scalp. Joe was in his mid-forties, dressed like he was in his mid-thirties, and played music as loudly as someone in their mid-twenties. He had a wife and three kids and a dream job but was proudest of his hair, which was long and thick and jet-black without the aid of Just For Men. When he noticed Artie in the doorway, dressed for the part of copywriter with his starched blue shirt tucked tightly into a pair of khaki pants, Joe lowered the volume on his stereo and waved him in with a gesture that, if performed by almost anyone else, would have been welcoming.

"Cookie Squares stuff," Artie said stiffly as he handed the

taglines to Joe, who just tossed them on the only bare spot on his desk. After a pause, Artie reminded Joe that today was his birthday, that he'd already worked with Annette on layouts, and that he'd more than made up for the hours he'd be gone today elsewhere in the week, since he had to go home right at five to bake his own birthday cake in time for a dinner. He was overflowing with unnecessary excuses and used a defensive tone for no reason, as usual, but Joe eventually shut him up with a flap of the hand.

"I remember," he said. "What the hell are you still doing here? Go home. Have a great birthday."

"Thanks, Joe."

"I pay you enough, right?" he asked, finally looking up from the pile of mock-ups with a hint of genuine concern in his eyes.

"What? Yeah. I mean, of course. I'm happy with my compensation. I told HR that at my review whenever that was . . . a few months ago, maybe? Is there a problem?"

"I'm just saying you can save time by throwing money at the problem. Can't remember the last time my wife baked a cake for our kids. The only food she puts in our oven comes straight from the freezer—it's like she's somehow got less time than I do. I'll never understand what she does all day. But what I'm saying is, just go to any bakery, and they'll make whatever the hell you ask for. Sharks or trucks or Ninja Turtles or— What is it you like?"

"How do you mean?"

Joe sucked in his lips and squinted. "Just go," he finally said with half a laugh. "Expense the cab home if you want."

"Subway's faster, but thanks. Maybe I'll buy my own cake next year."

"You won't regret it."

· · ● · ·

ARTIE'S FIRM, RKS, had been around for ten years, which was relatively young for the advertising business. It entered the landscape after David Ogilvy changed the game with his now ubiquitous marriage of sparse imagery and large blocks of text. RKS always strove to be off-kilter, more inclined to create trends than follow them. But like most enterprises with noble beginnings, it had already begun to fall into a stasis, albeit a successful one. They had their trophy clients, the ones that paid everyone's handsome salaries and kept the office more modern and comfortable than any other in the twenty-two-story building they occupied on Madison Avenue, but they hadn't created a truly noteworthy ad in five years, when Joe's overtly misogynistic campaign for a deodorant brand won so many awards he had to buy another shelf for his office.

Eventually Joe was promoted to chief creative officer, a job that was more about decision-making than creativity. With it came a light-filled corner office complete with ample space for even more trophies, a suburban living room's supply of seating, plenty of time away from the family he openly loathed being around, and a mini fridge filled with Diet Coke and Heineken. Unless, of course, clients were visiting, in which case it was emptied and restocked with Diet Pepsi and Bud Light.

Artie had never studied advertising—he was an English

major, to the horror of his parents—and applied for the job on a whim, after a man he made out with for six hours at an all-night dance party at the Holy Spirit told him that advertising was a much more reliable way to make money as a writer. Well, first he told him to work for a magazine, but when Artie said he preferred writing fiction, the man licked his lips and said, "Advertising is just lies, and isn't that a kind of fiction?" Artie found a sort of profundity within the man's gentle slurring, and thought a quick buck would be better than his miserable job in the human resources department for an insurance company. Joe was surprised by Artie's application, specifically its total lack of experience in the field, but impressed by his inclusion of short stories, some published and some not. Maybe Artie was the kind of writer the agency needed for a burst of creativity—someone who came from a different world, instead of the same cycle of colleges and programs from which everyone else in the department hailed. He was a white man who knew how to tie a tie, so at the very least he looked the part. The problem, though, was that he never quite felt it. And when Artie felt a needling of discomfort around his coworkers, he preferred to believe it was because of his lack of experience, not because of his lack of any overt sexual identity.

"Running home," he said to his office-mate and creative partner, Annette, almost out of breath from a jog past the framed advertisements lining the south hallway. "Just gave the lines to Joe, but he seemed swamped and pissed, so I doubt there will be any feedback until after the weekend. You gonna be OK with the layouts, or do you need me to stay?"

"All good," Annette said, still hunched over the drafting

table as usual. He sometimes wished he were an art director and not a copywriter—there was a more palpable drama to their creativity, whereas his own just looked like typing. When she finally looked up and locked eyes with Artie, her face particularly youthful and innocent, she laughed. "I mean it. Go home. Happy birthday."

He grinned and bolted toward the elevator with a quick slap on the doorframe. "You're the best. Thanks, Annette."

A few power-walked blocks south and Artie was on the D train heading toward the West Village. On the one hand, he loved his commute, four stops on a single train that didn't even have a bend in the tracks. On the other hand, he hated its efficiency, as it prevented him from doing much reading. So, for the better part of his time at RKS, he'd left for the office forty-five minutes earlier than necessary, providing him the time to take in a chapter or two on a Bryant Park bench every morning. Thanks to the comforting anonymity of a metropolitan crowd, it was private time that just happened to be in public, a daily ritual he treasured to the extent that he never told another friend or coworker about it, for fear that its peace would disappear once exposed to another living soul. How were any of his friends, none of whom had a clue about advertising, to know that it wasn't an industry of late nights and early mornings? The last thing anyone in his department wanted to do was catch a proverbial worm.

It wasn't until the doors were closing at the 14th Street station that he realized he should have gotten out there. On most days, Artie used the West 4th Street station in the morning and evening, despite it being farther from his apartment, as he enjoyed the walk up and down the West Village's mess of improbable lefts and rights. Emerging at 14th Street would have saved him a few precious minutes, the remainder of which he calculated in his head once aboveground and jogging to his place. His friends would be arriving by seven, which meant the cake had to be in the oven in twenty minutes if it were to be even remotely cool enough to frost by 6:50.

It was enough time, he thought, but cutting it close. Artie liked a buffer zone in most things, a kind of grace period to be certain everything would go as planned. It was the kind of character trait people didn't mind calling him out for to his face, an insult disguised as an intimate observation. The last time this happened, when he was the first to arrive at the Quad for a movie, Kimberly commented that it was classic Artie, early when he didn't need to be and also, somehow, anxious about being somewhere too early, probably because he was the kind of person who left places early, too. She hadn't said parties or bars specifically, but Artie knew that's what she'd meant. And so what if Artie preferred to arrive to places early and be in bed at a reasonable hour? Though there had been acid on Kimberly's lips as she'd joked about him in the otherwise empty theater, Adam laughed anyway at her comment and clapped Artie on the shoulder as they settled in their seats. "Classic Artie," Kim said. The words echoed inside of him, shaking loose intrusive thoughts as they rattled around.

Artie's apartment building was on the corner of Bank Street and Greenwich Avenue, in the northeastern corner of the neighborhood. He lived on the fourth floor, and his living room looked out onto Greenwich, not quite east, providing the perfect angle for a gentle morning sun. He'd moved the previous year, when the extra money from his advertising salary made him feel a little better about living on his own. It wasn't that he couldn't have afforded it before—plenty of people he knew lived in studios alone and paid rent on time without worry—but once again, the buffer. There was a larger one with RKS, so he finally moved a couple blocks away to an apartment with a real view and a real bedroom. He'd never been prouder of anything in his life than that view. It was the sort of thing people admired within seconds of crossing the threshold. He didn't have much stuff, but oh, did he ever have light. "Oh my god," they'd always say, followed by either "Your light!" "Your windows!" "Your view!" or "Your apartment!" He melted at their inevitable use of the possessive. To them, the light was his. The windows were his. The version of New York down in the street below, his. He wrapped himself up in their compliments every time, despite knowing they weren't really complimenting him but his city. No matter, it still made him feel like he'd made the right decision. He'd grown up in southern Ohio, surrounded by trees and brush, inside a tense and silent home where all the light was filtered through leaves whose fluttering made the air seem like it was simmering. Thanks to his parents, it often was.

Cake. He turned on the oven. He opened the box of Duncan Hines yellow cake mix he'd placed there before leaving in the morning and dumped its contents into the adjacent bowl. Eggs, oil, water. Stir, stir, stir. Spray both pans. Divide them as evenly as possible. Pop them into the oven, which wasn't quite pre-heated but close enough. He set an egg timer for forty minutes and ran into the bathroom to shower. Getting ready took longer than he'd anticipated, as he couldn't decide what to wear. This would have been easier if Kimberly were already here, he thought. Instead, he was just trying on outfit after outfit, staring at himself in the floor-length mirror nailed to his bedroom door as he contorted his body into all the awkward ways it managed to move, especially during a night out drinking, hoping it would look somewhat appealing in at least one of them. He was in black jeans and a white tank top when he took the first alarming sniff. There was no time to decide on a shirt; something was burning. Not just one thing, actually, but two.

He cracked the oven door just as the door to his apartment burst open.

Artie screamed *"FUCK"* as Kimberly screamed *"HAPPY BIRTHDAY,"* a shrieking harmony of thrill layered upon terror, fit for a thirtieth birthday.

"What's wrong?" Kimberly asked.

"I burned the fucking cake! The timer didn't go off! I set it! I remember setting it and literally saying aloud, 'I'm setting the timer,' so I wouldn't worry about not setting it! Why the fuck didn't it go off? Nothing ever fucking works."

"Maybe it's salvageable," Kimberly said as she walked into the cramped galley kitchen where Artie was still pacing in small circles, though a quick look at the charred, smoking round made her grimace. She was about Artie's height but broader, with powerful thighs, typically covered in short shorts, and a forceful chest, typically covered by a tucked-in button-down shirt containing a pack of cigarettes—the bulge of the pack adding a sort of finishing touch to her look. "OK, maybe not."

Artie tossed the second pan onto the stove, and Kimberly jumped at the clash of hot metal on hot metal.

"I fucking ruined them," he said, seeming to forget his friend's presence. "Of course I fucking ruined them. That's got to be a sign."

"A sign of what?"

"That this year is going to be cursed."

"Don't be stupid. We'll go out and buy you a cake. Or we can ask the waiter to pop a candle into a soup dumpling. The whole restaurant will sing!"

"I know it's fine and I know I'm being dramatic, but," Artie said, "you know."

"You had a plan and it went to shit, I know," Kimberly said.

"I didn't say it. You did."

"Of course I did." She extended her arms and turned her mouth into a big, theatrical frown. "Would a birthday hug make it all feel better?"

"I guess."

He hugged her, feeling the expected gentle press on her cigarettes, and it did.

"I hate it in here now. I don't even want to celebrate anymore. It smells like failure."

Kimberly turned her wrist and checked her watch with the theatricality of someone performing for the cheap seats. "Just so you know, you only get five more hours of this moping. Painfully depressive Artie needs to go back in hiding when the clock strikes midnight."

"At least give me until last call."

"Tonight is going to be fun," she said, rubbing his back. "I promise."

They'd just sat down in the living room with a pair of gentle sighs when a knock on the door startled them both, and they turned to watch Adam, in his leather bomber jacket and black jeans, looking like Tom of Finland visited an electrolysis center, step inside without waiting for an invitation. He was a boyish hunk, the friend who invited the most attention from strangers anytime they ventured out as a group, as well as the one who tended to disappear without saying goodbye. But Adam always put Kimberly and Artie first, even if plenty of others were in his social queue, and the three of them were mulling about in his apartment by 7:10, more or less on time. Artie appreciated their punctuality and recognized it as a kind of birthday gift. On any other Friday he could be waiting an hour or two for his friends to be where they said they'd be.

"Happy birthday, fag," Adam said, leaning in for a hug. "Did you burn something?"

"We're not talking about that," Kimberly said, bolting up from the couch as if the springs in the cushion suddenly decided they didn't want her there. "Shall we eat?"

"Yes," Artie said. "Where are we thinking?"

"It's your birthday," Adam said, already at the door, the burnt smell already a distant memory. "If you lead, we will follow."

They marched down the stairs and onto Bank Street. The air was ten degrees cooler than it had been when Artie got home, a welcome tease of brisk, newly autumnal air that wouldn't come in with full force for another month. Artie took a confident right toward 7th Avenue, as if he knew where they were going, and his friends followed without question.

Kimberly tapped him on the shoulder with a pack of Parliaments, and Artie took one with a wordless nod. He pulled a brown lighter out of his pants and lit the end, the hit of nicotine instantly dissolving his anxiety over the burnt cake. He looked south down the avenue at all the lights and signs and people, electrified by the very thought of being among such brightness and bustle. Inhale. Exhale.

He remembered the first time they'd all eaten dinner together, five years before, when he still shared an apartment with Waylon. Adam had arrived the previous night, after meeting Way at the bar where he worked, and though they never had sex again, Adam quite liked hanging around that peculiar man and his kind, interesting friends. When Kimberly came by to watch *Roseanne*, she didn't ask any questions about Adam's presence, only whether Chinese food would be OK with everyone. When they all took their seats around the coffee table, topped with several cartons of food, Artie saw the living room as complete. He and Way had lived in that apartment for over a year by that point, but it hadn't felt like home until that night.

After Artie's birthday dinner at Shanghai Lee, which was served fast and eaten even faster, Kimberly lit another cigarette on the sidewalk outside and said what all of them were thinking. "Julius'?"

"I thought you'd want to take us to the Cubby Hole."

"I wouldn't do that to you boys tonight."

"I could do Julius'. Maybe dancing after?"

"Maybe. One step at a time."

"Oh shit," Kim said, biting down on the tip of the Parliament and speaking through gritted teeth. "Since there's no unburnt cake at your apartment, where should we trek for dessert?"

"I'm over cake," Artie said. "Let's just go to the bar."

No gay bar was perfect, and all of them had their problems—racism, sexism, transphobia, and homophobia weren't absent just because a place was designated as queer—so when you found one where you felt comfortable, you nested. For them, that place was Julius'. They marched toward Christopher Street, and then turned on Waverly Place up to the corner door of their favorite bar in the neighborhood. There were queer spaces where you met people, queer spaces where you danced, and queer spaces where you fucked—all of them had their time and place—but Julius' was the kind of place where you talked. Not quite a dive and not quite a cocktail lounge, it was a relatively dark and quiet establishment best known for being the site of a "sip-in" in the '60s, when gay men refused to leave without being served in protest of the State Liquor Authority's anti-queer practices. Despite its long and storied history, the likes of which you could almost feel pouring out of every piece of wood, Julius' had a way of making patrons feel both younger and older than their years. It was a kind of agelessness that seemed to make the bar say, *I've been around long before you, and I'll still be here long after.*

Like most other nights, the regulars, Brian and Todd, sat at the short end of the bar, a perfect vantage point for keeping an eye on their turf, as well as the bartender's phenomenal ass.

They all nodded at the two men, who must have been about sixty-five, as they claimed the four-top by the door.

Adam gave his chest a declarative pat. "What does everyone want? First round's on me."

Kim scoffed. "Second, third, fourth, fifth, and everything after on everyone else, right?"

"It's mind-boggling that you color a gift as generous as alcohol with cynicism."

"I'm just saying I think it's very convenient and even a little sneaky that you always buy the first round. As if it's some grand gesture. As if it prevents you from ever having to buy another one."

"I don't get the first round because I plan on leeching from everyone later in the night, I always get the first round because it means I get to start drinking a few seconds before everyone else."

"Either way, it's selfish."

"Now, that I won't argue with."

As Adam flirted with the bartender and put in the order for all their drinks, it struck Artie that these nights where it was just the three of them, no significant others or flings or straight friends or coworkers, were becoming more and more infrequent. And that one day, probably sooner than he hoped, they might only get together on birthdays. He scanned the room with the intention of committing the moment to memory, taking in every detail: the song playing ("Erotica"); the temperature (a little chilly); the bartender (Orlando, his real name, somehow); the conversations being had beside him (Brian and Todd were expressing their hatred of Ed Koch, the city's closeted former mayor, rather loudly, even for them); his horniness (debilitating); the youngest people in the bar (a group of five young men who couldn't have been more than twenty-two); and, finally, the best-looking person inside. It was a solid night, with plenty of attractive people out and about, perhaps dressed better than normal because of the autumnal layering—all those sweaters being dragged out for the first time in half a year and itching for a place to be shown off. But there was only one person in the crowd who stopped Artie as he surveyed the room, someone whose beauty could control the tides.

Sitting alone at the bar, at the end of the long side, drinking something brown and reading something old, was a man—he was more of a gentleman, really, the more Artie stared. He looked tall, taller than Artie, and slender. Maybe fit. Probably fit, with dark stubble covering his tight neck and chin. His hair was sloppy but intentionally so, flopped over to one side in a kind of scholarly way. Though the hairstyle was that of someone who looked down on vanity, his clothes were the opposite. His loafers were shiny, his pants hemmed just above the ankle, and his shirt, Artie couldn't help but notice, fit him like it had been custom tailored, every stitch and fold accentuating the curves of his upper body in a kind of manner that mocked the observer. His clothes were immaculate, impossible not to envy, but they also dared you to imagine the body underneath. As Artie was busy imagining, the drink Adam placed in his hand slowly teetering down as his wrist lost its tension, Kimberly slapped the back of his head.

"Easy there, birthday boy," she said. "You're making the three of us look bad."

Artie stirred and turned back to his friends. "Sorry, I was just—"

"We know what you were doing. The whole bar does."

"What do you expect? What does he expect? You don't read at a bar during prime time. You read when it's light out. When you're one of the only ones here. If you read during peak hours, you're just asking to be stared at."

"So you're saying you did exactly what he wanted?"

"What I'm saying is he shouldn't have done it in the first place."

"Since when did you become the arbiter of bar decorum?"

"Since that guy broke my rules," Artie said, taking a punctuation gulp. "Flagrantly, I might add. Have either of you ever seen him before?"

"I haven't," said Kimberly.

When both their eyes turned to Adam, he just shrugged. "He fucked me once."

"When?"

"I don't know. A few months ago. Weird guy, but great apartment."

Artie collapsed into his chair, took a quick reminder of a glance at the best-looking man in the bar, then turned back to Adam. It should have been easier by now to be comfortable with a casual fuck here and there, but every encounter, even ones practically free from risk, required too much mental preparation. He wished Adam's rationality—that ability to put faith in himself and others—were contagious. Instead, Artie stuck with his own kind of affliction, worrying himself out of 90 percent of his desires and regretting it 100 percent of the time. "What's his name?"

"Abraham. Not Abe, *Abraham*. Seems like it's, I don't know, a point of pride. Him getting deeply annoyed by me calling him Abe was the most memorable part of the night, if you can believe it."

"And you never felt like calling him again?"

"I never called him *once*! I saw him here, and we went back to his place. Not one for the regret pile by any means, but, like I said, weird. Closet case, that's my guess."

"Huh," Artie said, deflating once more. Artie was never bothered by news of a shared sexual partner, and instead found it sort of lovely to live in a community where sex could be had as comfortably as it could be spoken about. But he always seemed to be the last to arrive. For once he'd like to have been the first to experience something. The first person in their group of friends to have met someone, felt something, experienced a thrilling moment. But it never seemed to happen that way. Even his last actual boyfriend, who could have also counted as his first, had dated Adam for a few months. What's worse, it ended in the same fit of ugliness. Both Adam and Artie ended things with Theo after a series of drunken phone calls and an eventual confrontation outside Theo's Chelsea apartment, because he wanted to save his neighbors the noise.

"I'm not going to say, 'I told you so,'" Adam said as they commiserated the next day. "I'm just going to say, 'I'm sorry it happened to you, too.'"

But Abraham already having a chapter in his and Adam's shared history didn't stop Artie from approaching him later that night, after Kimberly brought the second round to the table. "I'm going to sit down next to him," Artie said, as confidently as he could, "and ask what he's reading."

"That's the worst thing you can say to someone who's reading in a bar!"

"Exactly," Artie said, a shit-eating grin appearing on his face. "When he protests, I'll explain the rules."

"*Your* rules, you mean."

"Whatever."

He downed about a third of his martini and marched over to the end of the bar, where Julius' single open seat just happened to be to Abraham's right.

A deep breath. An unpleasant tightness in his back. A coy smile. And then, a terrible line: "So what're you reading?"

Abraham kept his eyes on the page. "*The Talented Mr. Ripley*," he said. "Patricia Highsmith."

"Incredible book."

Abraham nodded but didn't look up.

"I, uh, thought you'd be mad at me for interrupting you."

"Then why'd you do it?"

"To make a point."

"Which is?"

"That it's impolite to read in bars during peak hours, and in case you haven't been checking your watch, it's after nine. Bar reading is reserved for slower times of the day."

"I don't really have the time in my day to come here outside of what you call 'peak hours.' To me, they're just the hours I'm not at work."

"And what do you do for work?"

"Listen, I'm trying to read."

"I know, we established that."

Abraham placed a bookmark imprinted with the Strand's

logo deeply into the crevice of the pages and calmly shut the book. "I can see you're persistent," he said sternly, but Artie noticed the edges of his mouth soften as they locked eyes.

"Typically? No. After a martini? Yes."

"I'm a lawyer."

"That explains the lack of free time. What kind of law?"

"Family. Divorces and marriages and deaths. Prenups and estate planning, that kind of stuff."

"Sounds depressing."

"It can be," he said, finally taking a sip of what Artie now realized was a Manhattan. "What about you?"

"I'm a writer."

"What kind of writing?"

"I write copy for an advertising agency."

"So you're a *copy*writer," he said, lingering on "copy" so that the job would be split in two, violently halved by a guillotine's blade. As if "copy" were an embarrassing qualifier.

"No, I'm a writer."

"That makes it sound creative."

"I'm in the *creative* department."

"Don't be daft. You know what I mean."

"I'm not sure I do, but I know you're not British."

"Do you write books? Stories? Plays?"

"In my spare time, sure. I'm working on a novel, actually."

"How long have you been working on it?"

Artie shrugged. "It's been a few years."

"Do you have an agent?"

Artie held in a scoff. "No."

Abraham raised his hands in front of him, palms up in a

cruel act of dominance dripping in egotism. "Just say you're a copywriter next time. It's easier."

"But it's not the truth."

"I'm trying to be helpful."

"Well, it's coming across as condescending."

"I just think 'writer' is one of those jobs people tend to give themselves without actually putting in the work. When I say I'm a lawyer, no one questions what I do or how often I do it. I practice the law and I get paid for it. When someone says they're a writer, I don't know what the hell I'm getting myself into. I'm rarely convinced they're even literate."

"Well, maybe I ought to write a short story about this abysmal conversation we're having."

Abraham flashed him a smile. "You should! Submit it to *The New Yorker*, and if they publish it, you won't have to lie when someone asks you what you do. And if they reject you, I'd settle for a zine."

Artie gritted his teeth and looked deeply into Abraham's eyes. He hadn't felt this kind of attraction to someone in ages, maybe ever, especially to a man who was being so openly hostile. So he smiled, to test the waters, and when Abraham didn't smile in return, he scooted his stool back.

"I'm sorry I interrupted you. Artie Anderson, by the way. Not that you asked."

"Don't worry about it," Abraham said before cracking the Highsmith back open. "Abraham Ford. Not that you did, either."

Artie returned to a rapt audience around the little table. Kim's mouth hung open, her jaw dangling there in an awkward silence until bursting into a laugh. "What did you say to him?"

"To hell with what you said to him," Adam said. "What the hell did he say to you?"

Artie sat back down and squeezed every muscle, hoping to make his body as small as he could. "Neither of us said anything worth repeating."

"Let me guess," Adam finally said, adjusting himself in the chair. "He said something sort of dismissive of you, but with a slight wink, so you thought, *Oh, maybe we're flirting.* So you flirted back. Then he said something objectively condescending, and you lost your hard-on upon the realization that he never had one to begin with."

Artie placed the martini glass to his mouth and tilted it up nearly 180 degrees, straining his neck and affirmatively pointing at Adam as he gulped it down. Adam and Kim both laughed until noticing Artie wasn't joining in. He seemed to have gone elsewhere, repelling deep into the innermost recesses of himself, and Kim touched his shoulder to nudge him out of the pit before he fell too far. The night was still young, after all.

"Fuck him," she said in a tone she thought too kind, so she repeated it. Sternly. "Fuck him. I'm serious."

Artie shrugged. "It *was* rude of me, he was right about that. I interrupted him."

"What else did he say?" Adam asked, almost eagerly.

"It doesn't matter," Kim said. "What matters is that the birthday boy's drink is empty. And what matters more is that so is mine."

"I hear you loud and clear," Adam said, giving Artie a gentle rub on his back before heading to the bar. As he approached Orlando, Kim scooted a little closer to her friend.

"You don't have to tell me what he said," she whispered. "But if you want to, you can."

"He said I'm a liar," Artie said without thinking, as though he'd been waiting to let it out. As though it was the only thing on his mind.

"A liar? What'd you say that would make him think that?"

Artie explained the exchange as succinctly as he could, both to tell the story before Adam returned and to prevent himself from crying. He was often incapable of speaking about his feelings for more than a few sentences without letting them collapse around him.

When he stopped, Kim just shook her head. "Well, that's bullshit and you know it. No one who speaks to someone like that is worth any of your consideration. And they're especially unworthy of your tears."

"Thanks," Artie said. "But there's one problem."

"What?"

"He's right. Everything he said. He's right."

And there it was. The trickiest part of every friendly pep talk, when nothing the comforter could possibly say to the person needing comfort would be the correct thing. Kim knew this well, so she nodded and rubbed Artie's shoulder, a reminder that she was there, even if she was silent. He thanked her again, then shook away the coming tears when Adam appeared with another round.

"Orlando noticed your little run-in with Abe, so he threw in a round of shots on the house."

"That was nice of him," Artie said, forcing a smile as he snuck a glance in Abraham's direction over his left shoulder.

The stool was empty, but his drink was still on the bar, covered in a napkin beside the closed, curling book. His eyes narrowed, and he whipped his head to Kim. An unlit cigarette was in her mouth, and another between her fingers, filter toward her friend. He grabbed it, mouthed a *thank you*, and kissed her on the cheek.

After the first drag, he went verbal. "I'm such an idiot."

"No, you're not. You're just thirty."

Abraham left after finishing his drink—Artie couldn't help but notice his brisk departure—but his presence lingered at the table of friends for the remaining hours of their celebration. Kim and Adam knew better than to breathe his name again, and they discussed everything but romance and sex out of kindness to their friend. Kimberly complained about her job as a photographer for various music publications. Not the work itself, but the slow, though exorbitant, payment. Artie could never believe how much she was compensated for attending live shows and getting as close as possible to the artists, many of whom he loved and would have killed to see in concert, but let her vent about the process of being a successful freelancer. Adam and Artie lamented the impending closing of their favorite club, the Holy Spirit, where they would spend at least one long night a month dancing from one to eight a.m.

"I can't believe it's finally going away," Adam whined, the extent of his drunkenness made apparent by the raised volume of his voice. "Can you imagine? One day someone's going to be selling their paintings to Wall Street guys in the same spot where I used to stuff ethyl rags in my mouth." He sighed. "I can't believe we've all been here long enough to lament about how New York City is changing. Do you ever wonder what it'd been like if we'd moved here five years earlier?" he said, looking toward the bar but not at it; maybe he was trying to see behind it, or through it, at the bar it once was.

"Yeah, we'd be dead," Artie said grimly, with a smile that quickly faded. *But we're not*, he wanted to say. *We're here. And we have the audacity of being miserable about it.* Of course, he kept such saccharine platitudes to himself. "Well, maybe not Kimberly. Congrats to the immortal lesbians!"

And then the night took the turn it typically did around this time, after that many drinks and the inevitable comment. AIDS had killed so many of their friends since they'd arrived in the city, wide-eyed and deliriously horny. That it hadn't come for the three of them felt less like a blessing and more like dumb, soul-crushing luck. They'd spent the bulk of their twenties protesting against Koch, attending as many Monday night ACT UP meetings as they could, delivering free meals for the People With AIDS Coalition, calling their congressmen and senators, engaging in civil disobedience, getting arrested for civil disobedience, attending funerals of lost members of their community— even ones they'd never met. Most of it was selfless. Nearly all of it out of compassion and anger and empathy and desperation. But part of it was guilt. Guilt for being one of the few who remained. Guilt for spending even a moment celebrating, or even a moment wanting to. All of them felt it right then, and sat in silence as it passed, after which they'd try to make it through another day until it returned again, never changing course, orbiting them with the consistence and pull of a moon.

"I think I'm ready to go home," Artie finally said. Everyone stood without responding, thrilled that he had finally called it a night.

Outside Artie thought he saw Abe across the street from Julius', crouched on the curb, still reading, and pulled out a cigarette as they walked to prevent himself from calling attention to the mirage. *Just make it back to the square without further incident*, he thought, finishing a second one by the time they were all at his door. "Thanks for a great night," he said after hugging Kimberly and Adam, swaying a little from the booze and the nicotine. "And for making me forget about the cake for a few hours. Love you dearly."

Kimberly stumbled away first, waving back to them as she turned the corner toward home, but Adam stayed behind. "I know it's maybe not the time, and that we're both drunk," he said once Kimberly was out of sight. "But if you want to stay up a little longer, I've got a pack of cigarettes in my desk drawer."

"I think I should go to sleep," Artie said, his eyes welling up with tears. "But thanks."

"Hey. You all right?"

Artie nodded, then put his head down.

"You sure?"

"Do you think I'm a fraud?"

"A fraud?"

"You think I'm worthless? A liar?"

"You're asking a lot of questions, but I think the answer to all of them is no," Adam said before asking a question he already knew the answer to. "Is this about Abe?"

"Abraham," Artie said, elongating each syllable in a whiny voice. "Sorry, I'm actually going upstairs now before I fall asleep

26

on the sidewalk, and I swore I'd never do that again in, like, 1986."

Adam laughed and gave his friend a long, shoulder-crushing hug. "Happy birthday, you old fruit. And let me bake your cake next year. Ovens are not your friend."

Artie kissed him, a friendly peck on the lips. "I can't believe it only took a day and three hours of being in my thirties to cry in public," he said. "Night. Love you dearly."

"Love you dearly," Adam said before rounding the corner and walking the twenty or so steps it took to get to his own front door. Artie shoved his key into his front door and turned the handle. Once in the vestibule, he noticed the lack of the heavy slam behind him and turned to see Abraham with his hand holding the door open, his slender frame now more imposing than before.

"I thought I saw you out there. You followed me home?"

"Technically, yes."

"Should I be afraid, or did you just come to insult me again?"

"I wanted to apologize, actually."

"Really? You don't seem like the type."

"Well, maybe you should get to know me."

Artie nodded. "Come on up, then," he said. "Let me find out who you really are."

2

2022

ARTIE TAPPED ON the oven light to examine the progress of his birthday cake, a largely futile act considering the warm yellow glow made everything that needed to be baked until golden brown look perpetually golden brown. The pair of nine-inch pans were filled with identical amounts of batter, measured by weight, of course, and sat in the center rack of his oven, where hot air whirred over and under and all around them thanks to a noisy convection fan in the rear. Not long before purchasing one for himself, Artie read that convection ovens were better for baking than their traditional counterparts, and even watched a few videos of erratically gesticulating men who claimed to be engineers explaining the process in detail on the internet. Circulating the air inside an oven prevented hot spots, they said. The air in normal ovens is stagnant and lazy, but if you keep the air moving, your cakes and cookies and pies will bake evenly, uniformly, beautifully. If you keep the air moving, you'll have a better end result. If you keep the air moving, the birthday cake you bake yourself this year will be the best one you've ever baked before. Artie so wanted to crack open the door to get a clearer peek at the color but knew that no oven, not even one shipped from Italy, could break the laws of physics. Precious heat escapes with even the quickest of looks, so he squinted and waited for the timer to ding. *This will be the best birthday cake I ever make*, Artie thought. Which meant, he suddenly realized, no future cake would be any better.

He sipped from his tumbler of iced coffee and rested his body against the butcher-block counter across from the oven. Vanessa and Halle wouldn't arrive for eight hours, enough time for the yellow cake to cool completely, and for the chocolate frosting to be made and then scooped and smoothed onto each layer. He would wait until they were in his presence to add the candles, and they would smile politely as he pressed both numbers down into the mounds of creamed sugar and fat, fully aware that Artie had waited for them because this specific part was the saddest to do alone. And Vanessa and Halle would find all of it a little pathetic but also a little lovely, as they did every year, and he would find it all the same. Then they would agree that the three of them should get together more often, as they did when Halle was a girl, and then they would leave, setting a timer for another year.

Candles! Artie yanked open a drawer filled with pens and scissors and stamps and clasps and other household miscellanea and dug around for his bag of wax numbers. He'd thrown out the big blue 5 the year before—a grim, melted visualization of ten years come and gone—but plenty of others remained, warped by fire to varying degrees. Inside he found a green 6 and the white 0, both covered in dust and crumbs and scratches from all that time spent rustling inside of a drawer, and set them on the counter. The oven timer buzzed just as he decided to throw out the whole bag. It was time for a new set, or at the very least a sparkling pair for this year's particular celebration. The cake was still steaming on its cooling racks as he locked the front door behind him and stomped to the elevator.

"Arthur," a voice called from down the hall, as if it came from someone lying in wait. "You going down?"

Artie fought the urge to remind the woman in 16G that they lived on the top floor and that the elevator only went down from there, and instead walked in the direction of her wobbly voice. "Sure am, Gina," he said. "Can I get you something?"

"Would you mind using those big arms of yours to bring my cat food up from the basement? I keep calling UPS and telling them to bring my packages to my door, but they never listen. Don't know why I even bother. They just drop them off in a pile with everyone else's. If I break my back, I'm good as dead."

"You're not going to break your back, Gina," he said, giving her a close look and, somewhat reluctantly, realizing that his arms weren't that much bigger than her own. "You're very healthy."

"If I can come to terms with the fact that I'm going to die with a broken back on the floor of this apartment, then so can you," she said. "So can I at least depend on you to get my cat food?"

"You can always depend on me, Gina. Do you need it urgently?"

"Take your time. I'm sure you're busy scooting around the city doing whatever you do. I'll be here when you get back. Just make sure it's not after nine. After nine I'll be in bed. I won't be asleep until later, I barely sleep these days, but just come before nine."

"I'll be home shortly."

"Please do not rush because of me. A young man like you probably has plenty to do."

Artie winced at the descriptor and considered correcting her, but the conversation had already run its course. Outing himself as a newly-sixty-year-old would certainly leave him breathless. "Well, expect a knock in an hour or so. How's that?"

"Perfect," she said, flapping off a little wave before closing the door and twisting its two ancient locks, which echoed loudly across the concrete walls of the dimly lit hallway.

Artie rode the elevator down, greeted Dennis, the doorman, and stepped onto the sidewalk, where he inhaled two lungfuls of the West Village with closed eyes and a subtle smile. His apartment building was tall and broad, smack-dab in the center of Lower Manhattan's most discombobulating tectonic disaster, where boring right angles collided with degrees of character and intrigue, and order gave way to instinct. When he caught someone stopped in the middle of the sidewalk, looking down at their phone and rotating slowly from one direction to the other, he felt pride in the Village's atypical grid. This neighborhood had a learning curve, and it required a kind of metropolitan grit

of those who were forced to navigate it. *Best of luck*, he thought
as he saw the lost ones trying to find the bar or the apartment
or the corner where they were supposed to be meeting their
friends. *I'd help you out, but doing it yourself will help you commit the streets to memory. It may even build character.* It certainly had a hand in building his own.

When Artie first moved to the neighborhood, in 1986, the
store where he was headed had been a gay bar called the Rod.
He visited only twice: the first time, to see if it lived up to its
name, and the second, to revel in the fact that it did. Like most
businesses in the city, it eventually closed and reopened as yet
another version of something there already seemed to be enough
of, but the evolution the Village had gone through over the past
three decades cut deeper than an Italian restaurant he never
liked turning into a vape store or Chase bank. The neighborhood used to be humming with noisy queers and noisier artists,
and every turn of a corner represented a new potential thrill.
But now leather bars had been replaced by restaurants with
four-week waits. Queer bookstores were demolished to make
way for boutique hotels. Private jerk-off clubs had become real
estate offices occupied by people who'd bristle at the thought of
such a place. And the Rod, a bar for which Artie held only a
modicum of nostalgia, was now a place to buy overpriced
kitchen supplies called Offset. That it was generally staffed with
good-looking young men was a happy coincidence.

He took a right on 8th Avenue and walked southwest, then
jaywalked between a smattering of crosswalks until he was
walking due south—strange for streets in Manhattan—after
which he took a quick left on 12th Street, which wasn't one but

two blocks north of 11th Street. Offset was at the corner just before 12th started pointing in another direction, steps away from the border of a new neighborhood, with its own histories and inhabitants and traversal idiosyncrasies. He might as well have been at the edge of the earth.

"Hello," he said to the employee restocking wooden spoons by the front door.

"Morning," they replied without turning, too focused on fanning out the spoons just so. "Can I help you find anything?"

Struck by the care with which the young person was arranging the utensils, like they were delicate flowers and not hunks of teak, Artie feigned obliviousness and let the handsome young person direct him to the candles.

"Follow me," the employee said.

In the back of the store, beside baskets filled with the kinds of single-function kitchen supplies Artie found impractical and poorly made, was a baking-decor section overflowing with cookie cutters, cupcake liners, food colorings, edible toppings, stencils, airbrush kits, and, in a row to themselves, a robust selection of candles. The sign hanging high in the corner said, in a whimsical font, "Get Baked!" There were packs of sticks—white and black and red and green and pink and blue and rainbow (classic and pastel)—and then, to their right, a metal bucket of numbers, all loose in an enticing pile. They were all between one and three inches tall and came in varying colors and fonts. As he riffled through them, he was struck by the appealing tactility of the experience, and he wondered how many other people had dug through the same pool of ages, and if their combined purchases had accounted for every age ever reached.

33

Or, he thought, at least up to 100. People who lived to be 115 always seemed to live in a small town he'd never heard of on the other side of the world. Never in New York City. He fingered an 8 and wondered if he'd make it another twenty years. Without answering himself he found a 7 and thought it felt a little more achievable. Ten more good years, fifteen if he was lucky. He shook his head quickly to resist the urge to keep considering the future and grabbed two numbers that represented the absolute present. Since the candles, which were a galling, if predictable, twelve dollars apiece, wouldn't bring him to the fifty-dollar total he needed for another punch on his loyalty card, he grabbed a new set of tea towels and, why not, some new wooden spoons. And then, sure, a bottle of grenadine. Maybe two bottles of bitters, not that he needed them, but they didn't exactly go bad.

"$86.87," the cashier said, so Artie returned to the bucket of numbers and bought a 7 and, what the hell, he threw in an 8.

Artie could afford a couple overpriced candles. He had steady work as a ghostwriter, minimal expenses, and, most crucially, an apartment he owned outright. Sure, it had been given to him—he could never have afforded a place like that on his own—but it technically made him just another white gay property owner who lost his edge as his neighborhood lost its own. As others were displaced, he could afford to stay. And though his zip code contained its fair share of rich, influential queers, all it took was one afternoon stroll spent dodging Instagram influencers and straight couples draped in yards of linen to realize the neighborhood's queerness had been largely relegated to paperback-sized rainbow flags dangling in the windows of businesses that catered exclusively to people with money, not personalities. After handing over his credit card and smiling a little too brightly at the cashier, who had the face and arms of an actor and the hairline of one who had just started auditioning for father roles, he imagined what his younger self would think of him. What would Kim, Adam, and Way have said if they'd seen him now, transparently swooning over a young retail worker while spending one hundred American dollars on kitchen items he didn't actually need? Before imagining the particulars of their gentle ridicule, he pushed the thought out of his head and walked home.

In the elevator of his building, he cradled a box of cat food in his left arm and slowly lost feeling in his right fingers as the black nylon tote filled with Offset purchases pulled down on his palm.

When Gina opened the door and saw him holding both items so casually, confidently, she clasped her hands together and squealed. "You remembered! Would you mind bringing it in?"

He lied and told her he didn't. Once the box was perched atop a stack of so many others, half of which he'd brought in himself, she asked him to stay for a chat. Knowing she was incapable of brevity, he politely declined and said he was expecting company soon.

"It's good to have people over," she said with a knowing nod, her disappointment almost imperceptible.

"Until next time," Artie said.

He waited for Gina's locks to rattle his eardrums before pausing at the mirror in the building hallway, where he took in this slightly older version of himself. In the floor-length mirror in his bedroom, he looked confident and five years younger

35

than the age on his passport. In this one, with its speckled, foggy edges and the hallway's energy-efficient overhead lighting, he simply looked like his father, tall and long-limbed with a stony, stretched-out face containing small, sunken features. Enough of that. He stomped to his door, went inside, and unpacked all his new things.

It was golden hour when he sat down on the couch and sighed, ready at last for company to arrive. He opened one of his apps and scrolled through faces of people he would, if past was prologue, find it impossible to message. Though he was not technically celibate, sex for Artie happened about as frequently as a flu shot. He'd expected that his PrEP prescription would finally open his life to casual hookups—the ability to fuck without fear—but in five years he'd had sex only a handful of times, and when he came, he didn't feel relief, only regret over people he could have known and the pleasures he could have had when he was younger. But still, he liked to scroll and chat, because it temporarily convinced him that his queerness hadn't become entirely theoretical. He exchanged a few vaguely flirtatious messages with a forty-year-old tourist named Hugh until, poof, he went offline. Only slightly disappointed, Artie looked up from his phone and noticed a blue-orange glow now filled the room, giving the countless framed photos a short-lived third dimension: a whole wall of dead friends and family, brought to life by the setting sun. His parents kissing under ancient mistletoe. A shirtless man in repose. Old friends smiling. Older friends not. Friends who died before they'd become old of any kind looking off to one side, oblivious to Artie's lens. And then, in the center, Abe. He had taken more flattering photos of Abe in the dozen years that they knew each other, but few where he was smiling. And just one—this one—of him laughing. He'd been dead longer than Artie had known him, and just as long as he'd known Halle. Artie often wondered what Vanessa told Halle about her father, and made sure that she would get nothing but good stories under his own roof. Under Vanessa's, he imagined she'd only get pain, or at least discomfort. Under Artie's, well, she would only get laughter. It cut his selection of stories by more than half, but he felt those provided some kind of balance through an unofficial fairness doctrine. They weren't related by blood, marriage, or even state law; they were only bound by the very fact of Abe. Halle's father. Vanessa's husband. Artie's—

The doorbell buzzed before he could decide. It had been eighteen years since his death, and Artie still didn't have a name for what Abe was to him, but there was no time to figure that out tonight. He put the finishing touches on his smile and opened the door.

"Happy birthday," they both said as more statement than exclamation. Vanessa, stiff and draped in linen, still had her sunglasses on and, clutching an unwrapped gift box of champagne, hugged Artie limply with her free arm. Halle held a large box, clearly wrapped by a professional, and kissed him on the cheek.

"Right on time," Artie said. "Come on in."

It was the first day of fall, but the warmth of late summer still lingered, so there were no layers to shed or umbrellas to store. Once they removed their shoes, which they did without prompting, Artie led them into the kitchen, eager to turn the dessert on his breakfast table into a birthday cake.

"No color this year," Halle said. "I expected you to go crazy. Funfetti or something. A bunch of little sculptures out of fondant."

"Well, I got new candles and they're a little loud, so I thought I'd keep the rest a little simple. But I've been known to screw up even the easiest cakes." He held a hunk of wax in each hand and, pretending to be thrilled by the number they made when combined, hovered them over the cake in search of its center. When he was more or less confident in the placement, he pushed down. *Now it's official*, he thought.

Pleasantries. Compliments. Commentary. The same conversational beats as usual, but this time, what was hovering just above it all, uncertainty? Anxiety? Actual fear? Halle typically began their dinners with a rundown of her recent personal and professional grievances—her complaints were a kind of performance art—but tonight she avoided all personal anecdotes and kept the focus on Artie. What had he done all week? What was he working on? How was Gina down the hall? He answered every question she had, but being under the spotlight for so long was starting to make him sweat. When the tone of her voice lost all of its feigned brightness, he knew she was finally ready to discuss herself.

"We have some news," Vanessa said, delicately folding her arms. Artie lifted his fingers from the candles, not entirely happy with their position but too distracted by his sudden anxiety to get them precisely where he wanted. He noticed Halle shaking her head and read it as a plea for her mother to stop, but she didn't. "We were going to wait until sitting down at the restaurant, but I think it's best to bring it up now."

"Mother," Halle said in a guttural groan.

"What is it?" Artie asked. "Are you both OK?"

"We're fine, everything's fine," Vanessa said, reaching toward his hand. "Better than fine, actually. Halle?"

Halle buried her head in her hands. "You are," she said, her voice muffled, "completely impossible."

"Can one of you say the thing that needs to be said, please?"

Halle pulled her hands down and shook her head. "We're moving."

"Who's 'we'?"

"Me and Nolan, and Mom and Danny," Halle said. "To Washington."

Artie didn't move. "State or city?"

"State. Seattle."

"Why?"

"Artie, I didn't want to tell you like this, or right now," she said, shooting a glance at her mother. "But I'm pregnant. And Nolan wants to raise the baby near his parents."

"What do you want?"

"Well, I want to, too! But I feel bad . . ."

"But wait, oh my god," he said, trying desperately to shake the selfishness out of his head. "You're pregnant! I should be congratulating you." He grabbed her tight and took a pair of deep breaths to try to will the tears back from falling. When he pulled away, he was pleased to find he'd succeeded. "When are you due?"

"February twentieth."

"A Pisces! So this is, wow, you're pretty far along," he said, his eyes drooping slightly after doing the math.

"I'm about sixteen weeks in, yeah. I really haven't told many people, it's been so hard, combined with the move."

"And when do you and Nolan think you'll get out of Dodge?"

"Next week."

Artie exhaled loudly. "Next week?"

"Well, we already bought a place in Seattle. Sort of an impulsive thing. His parents looked at it, gave us the all-clear."

"You bought a house you haven't seen in person?"

"They know exactly what we were looking for. It's near them, just a ten-minute drive. We trust them."

"She likes his parents more than she likes her own mother," Vanessa said, forcing out a little laugh at the end.

"Mom," Halle said sternly, as if rehearsing her impending parenthood.

"When will you know the sex?" Artie asked, hoping to break the tension.

"We don't want to know."

"Any hopes? Any names?"

"Nolan really wants a son named Nolan. I am being completely serious when I say I couldn't care less about the sex, but that I love the name Teddy, whoever the baby ends up being. Theo. Thea. Ted. Or just Teddy! No edits! They'll have so many options."

The tears, sick of being held in by his breathing exercises, finally revolted and burst out of him. Artie laughed at his own embarrassment, and Halle rubbed his back, laughing along and telling him everything would be fine.

"I know it will be," Artie said. "And if it isn't, that'll be fine, too. It's going to be fine. I'm just, I just wish Abe were here. I wonder what he'd say."

"He'd say, 'You're only twenty-four. Don't even think about kids for ten years.'" Halle rolled her eyes and turned back to Artie.

"You're probably not wrong. He'd make a joke about Nolan's parents—call them 'ordinary' in a cutting tone or something like that. He'd pressure you into thinking about schools way too early. He'd *demand* that the baby get *your* last name. But then he'd give you a hug, he'd tell you how much he loves you, and all the rest of it would all just melt away. I hope you know that."

"Of course I know that."

They hugged again, longer this time. With his chin on Halle's shoulder, Artie caught a glimpse of the 6 atop his birthday cake, slowly tilting to one side as Halle expressed her surprise and excitement. Before they separated, he saw it fall with a silent plop, and all that was left was the 0.

·•◦●◦•·

THE CAKE LOST its sheen sitting out overnight, uncovered on his kitchen island. Dinner with Halle and Vanessa had been atypically uncomfortable and brief, an hour of superficial chatter about moving and children and the differences between the East and West Coasts. Halle and Artie were making too transparent of an effort to make the night feel normal, making their socializing feel more like group labor. Once Vanessa paid the bill, as she always did, they did not come back after dinner for a slice of the cake waiting in the kitchen—the birthday tradi-tion he'd had for most of his life—or even an espresso, and Artie couldn't bring himself to pierce such a beautiful object once he was alone with it, a little drunk, and getting a little drunker. He was surprised to see it glowing on the quartz when he woke, the morning sunlight reflecting off the walls and glass-front cabinets onto its edges. He was sober now, and hungry. Hungry and sad. Hungry and sad and hungover and uncaffein-ated. Hungry and sad and hungover and uncaffeinated, and when the phone rang, he covered his ears in agony.

The building's concierge was on the line. "Halle's here, Mr. Anderson," he said, a note of concern in his voice. "OK to send her up?"

"Uh," Artie said. "Sure. Yes. Of course."

He ran to the bathroom to wash his face and comb his hair just in time for Halle's knock to summon him to the front door. When he opened it, he stood still for a moment as he took in the sight of her, still in the mass of wrinkled clothes she wore to bed. Through tears and small gasps that made her seem ten years younger, she asked, "Can I come in?"

He walked her to the kitchen and gave her a hug. "Hal, is something wrong?"

She gasped once more when he let her go. "I was about to ask you the same question."

"I asked first," he said, smoothing out his hair and pulling two bar stools out for them both. "What's up? I haven't seen you this early in ages."

"I just, I just feel bad about last night," she said. "The way

Mom told you. The way we both just blindsided you. It wasn't fair, especially on such a big birthday, and I am so sorry."

"Oh, don't apologize for that. And, come on, sixty isn't *that* big of a number," he said, the lightness of his tone doing nothing to ease Halle's misery. Was she even listening to him?

"I wanted to tell you earlier, and I should have, but I just, fuck. I don't know why." Her head collapsed for a moment, and when she looked back up, she noticed the cake. "And you didn't even get to eat your birthday cake," she said, almost wailing.

Artie leaned over to hug her and started to laugh. "Oh please, don't worry about the cake. I'm proud of you for trying somewhere new. Maybe it'll be the best decision you ever made in your life! Think about that!"

"What if it's the worst one?"

"Then you make a new one. That's how life works. You just keep making choices until you're dead. Some of them are good, some of them aren't, but isn't it exciting that you get to make them at all?"

"You're so annoying," she said, finally smiling. "But really, I feel like shit, and I want to apologize again. Will you accept it?"

"I still don't think you need to, but if it makes you feel better, then yes. And for the record, I accept it *begrudgingly*."

Halle nodded. "Can we have some cake?"

"I was hoping you'd ask. Want a coffee? Or are you not allowed because of your *condition*," he said, approximating Gloria Swanson.

She laughed, to his delight. "Don't start with that. And yes, I'm allowed one a day."

Though hours spent uncovered had left the frosting more hardened than Artie would have liked, the cake itself was still perfectly moist. The two of them picked at their generous slices and sipped their Americanos slowly, as if knowing this would be the last meal they'd share for a long while. Artie veered and maintained the spotlight of the conversation on Halle and her big move. Where she and Nolan would be working. What color they'd paint the nursery. If she'd finally get the border terrier she'd always wanted but felt guilty about owning in the city. It wasn't until the two blue-rimmed plates were covered in nothing but a sprinkle of crumbs that Halle surprised Artie by commandeering the spotlight and directing it toward him.

"I don't want to be weird," she said, "but can you tell me a little about Abe?"

"You act like I haven't told you plenty over the years."

"You have." His silence forced her hand. "It's just, even now, I don't really know what he was *like*. With you, I mean. I know what my mom told me. But all you've ever said is that he was smart and handsome and severe. You always use that word. 'Severe.' That's as descriptive as it's ever gotten."

"I guess it's hard to describe a person to someone who's never really known them."

"Isn't that literally your job?"

He was taken aback by her wit and accuracy and scoffed with a kind of delight. "I guess you're right. What do you want to know?"

"What do you think I should?"

44

"You're acting like there's something that's off-limits."

"No, I only mean, when you remember him—outside of me, keep me out of it—what do you think of?"

Artie shut his eyes and called for Abe as he usually did, politely and as if he were interrupting his stay, wherever that might be. In no time, there he was. It was Artie's clearest memory of him: stoic in profile, eyes toward a book, then turning to the door with a smile, happy to see Artie in the frame.

"He had a beautiful smile," Artie said. "That's one thing."

"Perfect teeth?"

"Well, sure, but that wasn't what made it beautiful. He didn't smile often, so when one appeared on his face, it was cause for celebration. It was like he thought you did something right, even if that just meant being there."

"Why do you think that is?"

"Why do I think he didn't smile? I don't know."

Halle's eyes narrowed.

"Abe wasn't like me."

"He was butch, you mean."

Artie laughed. "That's one way of putting it. Sure. He didn't tend to show much emotion beyond, oh, I guess contentedness. He seemed so in control of his emotions. And as someone who never felt like I was, I found that very sexy. Sorry. I found it . . . attractive and aspirational."

"Do you still?"

"What do you mean?"

"Do you still find it attractive that he was cold?"

"I didn't say he was *cold*, I just said he was more restrained than I am. More restrained than you. And to answer your question, I don't know. I think a lot of it had to do with his parents, your grandparents, who were dour, deeply serious and unpleasant people who worshipped academia and feared hell. And that is, let me tell you, a bizarre and noxious mix. He grew up idolizing his father until coming to terms with his sexuality, and by that point it was too late."

"What was?"

"He'd become a person. Specifically, he became a version of his father."

"Don't we all become versions of our parents?"

"Sure, I guess. You're interrogating me a lot like your mother used to, now that you mention it."

Halle laughed. "I'm serious. Mom has never talked about them, Abe's parents. I had no idea they were so . . . dreary."

"A lot of people were at that time, especially where he grew up. Haven't you read Richard Yates?"

"No."

"Don't bother. What's with this sudden interest?"

"I don't know. I guess it's the baby. Finally leaving the city. "

Artie sighed. "I'm an idiot. Of course you feel some kind of pressure to learn more about him. But there's no rush. You don't need to soak it all in before you go. I'll be here, so will your mom, so will all the stories."

"Also, and maybe this is the real reason I came by, but I read *Four Squares* last night after we got home from dinner."

"So that makes about, hmm, let me think . . ." Artie said, counting invisible numbers between them with his fingers. "Thirty-four readers total. And you're probably only the third to read it twice!"

"The first time barely counts. I was in middle school. I thought it was so amazing that someone I knew wrote a book with their name on it, but I was definitely too young. I thought it was just a story about someone making friends. I don't know that I really *got* it."

"What did you think now?"

Halle took a moment to piece her comments together as respectfully as possible, and Artie was pleased to watch her think so carefully about something he wrote. Something he lived. "Well, I obviously understand the context now," she said with a slight shrug. "The undercurrent of death was lost on me then. The title also hit me harder, I'd definitely never read too much into it. And I thought more about my friends here, how I've never had to move somewhere far away from home and make friends as an adult like you did in the book."

"It's fiction, you know, there's no 'me.' The character's name is Peter, not Artie."

"Right," Halle said with a laugh. "But still, it made me think about how lucky you—I mean, how lucky Peter was to find them. And whether I'll be quite as lucky as he was."

"If I can do it, you can."

Halle smiled. "Peter too."

"Ha ha, you got me."

"Were they mad that you wrote it?"

"Who?"

"Your friends. Whoever the real Patricia, George, and David are."

"*Were*," Artie corrected her, hoping the tense alone would suffice. "And no. They weren't mad. They were happy for me, maybe a little confused by it all, the impulse to tell a story about myself, even a fictionalized one. The impulse to tell a story at all, really. But they all supported me throughout the whole endeavor. Not everyone in my life did."

"Why didn't you ever write another one?"

"I write books all the time."

"Another *novel*. You knew what I meant," she said with a pithy laugh.

Artie shook his head silently and found a simple, if incomplete, answer. "It's easier to tell stories when they're not your own. At least for me." He watched her nod and attempt to process his answer. "You OK?"

Halle slumped in her seat, as if a sleepless night had finally caught up with her. "I've just been thinking a lot about him lately. I feel like I never really knew much about him, I never asked questions before, and now I feel guilty for not caring more. For waiting too long."

Her confession was nearly enough to topple him off the stool and onto the marble floor below them. He was struck by how well he knew the feeling she described. That nebulous, all-encompassing guilt that makes you feel miserable despite your inability to figure out why. It's a guilt you're certain of, one you do not question, and you spend countless amounts of your mental energy unpacking and deciphering and dwelling over it. It's the guilt of someone with no confidence and many regrets. The guilt of someone who feels like every action they make is the wrong one, too selfish or too easy. But it wasn't just the feeling itself; it was the knowledge that he shared it with her. Not Abe and Vanessa—they were too self-assured and practical and, frankly, oblivious to succumb to that kind of guilt. She shared it with him. He and Halle finally had something fundamental in common, not an interest he deliberately imposed on her, like musical theater (it didn't take), or one learned from exposure, like baking (her cakes rivaled his at this point). This connection felt genetic, like something buried inside her DNA. He wondered if this was how it must feel to be the birth parent of a child, if you scrutinized their every action and character trait in order to figure out which ones they got from you or the other one.

He remembered seeing Halle for the first time, just after Abe died. He remembered the way she nervously clutched her mother's leg as Vanessa looked down at him with such pity. He'd felt just as much, if not more, for Vanessa, but tried to hide it in his face. If only she'd extended the same courtesy. There she was, a newly widowed single parent with a six-year-old, and she felt sorry for the fag who lost a boyfriend. But it was that same pity that made her so willing to let Halle be a part of Artie's life. She looked at him and saw a man who was completely alone. A gay man incapable of finding a husband, thanks to the law, and his own child, thanks to his fear of single parenthood. She had a child; he had nothing. That's the way she thought, and though he resented her for it, he let her think it in order to stay close to Halle. The one piece of Abe he had left. When Halle moved into her dorm room twelve years later, only a few stops north of Vanessa's apartment on the 1 train, Artie was the only one among them who cried. "You'd think that when they snipped the umbilical cord off of me, they just attached it right to you," she told him, perhaps much less viciously than he had interpreted it. He thought of that often. He was thinking about it now.

But now wasn't about him. It was about his niece, who wasn't even that. At Vanessa's request, one he quietly thought to be rather generous, he'd always referred to her as though they were family. But at this moment the whole facade seemed to crumble, if only for a moment. Right now, he was simply talking to his friend, which, he thought, must be enough.

"Do you think I'm being ridiculous?" she asked.

"No. Not at all. But don't feel guilty. I'm glad you're asking now. Anything you want to know. Anytime. But maybe not before noon next time."

She finished her coffee and placed the small mug on the counter without making a noise.

"Thanks for the chat."

"I'm glad you finally wanted to start it."

"And thanks for the coffee."

"I'm glad you finally acquired the taste for it. I was worried it wouldn't take, and I don't know that I would have been able to live with that."

Halle didn't laugh. She didn't even look up. "I just . . ." she said, before crying once more. This time it was more pronounced—her shoulders shook, and she kept her face to the floor, so the tears didn't even have cheeks to slide down gently. They just fell straight down, plopping on the floor as Artie rubbed her back.

"What it is, Hal?"

"I just wanted to tell you," she said.

"You wanted to tell me what?"

She looked at him and squinted, then rubbed her eyes. "That I'm going to miss you."

"I'm gonna miss you, too. But you'll visit! Right?"

She offered him an unconvincing nod.

"Well, there's always a room for you. And a hotel for your mother."

She laughed, a real one this time, and pulled her phone from her pants. "Oh shit, I have to go. I promised Nolan I would help with the packing."

He walked her to the door, and they shared one final hug. After a brief speech about how exciting this should all be for her, and a final urge to call whenever she'd like—for whatever reason, knowing she could always tell him things in confidence— she gave him a parting smile and took a deep breath. He expected something rough, but not as rough as what came out of her mouth.

"What're you going to do without us?"

"Don't worry about me," Artie said. And as she went down the hallway, then out of the building, and then, only a few days later, to the other side of the country, Artie began to wonder who would.

·· • • • ··

HALLE AND VANESSA'S announcement had blown through Artie's life like a hurricane, and the next month reminded him of those first weeks after Sandy. The morning after he believed that the city had missed the worst of it, only to discover in the coming days and months and years that the damage had indeed been substantial, only out of sight, wreaking havoc on the city's old and already crumbling infrastructure. Once the women were gone—both of their apartments emptied and sold, all property ties cut—Artie looked at what was left of his own life and saw its foundation for the first time in years: corroded and crumbling, not by force and salt water but simple lack of care. For years he'd put his trust in the persistence of a life he'd stopped maintaining long ago.

Without Halle and Vanessa, his life, he thought now, consisted of his apartment (where he worked), his work (which he did alone), the occasional errand he ran for Gina (who thought he was twenty-five and straight), and Nikki (his agent and only friend, though more prominently the former). They were drinking on Thursday night at Julius'. The bar was reliably relaxed and filled with an older, local crowd before six, around the time of their arrival, but had a tendency to flip into an overstuffed meat market later in the evening, especially on weekends. It was one of Artie's favorite places in the city; he felt, like countless others had for decades, that it was an extension of his home. He still came there to read, sometimes even work, at least three times a week. Some nights, like this one, he even invited Nikki.

"You need friends," Nikki told him, finishing the final sip of her martini with a dramatic swig such a small amount of liquid didn't deserve. A third-generation literary agent, she dressed like one from another time, in smart blazers and pleated pants, because her money and career came from one.

"I have friends," he said. "It's just that two of them don't live here anymore."

"Which leaves you with one."

"You're enough of a friend."

"You're sweet, Artie, but I'm not. Also, not to speak for gay people, especially in a gay bar, but you need gay friends. Or bi friends, or queer friends, or simply single friends. I haven't kissed a girl since college."

"And you *didn't* like it, I know. I also know I need more friends. I didn't need you to say it. I just wanted to complain?"

"You made that clear when you asked me to hang out, but isn't it my job as your friend to let you know when you need a little more than what you're asking for? And isn't it my job as your agent to do what I can to make you as productive as possible? So I'll say it again, not only because I think you *did* need me to say it, but because I think you wanted me to: You need gay friends. I can't believe I'm telling you this with Donna Summer literally playing in the background."

"Fine. But you know it's not as easy as just deciding to. I can't remember the last time I made a new friend. An actual cultivation, you know? An emotional investment in someone. Isn't that crazy?"

"You come here all the time, and you've never made one friend?"

"I come alone."

"When attractive, well-dressed people go to bars alone, people talk to them."

"Not when you bring a book."

"In my experience, *especially* when you bring a book."

"Maybe I'm putting the wrong energy out into the world," he said, turning his head to the wall of the bar, where he scanned the bottles as if the right energy might be trapped inside one of them. Maybe he could pour out a shot of it when he needed it.

"I think the problem is that you're not putting *any* energy out." Nikki regretted her comment immediately, so she kept talking. "I don't mean to cross a line, but is dating out of the question? I haven't heard you talk about a guy since—"

He interrupted her. "Dating is out of the question."

"Is questioning *why* out of the question?"

Artie nodded.

"Well, sometimes it feels like you're punishing yourself."

"Maybe I am."

"Have you tried a hobby?"

"I have hobbies."

"I don't mean reading or cooking meals for one. That's routine. I mean a hobby where you interact with other people in other places. Or at least on a screen. A regular vacation from your own mind."

"It would eat into my writing time, and I like my schedule. It's perfect."

"OK, what about that old gay place you're always donating money to. The one you told me and Nick to give to a few years ago. The senior citizen center."

"GALS? What about them."

"I don't know. It's something you care about. You could give them a little time in addition to a little money."

Artie shrugged. "I'm practically old enough to be a member. That would be weird."

"Would it?"

"Maybe not, I don't know."

"At the very least, you should take some time off. I know you can afford it."

"I'll think about it."

"Good," Nikki said. "Oh! I have to tell you what happened to that bitch I work with, Lena."

This was how it usually went when the two of them hung out socially, with Nikki making just enough of an effort to talk about Artie for him to feel like an attempt had been made, only for her to make a sharp turn into the subject she most preferred: herself. Up to date on Artie's silly little single-gay-man problems, Nikki talked about her issues at work, where a new hire in her thirties was trying to usurp power. Artie listened intently and nodded at all the right times. He smiled when he needed to and rarely lost eye contact. He laughed at a story in which the young nemesis shared her screen during a Zoom call and unknowingly revealed she had been scrolling through a good-looking new male coworker's Instagram photos. He didn't even check his phone. Tonight had swiftly become about his friend, and he was happy to be relieved of the spotlight, even if it meant ignoring the glances from a handsome stranger across the bar. That was his decades-long penance, he thought, pretending not to be seen.

When they hugged goodbye outside the bar, the bouncer politely asked them to step out of the way. Jolted out of a tender moment that almost made Artie tear up, he shook his face into seriousness.

"I have faith in you," she said before hugging him again. "Good night. I'll text you next week. Maybe you can come over for dinner, I'll make Nick cook."

"I'd love that. Night."

The walk home should have taken six or seven minutes, but

Artie zigzagged it out to a distance more reasonable for his state of mind. He needed to think, and there was no better place for it than on the sidewalk. As he looped around Abingdon Square, Jackson Square, and finally down the cobblestones of Gansevoort, he imagined someone building scaffolding around his life. He saw his silhouette, surrounded by metal pipes and wooden planks, and wondered where the workers ought to begin. By the time he approached the awning of his building, where he waved at Dennis, he'd given up. But at least he'd made some progress, he thought. Construction hadn't yet begun, but all he had to do was give the word.

Seconds after he stepped out of the elevator and onto his floor, locks started rattling at the end of the hall. "Arthur," Gina shouted once the door was open. "Come inside. I have to give you something."

Gina rarely invited Arthur in unless he was delivering one of her packages, and even then, he rarely walked beyond the cluttered foyer, but tonight, while he was totally empty-handed, she gestured for him to follow him into her living room.

"Sit down, sit down," she said, and when he did, her cat, a slender, long-haired silver thing that looked like it was all too familiar with its species' history of being worshipped, sat right down on Artie's lap. He reluctantly pet the cat and scanned his surroundings while Gina puttered around loudly in another room. The apartment didn't smell like cat, nor did it smell like a home filled with old, decaying things. On the contrary, it smelled like lemon. Whether lemon tea, lemon candles, lemon air freshener, lemon extract, or maybe lemon cleaner, Artie couldn't tell, but whatever the case, the smell was pleasant. He took deep breaths as he looked at the old family portraits on the wall, the doily under the forty-year-old television, the surprising lack of dust. When was the last time he'd been this far inside, he wondered, settling on a decade before, when Gina came rushing back to his side.

"Look at this," she said, handing him an unframed black-and-white photo. "From the day me and Luther moved in."

Artie took his hands off the cat and held the eight-by-ten image gently by the edges. It was his building. *Their* building. Its facade, a forty-five-degree turn from all the buildings surrounding it, as beautiful and dramatic as ever. The pair of cars parked in front suggested the photo was from the mid-'50s, but the back of the man in the foreground, draped in a giant wool coat, looked timeless.

"Did you take this?" Artie asked, his eyes still on the man.

"In 1958," Gina said. "I found it earlier today. Can't believe I never framed it."

Artie thumbed the man's coat, half expecting to feel wool against his skin. "Is that Luther?"

"That's him."

"Wow. It's a beautiful photograph."

"Take it!"

"What! Gina, I can't take this."

"That's why I called you in here! Take it. Frame it. Hang it up somewhere you can look at it. Or don't! I'm not telling you how to decorate your own house."

The cat jumped off his lap, sudden and graceful, and disappeared as Artie considered Gina's gift. "I appreciate that. Thank you so much. I'll absolutely frame it."

"Good. Now, go on, I'm sure you've got a date you're missing because of me. A girl you gotta take out dancing."

In all the years he'd listened to Gina's commentary about his dating life, he'd never corrected her, but the moment felt uniquely special, like a moment for him to show her the respect and kindness of being totally honest. "No dates with girls for me," he said, flashing a smile. "I just date men, though not too often, I must say."

Gina squinted for a few seconds, then shook away her tension with a shrug. Artie didn't know what to expect, but it certainly wasn't the words that came out of her mouth next. "Well, that makes sense," she said, patting him on the back.

"It does, doesn't it," he said, rising and shuffling to the door alongside her. When he turned to say goodbye, her arms were already open wide, inviting him to hunch over for a hug.

"You have a nice night," she said.

"Thanks again for the photo, you've got quite an eye."

She waved off the compliment and shut the door.

After a quick scan of his bank accounts with the photo of his apartment building propped against the wall behind his desk, Artie decided that he could take a break from more work for the next few months, if not a little longer. His last project, a self-help-cum-memoir for a famous tech CEO, had paid almost double his normal fee thanks to the credited writer's hefty advance, and had been much easier to write than Artie or his agent had expected. His process typically began with a long meeting with the author and their editor. Broad-strokes stuff during which the proposal was sifted through and discussed at length: *Here is the book we sold.* Next came interviews with the author, which, depending on the amount of time they had to spare, could be anywhere from two hours of audio for a more rushed vanity project to over a hundred for most memoirs. He then had between two and six months to deliver a finished manuscript to the author's editor, who then shared it with the author, mostly as a formality. Then he was paid a second check. After revisions, he was given his third, and final, lump of cash, and the author received everything else, if there happened to be anything else to give.

Artie had once been ashamed of his participation in this little sub-industry. He knew some people considered it a deceitful practice that corrupted the art of writing into something purely capitalistic, which was precisely what he thought he could escape when leaving advertising behind. But then, when he needed money most, the capitalism of it all stopped bothering him. This wasn't art, anyway, he thought, assuring himself that he would have plenty of time to make art on the side. But when he did have the time, he just used it to take on more work. He'd never worried about money before Abe died. Before they'd met, he'd made just enough to get by without too much complaining. When they were together, there had been plenty to spare. But after Abe, he saw himself alone forever, which he could live with, but what about dying? How would he afford to live when he could no longer work? How would he take care of himself without a family to lean on? That he never stopped asking himself those questions would account for the speed with which he became one of the most sought-after ghostwriters in the industry—reliable, talented, and arguably most important: fast. Artie wasn't just good at capturing someone's voice; he could do it on the first try and deliver weeks before his deadline. He thought of his own reputation now, drunk on two dirty vodka martinis and staring into the glowing, Tetris blocks of food inside his refrigerator. Maybe that was the problem with his energy. When your job is being anybody, doesn't that make you a bit of a nobody? He pulled a leftover chicken breast from the center rack, dumped it onto a plate, and sprinkled it with a few drops of hot sauce. He was sad and tipsy on a weeknight, and thought this dinner, which he ate standing at the kitchen island, was the most he deserved. That night, as he tossed and turned from the late-night meal and alcohol vigorously churning inside his stomach, he dreamed of the person he always dreamed about in times of stress and panic: He dreamed of Abe. In his dream Abe was moments before death, dangling off a bridge as Artie watched from the road, unable to pull him back up. If only the real story had been as interesting.

· · ◦ ◉ ◦ · ·

HIS SECOND ESPRESSO was brewing when Artie heard a commotion in the hallway the next morning. Banging, then a jingling of keys, and muffled voices on a radio. More confused by the noises than nervous about them, he stepped outside and looked toward Gina's door, cracked just enough for him to see movement inside. He crept toward the fluttering sunlight and pushed it open. "Hello?" He cleared his throat and repeated his greeting with more authority.

"Sir, please step back into the hall," a police office said after entering Gina's hallway from the living room.

"I live down the hall. Is Gina OK? Did she call you? Did she fall?"

"Sir, please step back into the hall," the officer repeated, startling Artie with his coldness.

Dennis, holding a large ring of keys, squeezed past the officer and escorted Artie into the hall. "I'll get him, Officer. Excuse me."

Dennis put his arm around Artie and walked his squirming body to the center of the hallway, in front of the mirror. "Artie, I'm sorry, but Gina passed."

"What do you mean? I saw her last night. We talked! She sounded normal. She gave me a photo."

"She had a delivery, didn't answer the phone or the door, so I called the police and they found her," Dennis said, giving Artie's shoulder a lovingly painful squeeze. "Just get back into your apartment. I don't want you to see them take her out."

"What about Walter? Her cat?"

"They haven't found him yet."

"Where could he be? He's gotta be in there."

Tears were finally falling down Dennis's cheeks, but he maintained a humble authority for the sake of his friend. "Come on, Artie, please, let me walk you back to your apartment."

They stood silently in the living room for a few minutes, neither of them certain how to react to the news, until one of the officers called for Dennis from the hallway. Before stepping out, he grabbed Artie's shoulder and gave it a friendly squeeze. "I'll keep you updated, OK?"

Artie could only nod. Another death on his floor of two

units. The second since he'd moved in. Unlike Gina, who Artie imagined was totally conscious and in control of her final moments, Abe had a heart attack in his sleep. Artie had gotten up, gone for a run on the treadmill in the building's gym, and bought a latte across the street before noticing his partner was unconscious in their king-sized bed. He'd had an entire pleasant morning to himself before thinking anything could be wrong, or even different. He'd always expected bad news around every corner, from every phone call, and could remember just four months—the most wonderful of his life—when he was totally free from worry. But there it was again, right down the hall.

3

1992

JOE KNOCKED ON Artie's office door, two quick taps, and opened it wide. Artie looked up from his computer, swiveled in his chair. "What's up?"

"Artie, my man, swing by my office when you have a sec?"

"Sure, sure," he said. "Everything OK?"

"Just come on over." Joe slapped the doorframe twice, a sort of inverse knock, and disappeared down the hall without closing the door. Artie couldn't decipher the move—was it hostile or thoughtless?—but he feared venturing to Joe's corner office to find out for certain. He collected a few printouts from earlier along with his notebook and shuffled past the other offices, stopping at his partner Annette's to offer a silent wide-eyed glance. An acknowledgment that Artie knew Annette had heard, and that he was nervous about the request. *Pray for me,* he seemed to be saying, suddenly convinced that prayer was something that could work. But Annette didn't meet his gaze.

"Hey, Joe," Artie said, clutching his notepad and pen tightly with his reddening right hand.

"Hey, hey," Joe said, his eyes fixed on the pile of renderings scattered all over his desk. "Shut the door behind you and have a seat."

Artie shut the door and made a quick scan of his options: A couch, a love seat, two armchairs, and a beanbag cascaded across the room like a seating accordion. He chose the end of the love seat and propped his elbow on the arm as if ready to take notes. "What's up?"

"How you doing?"

Artie's face twisted into something confused and uneasy. "How am I doing?"

"Yeah. You been doing OK?"

"I guess? I mean, I'm as OK as I normally am."

Joe looked up from his desk and began speaking as though he hadn't remembered asking Artie a question, let alone heard the answer. "I don't want to break your balls, you're my guy, but I think we're going to go with Rachel and Steve for the Cookie Squares campaign."

"Oh shit," Artie said quietly. "I thought we nailed it in the end, but I did like their work."

"Their stuff's great, it's going to be a killer launch," Joe said, the tone of his voice changing into something more soothing, almost parental. "But I'm just realizing, when's the last time one of your ideas was sold through?"

Artie's eyes widened, and his mouth fell open for a second or two before he closed it out of shame. "Well," he said, "I guess it was for the Frigidaire spot."

"So a year ago." He clearly already knew the answer, Artie thought. The prick. "And what'd you think of that spot?"

"Oh, uh, I was happy with it." Artie could see the dots Joe was aligning and quickly began connecting them. "But I guess the client wasn't." Artie's work for Frigidaire's newest side-by-side, a saccharine family spot where a kid is thrilled to be able to reach the ice cream because the freezer is no longer feet above him, was the agency's swan song for the client, which changed their agency of record after the contract ended a few months prior. The loss wasn't huge for RKS, but Artie had felt like his job had been on the line ever since. The problem, as Joe was now trying to explain, was that he wasn't working as if that were the case.

"You're coming in, I see you here normal hours, sometimes longer, but the work's just not the same as it used to be. Have you *felt* the same?"

Artie flipped his pen around his thumb and nodded.

"I took a big gamble with you, you were our first non-ad-school hire in a while, because I wanted to shake stuff up. Bring in a new perspective. I'm just not sure I'm seeing that perspective anymore. You know what I mean? I'm just seeing, hate to say it, the same old shit I could get from anyone."

"Oh, I'm, um, I'm sorry about that. I mean, I guess I just need to try to get back to that kind of thinking. I need to get back outside the box," Artie said, not quite certain what Joe meant and less certain that Joe knew, either. It had taken Artie months to feel comfortable at RKS, proving himself to not only his creative director but also peers, who'd gone into debt to get their graduate degrees at ad schools around the country. Now, three years later, he was starting to worry they'd all been right all along; he never really belonged.

"OK," Joe said, sounding slightly relieved. "I'm glad you think that. I wanna keep my team the way it is. Last thing I want is to make big changes in the fall, right before the holidays. That'd suck."

"Yeah, of course." Artie wanted to ask a question, anything to keep up the conversation's momentum so that awkward silences could be avoided, but that's all he had in him, an empty affirmative.

"So look, I'm going to put you on an RFP we just got for the New York Lottery. Would be good business, huge budget, reliable clients."

"Government contracts, government money."

"Exactly. I wanna get you and Bryan in to get briefed tomorrow a.m. Genevieve will let you know the details."

"Bryan? The new intern?"

"Yeah, and he's fucking brilliant. I think you two will kill this."

"I should probably let Annette know."

"Yeah, we already spoke about it. She'll be helping Stephen with the new Skittles campaign. They increased their buy, so there's a ton of new work in the scope."

Artie nodded. Candy was the dream account because it rarely followed the rules. Clients didn't merely accept experimentation when it came to candy; they demanded it. Every art director wanted to make commercials for candy. Every copywriter wanted to write copy for candy. It was weird. It was fun. It made being at work slightly less miserable. Candy was for creatives who were actually creative. Government work like the New York Lottery was for creatives who were merely competent.

"OK, well, that all sounds good. I'm excited to work with Bryan."

"You'll love him. OK, thanks for swinging by."

"Yeah, yeah," Artie said, standing up to leave. He turned to the window and wondered if the chain for Joe's vertical blinds would support his weight if he smashed through the glass and leapt down toward Madison Avenue. Dangling would be so much less traumatic for passersby than a full splat, he thought. Though a full splat *would* be nice.

"You all good?" Joe asked, stirring Artie from the details of his hypothetical public demise.

"Yep. And I'll get you the revised radio script for State Farm by end of day."

"Don't worry about it," Joe said. "I want you all in on the Lottery for the next few weeks. Laser-focused. Tunnel vision."

"Got it," he said, imagining himself split in two by a laser, his corpse then run over by a train in a tunnel.

When he walked back to his office, he noticed Annette's door was closed. "Fucking traitor," he whispered once seated at his own desk. "Fucking homophobes." His Cookie Squares ideas weren't going to win any awards, but they were certainly better than Steve's, which the client must have chosen because they were obvious rip-offs of a campaign for Fruity Flakes from two years ago. This had nothing to do with workload; of that he was sure. This was pure, unadulterated homo-fucking-phobia.

Nothing about his job had been the same since Genevieve spotted him leaving fucking Julius' on fucking July Fourth weekend months ago. "Oh!" she said upon seeing him walk out, drunk enough to lose the sheen of professionalism she wore so unconvincingly at the office. "I'm so surprised to see you . . . outside work!"

Artie blushed and introduced her to the person he had just successfully convinced to come home with him. "Genevieve! This is my friend Frank," he said. "Frank, this is my coworker Genevieve." When Frank extended a hand, Genevieve pretended not to see it. "What are you doing in the neighborhood?"

"I'm trying to find my friend at a jazz club, but I forgot how topsy-turvy I get down here."

"Maybe I can help. Where are you headed? The Blue Note?"

"No, no, it's fine, I'll find it. You just, uh, go on and do what you were doing."

Until then he'd kept his personal life off-limits at work. He didn't hide it, exactly; he just didn't show and tell. Easier to let coworkers think he was some kind of pathetic loser than what Frank described later as a ravenous bottom. Would they even know what a ravenous bottom was? And just because he was that night didn't mean he was all the time. Again, things they'd have no clue what to do with. But the problem after Genevieve was less about an inability to describe himself to his coworkers than it was Genevieve cutting him off at the pass before he felt comfortable enough to do it himself. He didn't want to imagine the things she said to the others at lunch, not to mention the way her story must have contorted and darkened and grown barbs by the time it made its way to Joe. Within days, Joe stopped dropping by Artie's office to chat. Even Annette, whom Artie assumed knew but didn't think would care, seemed to start caring anyway. She became more distant and less amused by his presence. For years Artie had been blaming every slight in his direction on homophobia, even when he knew it likely wasn't the case. But he was convinced he was correct about RKS. It was a straight boys' club. He always knew it, and he shouldn't have compromised even a single part of himself to be allowed to join it. Oh well, he thought. It looked like they'd be laying his gay ass off by Christmas. Ho ho ho.

When he looked down on 44th Street, he nodded at the heads of the pedestrians who didn't know he was there. Fuck them, he thought. Fuck himself for thinking he'd ever belong in this place. Fuck everyone. And fuck the idea of hanging off the edge, too. They all deserved the trauma of seeing him go splat.

· · • ● • · ·

HE DIDN'T PLAN on letting the bad news of his workday follow him into the weekend, but there's only so much you can hide from close friends with silence. By Saturday night, the anger and sadness he felt manifested through tiny, inadvertent changes of his face that only someone who could draw it from memory would notice—an extra fold on his forehead, his lower eyelids narrowed a millimeter more than usual, the edges of his mouth downturned just a hair.

As they sat at their favorite spot at Julius'—jammed into the front corner of the bar—Adam and Kim chose not to call attention to their friend's apparent misery. His pitiful attempts at engaging with them as if it were a typical Saturday night made it clear that his own feelings, obvious as they were, were not on the docket.

"I thought you said what's-her-name was going to join us tonight," Adam said as their second round of drinks was dropped off by the bartender, a short, muscular fifty-something named Cal whom no one liked as much as Orlando.

"Oh, yeah. Change of plans," Kimberly said. "I'm just going to meet up with her later."

They toasted, all of them making certain to clink their respective glasses with everyone else's before taking the first sips.

"It's starting to feel like you're ashamed of us," Artie said. "Are we that bad?"

"Oh please," Kimberly said, an atypical flush coming over her. "When's the last time I introduced you to someone I'm . . . whatever."

"You can say you're dating her," Adam said. "It's just a fact at this point."

"This is exactly my point. When's the last time I was legitimately dating anyone, let alone dating someone I wanted to introduce you to?"

Artie and Adam pretended to give her question an honest thought, despite the fact that the answer was obvious. "I guess Tiffany," Adam said. "Three years ago?"

"Yeah," said Kimberly. "And look how that ended up."

"Well, Tiffany was insane. Is this one?"

"Her name is Nancy, and no."

"Does she hate gay men? Will she hate us?"

"No. I don't think she even knows many gay men. Actually, she's . . . or I'm . . ."

"You're her first, aren't you."

Kimberly took a guilty sip from her vodka and tonic.

"So it's *serious* serious."

"This is why I didn't want to bring her tonight!"

"Didn't you two meet *at* the Cubby Hole? What's some new lesbian doing hanging out in a den of old dykes?"

Kimberly pushed her drink aside and dropped her head onto the bar with an exaggerated bang. "It was her first time there," she said, her mouth pointing at the floor. Adam and Artie howled, drawing the brief stares of people across the bar, who quickly turned back to their own conversations.

"Look at you, nabbing a virgin her first night away from home."

"She wasn't a virgin, Jesus."

"Biblically, sure."

"I don't want to talk about this."

"You always want to talk about your conquests, but not this one, let's unpack that."

"First of all, she isn't a conquest."

"And we're off to a *fascinating* start," Artie said, sinking deeper into his stool and holding his martini close to his mouth in a sort of conspiratorial pose. "So this one, this *Nancy*, is more important than your run-of-the-mill femme. Perhaps she's the one conquering you?"

"Stop!" Kimberly laughed, despite her own protestations. "I just want to make sure this is actually, you know, *real* before I introduce her. She could cut and run at any time. Go back to her ex, he's literally a corporate attorney. Loaded. I picture him looking like Michael Douglas, but meaner, if that's possible."

"So is that what tonight is about? Are you two having a *con-versation?*" Artie said, putting air quotes around the final word.

"Yes, at her place."

"Where does she live? The Upper East Side?"

"No, actually. The Lower East Side."

"Well, isn't that interesting!"

"God. Fuck. I don't want to fall for someone who just, I don't know, rode into town," she said, rising from the bar and losing the edge in her voice. "What if she realizes she wants to date other women and dumps me? What if she realizes she hitched her cart to a horse without checking out the whole stable?"

"First of all, I don't love farm metaphors and you're not a horse," Artie said, elbow now on the table, propping his head in his steady hand. "Second of all, sweetie, what if anything? What if you meet someone tomorrow who sweeps you off your feet? What if Nancy gets hit by a bus on her way home? What if you suddenly decide to try a dick that isn't made of rubber?"

"Well, that's never happening."

"You know what I mean. So you're taking a risk on some-one. She's taking a risk on you, too. That'll be true whether she's fucked all your friends or not."

"You're right, but don't make me cry in here. Humiliating."

"Everyone's cried in Julius'. It's one of my favorite places to cry, actually," Adam said. "I cried in the bathroom last week."

"Aw, baby, why?"

Adam had a way of teeing up a joke that was apparent to all of them by a certain ominous lilt in his voice, and neither Artie nor Kim expected his response.

"Inconclusive test."

"Shit," Artie said. "You didn't tell me about that."

Kimberly echoed his worry.

"It's fine, I got another one the next day. I'm negative. But *that's* when I cried." He took a sip from his drink without making eye contact with either of his friends. "When I thought I had it, I saw the end so clearly. More clearly than I've *ever* seen the rest of my life. I knew what I'd look like. I knew where I'd be. I knew who'd be there. It wasn't until I actually got my future back with that second test that I couldn't see it anymore. Isn't that crazy? I mean, isn't that so tremendously fucked up?"

His friends didn't try to mask their relief, but they did hold their tongues, knowing better than to ask why he didn't tell them sooner. This wasn't about their own feelings; it was about his. One of the toughest things about any friendship is remembering that the mere act of listening is often not only enough but also the totality of what the other person wants. Sometimes there is no follow-up question, no complementary personal anecdote, no soothing cliché that will do more than a silent nod or caress of the hand or pat on the knee.

"I didn't mean to drag down the mood," Adam finally said with a forced grin. "I'm really, totally fine. I promise. This isn't the first time, it won't be the last time."

"Well, I'm glad," Artie said. "But still, inconclusive. What a nightmare. I'm sorry."

Adam shrugged as the memory of Way fell upon all of them like an invisible dusting of snow. "Could have been worse. This is the world now."

They knew the world he meant. It was the world too many straight people had spent the first decade of the pandemic pretending didn't overlap with their own. Their world wasn't insular or even hidden; it was right there, within spitting distance of everyone else's. Worlds so close to each other that they shared an orbit, an atmosphere, an apartment building. The last time Artie emerged from a testing location on 19th Street, a passerby shouted, "Stay away from me, faggot." Since his childhood as the most effeminate boy in school, the word had struck him like the remnants of a broken glass: nonlethal but liable to scar, with emotional reverberations that linger long after cleanup. When a glass breaks in a room, you change the way you walk inside it; you keep your eyes peeled for pieces you missed, just in case one finally proves unavoidable and pierces your skin, drawing yet another stream of blood.

"Do we have time for another round," Kimberly finally said, "or should we head back?"

Artie fingered the rim of his empty glass and looked at his wristwatch. It was just after seven. "It's not too late. Let's do another here. We can make it back in time and order food once we're at Adam's."

He and Kim looked at Adam, whose opinion suddenly mattered most.

"Yeah, totally fine," he said.

"Abraham is coming, by the way."

"And that's how you change the subject. What the fuck, Artie? The guy who made you feel like shit?"

"He came over after both of you went home on my birthday," Artie said, watching Adam shake his head. "Oh please, don't act like you didn't enjoy sleeping with him just a little bit."

"I didn't say I didn't enjoy it, I said he was an asshole to you. Those two things are not mutually exclusive."

"You want me to disinvite him?"

Kim sighed. "Don't do that," she said. "I'm sure he'll be on his best behavior."

"He'd better be," Adam said.

Artie took a deep breath and held it, sucking his lips into his mouth and directing his gaze at the framed, fading photographs on the wall. "I'm not trying to replace him," he finally said, exhaling the rest of his breath with a sigh. "Abraham is not Waylon. He could never be Waylon."

Adam looked at Kimberly and shared with her a pained, loving smile, then offered Artie a generous nod. "We know," he said, reaching for his friend's trembling knee and rubbing it softly until it became still. "So what happened, apart from the obvious? Did he apologize before fucking you?"

"Abraham has a—how do I put this?—an uncomfortable relationship with the closet."

"Meaning he's not out of it?"

"He just doesn't know what he's doing. He doesn't know who he is. He's uncomfortable around queers. Gay men, especially. And that clearly manifests in aggressive and off-putting ways."

"So he apologized."

"In his way."

"OK, that's good," Adam said. "But don't let him break your heart. Please."

"I won't."

And with that, Kim felt Artie's knee begin to shake once more.

· · ● ● ● · ·

MOVIE NIGHT AT Waylon's started in the winter of '87, when a new neighbor, Lou, struck up a deal with a cable installer the week he moved in. The guy was going to charge Lou two hundred bucks for free cable. But if he could convince the guy across the hall as well, he'd do both for three hundred—a steal in every way. When Lou tapped on the door, Way cracked it with anxious hesitation until he saw his face and swung it open wide. Who was this handsome stranger who lived and slept and fucked just a few feet from him? Would he join their group of friends, or at the very least, would he want to go out for a drink? But Lou had the gruff, naive confidence of a straight white man, and Way's dreams were quickly shot. His offer, though, was instantly intriguing, and enough to make up for the lack of sex in their future—Way had always wanted cable.

"When would you need the one fifty?"

"He says he needs it now and that the offer's only good today. Ridiculous, I know, but I thought I'd at least try."

"I know Mr. Cable Guy is the one with all the power," Way said. "But I'd need to go to the bank to get cash. Think he'll wait fifteen minutes?"

"I'll spot you for now, but you're sure you're willing? You're not going to leave me with the bill like a fool?"

"I'm not dumb enough to make an enemy with a new neighbor the week he moves in," he said. "I'll wait at least a month."

His charms didn't seem to register on Lou, more proof of his paltry and steadfast Kinsey number. "Great," Lou said, reaching out his hand. "I think we've got a deal."

Way shook it, squeezing more tightly than he would have with a prospective hookup, and shut the door. Being attracted to someone who was more or less physiologically incapable of reciprocating was always depressing, but being the first of his friends with HBO? That lifted his spirits to the top of the Chrysler Building.

Their weekdays were filled with the work that made them money, the work that left them outraged, and friends who didn't go to Julius'. All of them had robust social lives outside of one another—groups of friends they danced with, protested with, saw plays with, ate dinner with, had sex with—but the four of them, Adam, Artie, Kim, and Way, were a team, and Waylon's apartment always felt like home base, the rare, treasured place where they could breathe a sigh of relief and simply *be* for a few hours. There was no better part of their weeks than sitting around his twenty-four-inch television, the most luxurious single item in his spartan apartment decorated with largely found and ingeniously fabricated furniture that always managed to look chic; eating Chinese food from Shanghai Lee or pizza from Not Ray's and whatever dessert Way had prepared alongside it, cookies or brownies or, his specialty, yellow cake; and going to Julius' afterward, where it was time to catch up on everything that had happened to them between that night's movie and the previous one. They were indiscriminate then, showing as much excitement for action movies starring Jean-Claude Van Damme as they did for rom-coms starring Julia Roberts. Watching illegal HBO felt risky but magical, like great sex with a stranger. For three years of Saturdays, not counting the weeks when boxing strong-armed its way into the nine p.m. slot, it was their unbroken routine, even after Way became sick. When Way's body seemed to become smaller with every passing minute and his skin became ravaged with KS, he still demanded that movie night go on. About these things he was equally adamant: He would not die in a hospital, he would not allow his parents to see him, he would not feel shame about having his friends clean up his soiled body, he would not miss *Gung Ho*. Or *The Naked Gun*. Or *Moonstruck*. Or *Cookie*. Or *Indiana Jones and the Last Crusade*. Or, finally, *Friday the 13th, Part VIII*.

Adam took over hosting duties the week after Waylon was gone, not allowing them to miss a single Saturday, even if it meant paying for HBO out of his own pocket. It was as if Waylon were playing a little joke on his friends in death. *If you want to honor my memory, you're gonna have to pay up.*

· · ● · ·

TONIGHT'S PREMIERE WAS an ensemble comedy that had made a good deal of money that spring but never interested any of them while it was at the multiplex. "I haven't cared about the sex lives of straight people onscreen since *When Harry Met Sally*," Kim said at the time.

But no one was in the mood to make better plans or to be alone that night, so there they now were, walking to Adam's apartment, smoking Marlboro Lights, and feeling as good as they'd felt about life and themselves since the previous Saturday. They turned the TV on with one minute to spare, knee-deep in a promo for HBO's upcoming slate of movie premieres, giving them a quick peek at their next few Saturday nights.

"Skip," Artie said upon seeing *Stop! Or My Mom Will Shoot.*

"Maybe," Adam said to *Sleeping with the Enemy.*

"Absolutely," Kim said to *The Hand That Rocks the Cradle.*

Adam pulled a stack of menus out of his junk drawer and splayed them on the coffee table, a stained and sanded piece of plywood resting gracefully on two piles of cinder blocks.

"We should order in the next fifteen minutes," he said. "Will Abe mind? Is he going to be eating?"

"I'm not sure why he's late. He said he'd be here," Artie said, rubbing his watch a little as he checked the time. "But yeah, no, let's just order without him."

Artie was the first to thumb through the pile, but he quickly threw the whole stack in Adam's direction. When it came to food, Adam was the one they trusted most, as he was the only one of them who could cook worth a damn. No one knew that better than Artie, who was often the receiver of Adam's abundance of leftovers.

"I don't think I have the brainpower to think about anything but Chinese food right now," Adam said. "So unless there are any objections, let's do Shanghai Lee."

Kim nodded and patted the air in front of her up and down as a way of shutting him up. "OK, it's starting." The sound of a buzzer interrupted the feature-presentation animation, and Adam bolted up to the panel beside the door in a panic.

"Hello?"

"Hi, Adam? This is Abraham, from Julius'."

"Come on up, movie's starting right now," he said, pressing the unlock button, unlatching the door, and returning to his spot on one of the two armchairs flanking a long, low sofa in three quick hops.

Artie met Abraham at the door, offering a gentle kiss on the cheek, and led him to his spot on the couch, where he and Kim soon sandwiched Artie. Abe's lateness, as they all quietly presumed, was intentional and clever, a way to ease into the night without instant interrogations.

The movie was a middling romantic comedy about two American women who travel to Italy together and fall in love with two Italian men whom they eventually discover are Americans impersonating Italians. The central question—are you really falling in love with someone if they're performing a character?—was an intriguing one, but the movie seemed to be unable to unpack why the answer is, in fact, yes. Is everyone performing, all of the time? Artie asked this question when the movie faded to black and Steve Winwood's "Higher Love" began playing over the credits.

"I think you're overanalyzing a movie starring Kirstie Alley and Teri Hatcher," Adam said.

"It was Andie MacDowell," Kim said with a scoff. "Her name was onscreen literally twenty seconds ago."

"I can't tell brunette women apart, sorry."

"But listen," Artie said, taking a final bite of his room temperature fried rice. "Those morons were pretending to be friendly Italian guys when in reality they were friendly American guys. But flip the movie around. What if you met someone and they were a hideous asshole to you. Like absolutely awful.

If you found out they were just doing some kind of unhinged gag and that they were actually nice guys, wouldn't you wonder, way in the back of your mind, if that introductory cruelty was somehow authentic? Would you ever really get over it?"

"Artie, listen to the song that's playing now," Kim said, grabbing the remote control and cranking the volume up a dozen notches. "This is not a thought experiment worth having."

"Are you referring to someone in the room?" Adam said, simultaneously picking at the remaining rice on the coffee table and stoking a fire that had been slowly warming them all up since the movie began.

"I mean, maybe I am," Artie said, turning to his right and facing Abe directly, their closeness electrifying both of them.

"I apologized to you within hours. In more ways than one, actually," Abe said with a smirk. "The guys in the movie took days to reveal themselves. And I don't think I heard an actual apology from either of them."

"And he wasn't playing a character, either. He really is an asshole," Adam added, softening the blow with the laugh.

"Let's not pile on the guy right away," Kim said, unable to hide her smile.

"I mean, I deserve it," Abe said. "I was an asshole, but only because I'm a terrible flirt. And I may be a lot of things, but I'm not a liar."

"You told me you weren't seeing anyone when we hooked up forever ago," Adam said. "And then I found out you had a girlfriend."

"I told you I wasn't seeing any other guys."

Adam rolled his eyes. "Oh, come on, you knew what I meant."

"I didn't lie to you, I answered your question. Go ahead. Ask me another one. I'll tell you the truth."

"Are you going to break my friend's heart?"

The room fell silent enough to hear the quiet cracking of Artie's nervous breath.

"No," Abe said, unfazed by the awkwardness Kim and Artie clearly felt. "I'm not."

"And are you seeing anyone else right now? Of any gender?"

"No."

"When was your last HIV test?"

"A few weeks ago."

"Do you go regularly?"

"Yes."

"Do you go to meetings?"

"What kinds?"

"ACT UP? GMHC? Anything?"

"No."

"Have you ever been to a march?"

"No."

"Why not?"

"That stuff isn't for me."

"Well, you're a man who fucks men, so I'd argue you're exactly who all that *stuff* is for. So why haven't you been in all these years?"

Artie waved his hands at Adam. "I think he gets your point, Adam. You're in Larry Kramer mode."

Abe touched Artie's knee. "Don't worry about me, this is healthy conversation," he said before returning his gaze, even more intense than before, back to Adam. "It's hard to risk arrest in my line of work."

"Maybe your legal prowess could be utilized elsewhere, ever considered that?"

"I'm sure it could. And maybe in another stage of my career it will be."

"So?"

"So isn't a question. So what?"

"I'm sorry, I just have a hard time understanding gay people who want no part in helping the cause. In helping their fucking community."

"I make donations to plenty of gay organizations."

"Great, you write checks."

"Yes. Plenty of them. I have for years. Why is that a problem, exactly?"

Adam abandoned the argument with a scoff and shook his head.

"I answered all your questions and you won't answer mine? Doesn't seem fair."

"Fine, you're not a liar, you're just exhausting, which must be why you're apparently so good at your job."

"And I'm pretty sure my being exhausting was worth it in the end," Abe said a notch more quietly, as if he were addressing just Artie.

"What's that supposed to mean?" Kim asked. Artie and Abe exchanged silent glances until, with a sigh, Artie finally explained, just as an episode of *Tales from the Crypt* began.

"I started making actual progress on my book," Artie said. "Thanks to Abraham's encouragement."

Kim and Adam raised their eyebrows in tandem, as if both pairs were being controlled by the same puppeteer's string.

"Oh, wow," Adam said. "What's it about?"

Artie shrugged and gestured around the room. "They say write what you know."

"You're saying it's about us?"

"It's about four friends in New York City, and none of them are breeders. Beyond that, it's fiction. Different names. Different apartments. It's all in the Village, but everyone lives on a different square. Abingdon, McCarthy, Father Demo, Washington."

"So you're saying it's *basically* about us."

"It's not about me," Abe said, asserting himself as the one who knew more than either of Artie's two best friends.

"Way's number four," Kim said, nodding without the need for confirmation.

"The great work begins," Adam said, breaking the somber silence in the most theatrical cadence he could muster while tipsy and full.

"Oh, shut the fuck up," Artie said, rolling his eyes.

"How far along are you?" Kim asked.

"Don't ask me that, please," Artie said. "All that matters is that I've started it. I'll finish it when I finish it. I'll finish it when it's finished."

"Can we at least have a title?"

"*Four Squares*," Artie said.

Kim and Adam shared a proud, if surprised, glance that seemed to say *Well, well, well* as Abe stroked Artie's thigh.

"Now that we're finished prying, I'm gonna have a cigarette," Kim said, breaking the tension. She stood up and walked to the window, which she pulled open with a squeak before awkwardly stepping through the opening and taking a seat on the fire escape.

When he heard the sound of her lighter, Artie joined her and shut the window behind them, knowing that by this point Abe and Adam would be able to get by on their own. He took a cigarette from the pack on the windowsill, lit the end, and inhaled. Staring down at the people below while blowing smoke in their direction, he said, "Do you think I'm making a mistake? Tell me the truth."

"I don't think you're making a mistake. I just want you to be careful."

"What do you mean? I've literally never had sex without a condom."

"Don't joke around. I just . . . Look, I know you're not a boyfriend guy, and I know dating is tough for you—"

"I can't wait to hear where this is going."

"Artie, I'm serious, I just don't know what you see in this guy. Sure, he's handsome, and Adam's already told me more about his dick than I care to know, but come on."

"Oh please, Adam is only combative because of his own weird rich-kid guilt. Abraham was argumentative, but he didn't start it!"

"Fair, but I'll say it again: I want you to be careful."

"I don't know what you mean! He makes me happy! I'm *happy*! I could actually finish this book! I never thought I would do that! I never thought I *could*!"

Kim took a deep breath and exhaled slowly, as if trying to bring down her heart rate. "I just want you to do things because *you* want to do them, not because the guy you're fucking will respect you for it."

Artie took a drag and nodded. "He may be a little prickly, but he makes me confident. I can't remember the last time I felt that."

"You're not bullshitting me?"

"I'm not bullshitting you."

"Good," Kim said before giving them a few luxurious drags of silence.

"Thank you for looking out for me," Artie finally said.

"Remember the first time we met?"

"The party in your old place on Third Ave, yeah."

"You complimented a photo I had taped to the kitchen wall. Over the oven. Remember that?"

"Yeah, it was of that woman in Tompkins Square Park with her dog. The beagle?"

"Close, border terrier. I loved that photo, and when you asked who took it, I was so excited to tell you it was me. *I took the photo you love.* Then you said, 'Oh, so you're a photographer.' Do you remember that?"

"I guess."

"Well, trust me, it happened. You just said it. You called me a photographer. You didn't ask if I *was* one. I never told you how much that meant to me, but it meant everything. It meant I was good enough. That I was the thing that I wanted to be, despite how little confidence I had in myself."

"I never knew that," Artie said, a wave of guilt hitting him like a warm blast of air from a subway grate.

"Why would you? I applied for the photo editor job like five days later."

Artie scoffed. "Holy shit."

"Yeah. Holy shit. Look at all those people down there. Do you think they're in this city because they want to be alone with their thoughts all the time? Because they want to dream in private? They're here because they want this," she said, gesturing back and forth between the two of them. "They want to meet people who inspire them and who tell them they're worthwhile. They want to be surrounded by people who understand them and see them in ways no one else ever did before. They want love. They want validation. They want to feel like they matter. Like what they want matters. I'm glad Abe made you feel like what you want matters."

He took another drag and nodded. "Good."

"Can I ask one more question about the book?"

Artie finished the cigarette with an obscene final drag. "You can."

"What'd you do to Way?"

"What do you mean?"

Kim narrowed her eyes and finished her own cigarette, snuffing it out on the rusted fire escape railing and letting the filter fall to the street. "Does he, whatever his name is in the book—does he, um, get a happy ending?"

"I'm not there yet."

"I don't mean he doesn't have to die. He died. People died.

People are dying. But, you know, can you do something nice for him?"

"Of course I can do that."

"Good. Thank you. I want to read it the moment it's finished. I don't even care if you charge me for the printing."

"Fine. You'll be the first," Artie said, and Kim believed him. "His name's George, by the way."

"Whose?"

"Way's. In the book."

Artie wrote every morning and, in anticipation of the layoff he knew would be coming by the holidays, during work hours. The first draft of *Four Squares* was completed by Christmas Day.

4

2022

THE GALS CENTER was in a nondescript office building in Chelsea, a few doors down from a bank and adjacent to a piercingly lit restaurant that specialized in photogenic lunch salads. Nothing about the exterior screamed gay or old or even inviting. The front desk where he signed in looked like most other reception areas in Manhattan, staffed by someone who was sick of being asked the same four questions every day, and the elevators were just as slow as he expected them to be after pressing the faded, formerly golden button. When he stepped onto the eleventh floor, he was greeted by a wall-sized GALS logo, with a different old queer person smiling inside each letter. It was a welcome change from the drab lobby, but he found the gayness of this place sort of artificial, a coat of cracking pink paint hurriedly rolled onto layers upon layers of gray.

As he walked past the photos, the face of someone far too

young to appear inside the acronym for Gay and Lesbian Seniors approached him. "Hi," they said brightly. "Are you here for dinner service?"

"No, I'm here for the monthly orientation? Is it not tonight?"

The young person cocked their head and narrowed their eyes the slightest bit, then took a quick breath. "Oh! *Volunteer* orientation! Is that what you're looking for?"

"Yes. I signed up online a couple weeks ago."

"Great. Duh. Of course that's what you meant. It's right through there—the computer room, we call it. It's getting kind of full, so if you don't see a free chair, just stand in the back row. Or maybe someone will be kind enough to give up their seat."

Artie was the oldest person in the room by at least twenty-five years, but nearly everyone he squeezed past and excused himself to was kind enough to pretend not to notice. A few of them had less tact, though as he saw their eyebrows raise and their lips purse, he couldn't blame them. Artie had always been dreadfully self-conscious, and the only way he could successfully assuage his anxieties around people was to convince himself that no one was thinking about him. That no one cared. So here he was at the intersection of two unpleasant and unavoidable truths: He lacked confidence and was convinced that he was being thought about. He wasn't just being seen; he was being perceived. Could there be anything worse? Sweat began to collect on his scalp as he found a nice place to lean in the back of the room, and when he smiled at a twenty-something, he was pleased to find them charitable enough to smile back.

When the program director, Ali, entered the room, backs stiffened and phones were immediately placed screen down on the tables. Their presence made the room take a breath—a quick inhale grabbing everyone's attention, and an exhale letting them all know playtime was over. For a person under five feet tall, they had a towering and imposing presence. Some combination of their clothes—a slightly oversized navy suit— and posture. They hadn't slouched since second grade, when their entire class had been given a scoliosis exam by the school nurse. When they were found to be suffering from the condition, they cried, not even knowing what it meant, embarrassing themself in front of all the children whose backs resembled yardsticks. From then on, they made the straightening of their spine a priority. *The* priority, in fact. No one would ever notice its gentle curve again. No one, of course, but them, who often thought it was the only thing they could see in their reflection.

"Thank you all for coming in this evening," Ali said in a clearly performative baritone as they picked the remote controls off the rear shelf. "Please sign in if you haven't already. I think I see the clipboard floating through the back of the room."

Artie darted his eyes around nervously, hoping the clipboard would make its way to him like trout in a gentle stream. As he noticed it moving away from him, Ali noticed his noticing.

"Make sure you send that the other way," Ali said. "The gentleman in the back seems to need it."

Artie waved a silent *thank you* in their direction and felt his heart rate increase.

"Statistically this will be the last time about 45 percent of you sign one of these forms. Of the 55 percent who become actual volunteers—this meeting isn't volunteering, by the way— only 30 percent will become active. I say this to let you know why we won't be doing any sort of icebreakers. So many of you will never be seen here again."

After a few muffled laughs, Ali gave a long, rehearsed speech chronicling the history of the GALS center. "GALS" was an antiquated acronym from when the center was founded, they said, explaining that bisexuals and transgender members of New York's robust queer community had long wanted the center's name to be more of a mouthful. In the end the money was donated by a straight philanthropist. "Find me an out billionaire and I'll be happy to find you more letters, or at the very least a Q," the inaugural president was said to have told a group of rightfully angry queers who interrupted an early meeting. "But until that time comes, we're the GALS." And so they were, even when the money came from different places. There's no changing a name, not really, and no one put up a fight for long. There was always something else to fight for anyhow.

By the very nature of being a place for aging members of New York City's queer community to find not just social services but also leisure, food, and companionship, it became a place for younger members of the same community—albeit a different branch—to find things of their own: a chance to give back, to assuage their own guilt for prior selfishness, to make friends, to keep the stories of elder queers alive, and, of course, to keep the damned place operational so that it would be accessible to them when they themselves would need GALS for its more explicit purpose.

There were over twenty-five GALS locations across the country, all with the same mission: to help make it easier for queer people to get older. This took various forms, from financial counseling to apartment hunting to health care guidance to weekly phone calls to nightly meal services (as well as home meal deliveries). Artie watched as the screen showed people younger than him interacting with people older than him and felt stuck in a humiliating generational purgatory. He had no business being in this room, in this place, at least not for a few more years, when he inevitably found himself even more miserable and friendless than he was now. He'd already accepted the fact of his quickly dwindling sex appeal, but found it harder to acknowledge that at some point the words would dry up. There would be no more books and no more essays; there would be no more stories to tell strangers, or even himself. Only then would he enter the GALS center as a member, he decided. And he wouldn't return until then.

"In the next few days you'll be receiving an email from GALS asking you to create an account for our online portal, where you can sign up for programs, check the calendar, and connect with other volunteers. All extra-center communications between volunteers and members will happen at the discretion of the members. Out of politeness to them, please don't offer your number or Facebook or Twitter or WhatsApp or whatever. Please come to consider this as their second home, and be as respectful of their boundaries above all else. Having said that, if you meet a Chatty Cathy who wants to exchange numbers immediately—and believe me, there are myriad Chatty Cathys—by all means, text away."

Ali then went on to describe the expectations for all the major programs, explaining that people with cars should consider meal deliveries, and people who didn't feel comfortable lifting fifty pounds should steer clear of weekend activities at their annex downtown, as those events required loading and unloading furniture and decor. All of it made perfect sense, so much so that Artie wondered why this hadn't been done over email. As a writer, he so rarely found himself as a participant in meetings, let alone inside conference rooms. It lacked the efficiency he craved and cultivated in his own life, but in this moment he tried to think of it as something novel to be cherished. *Oooh*, he thought. *Look how strangely the corporate half lives.*

"I'm surprised to see you here," Ali said to him as he approached the door.

"Why's that?"

They paused, stiffened their back, then quickly softened. "We don't get too many elders coming in to help elders."

Artie laughed a small but genuine laugh. "I suppose I am technically an elder, aren't I?"

"What're you, sixty?"

"Exactly, actually. Thanks for confirming that I look it."

Ali twisted their mouth into something between a smile and a purse. "When you work around people obsessed with their age—and believe me, the volunteers are as conscious of it as the members—it becomes second nature."

"Ever thought about being a bouncer? You'd be great at spotting fake IDs." He smiled just long enough to see that Ali wouldn't be joining him, then quickly lowered the sides of his mouth.

"No," they said gravely. "I have a job already."

"Right, right. You've been here long?"

"A little over a decade," Ali said, narrowing their eyes a little as if trying to bring the whole of Artie into focus.

"That's great. What a tremendous place." They nodded before looking at the elevator bank in the lobby to Artie's left. "But I should get going."

"Of course. Thanks again for signing up today. Hope to see you soon."

"You will, you will," he said, not quite convincingly, as Ali turned to leave him. "I'll be one of those thirty percenters, believe me."

"Hope so," Ali said, disappearing down the hall. "The members might enjoy having a volunteer their own age."

When the elevator door closed on Artie, he exhaled so loudly that the young man beside him stepped to the side. Probably afraid of catching some old gay man's disease, Artie thought. He couldn't believe he'd agreed to return, but though he dreaded seeing Ali again, he had the sudden urge to ask how old the man beside him was. Twenty-five? Twenty-seven? Certainly not over thirty. Artie sighed again, and this time the man didn't even blink. Artie had gone from man to ghost in record time.

·· • ● • · ·

A WEEK LATER Artie woke to the sound of drilling in Gina's old apartment. The apartment was sold and emptied in days, and Walter had not returned. A week ago the sounds and stirs were the biggest annoyance he'd faced in ages, and he said as much to the condo board, who calmly reminded him that the newly married and newly moved-in Mrs. and Mrs. Greenhill were well within their rights to begin making noise at eight a.m. on weekdays. He checked the bylaws himself, still in the folder where Abe had carefully organized them so long ago, and sighed at the confirmation in black and white. Damn them, he thought. Damn the bylaws, he thought next. Damn Abe, he thought eventually, as always. He tried earplugs one night but slept through his 8:30 alarm, and after a few more days of the noise, he started to appreciate the wake-up call. He pulled his phone off the nightstand and began to tap and scroll, tap and scroll. In his inbox were several promotions for sales from retailers he'd shopped at once or twice before. A neighbor on his building's email list attempting to sell a hideous old couch. Below that, an invitation to join the GALS online portal. He shoved his back against the headboard and tapped the link. It was official, he thought. He was a volunteer.

The form asked for contact information, a short bio for the directory, and, to Artie's dismay, a photo. Why did he need to be seen to put in the work? Why did his face matter as much as his intentions? He flipped through the Favorites album in his photo app and found the same photo he used for his Gmail and LinkedIn accounts. Twenty years old and taken by a professional in Chelsea for $150, it was a wordless lie. His hair had gone fully gray since then, his glasses frames changed to a pair that was decidedly less hip, and he was now officially gaunt. Not skinny, not thin, but gaunt. He clicked the button marked UPLOAD.

Looking back on this moment, Artie would realize the activity had chosen him and not the other way around. It made him feel better about what came of it all, especially in the grueling few days that followed. There were multiple volunteer opportunities available that week, all of which were within his capabilities, but Artie wanted to make up for lost time, so he chose the one happening soonest: movie night. Tasks included: setting up the room for the event, signing in guests, helping members find seats, preparing the film, operating the vintage popcorn maker, and, of course, cleaning up. Sure, he thought. This is a perfect way in. He'd even get something akin to a two-hour break during the movie itself. He clicked the button marked SIGN UP, followed by the one marked CONFIRM.

·· •●•· ·

NO ONE ASKED him to bring anything, and they certainly didn't request that he make a cake, but overcome by the excitement of this new phase in his life, he baked one anyway. Three layers, white cake, chocolate buttercream frosting, and rainbow sprinkles covering every square inch of the exterior. Though worried it was a little on the nose, he knew it was also delicious, which more than made up for his lack of subtlety.

When he walked into the center the following afternoon, brimming with pride over the cake in his left hand, he'd expected the kinds of salivating glances and charming commentary one might get in an office, but no one said a word. Not as he signed in on the clipboard, not as he strolled past the members reading in the main rec room, not even as he pulled the lid off after placing it in the center of the long table along the far wall.

Finally, a voice: "Where's orientation?"

Artie turned and saw two young men, svelte and fashionably

dressed, both with the same confusing but sexy haircut, standing shoulder to shoulder in front of the elevator bank. The one on the left leaned toward Artie slowly, as if approaching a dog that might bite. "Sir? Do you know where the orientation room is?"

Artie shook his head and knocked himself out of the trance of youth, the way a perfect hairstyle seemed to pour out of their scalps effortlessly, and gestured toward the computer room to their right with his chin. "Right in there! Looks like you're the first ones."

"Thanks," the one on the right said; then off they went, gliding into the room like two bodies controlled by a single brain. Artie smiled at his own helpfulness, then felt the corners of his mouth turn back downward as he considered the age gap between them and him. Another voice disrupted his melancholy.

"Did you bake that at home?" they asked.

Artie spun around and saw Ali, a stench of disappointment emanating from their every pore.

"I did, last night. But I frosted it this morning."

"Did you bring it for the event, or are you just carrying it around for random and/or unrelated reasons?"

Artie looked at them quizzically, as if expecting a punch line. When none came, he told them it was for movie night.

"Well, see, we can't serve food prepared outside the center."

"What?"

"It's the law. All food for members needs to be prepackaged or made in the kitchens here. Outside food is a health risk."

"So what am I supposed to do with the cake?"

"Take it back home when you leave, I guess? Give it to some-one on the street?"

"Would *you* like a slice?"

"Just put it away in the kitchen for now so the members don't see it and get upset about not being able to have any."

Artie nodded as Ali stomped back to their office. With a sigh, he covered the cake with its lid, then turned to find a man, clearly a member, staring at it wantonly.

"You make that for us?" the man asked, staring at the tower of chocolate as though it were pulling him to it.

"Yeah, I didn't know I wasn't allowed to serve it."

"Did you bake this last week?"

"Last night," Artie said.

"Well, it looks about as dry as my damn elbows," he said, then turned to face Artie after his eyes turned kind and opened wider, like the spell of the cake had been broken. "Pretty, though."

"Thanks," Artie said. "I'm Artie. New volunteer."

"I'm Gregory. Ancient member. Too bad I can't have a slice, it may be my last chance to enjoy solid foods before they shove in a feeding tube."

Artie laughed, despite a subtle and peculiar feeling that suc-cumbing to such grave humor would be rude.

Gregory Deveux was tall and lean, a few pounds away from frail, and seemed to delight in Artie's laughter. Although at least eighty, he didn't look much older than Artie, and credited his youthful skin to "melanin and bad luck." Gregory was the kind of old person who loved to harp on about how much they hated being alive—the aches in his joints as well as those in his heart. But his gruffness was just a facade. He didn't actually hate living; in fact, he enjoyed it more often than he didn't, but found that jokes about death tended to go over well with folks who were far from it. Before Artie had the chance to fully introduce himself, Gregory was telling a story about a cake he'd once eaten at a birthday party on the Upper East Side in 1972. Gloria Gaynor had been invited, but she couldn't make it for reasons he could no longer remember. Artie spotted a hopeful, fleeting joy in his eyes as he recalled the experience: the maximalist decor in the apartment, the champagne served in fine crystal, the green suit he wore and the brown leather shoes he had shined for the occasion. It was a look that communicated that maybe all of it, even the ever-encroaching end of it, continued to be worthwhile.

"Artie? There you are," said a forty-something man behind Gregory.

Artie had noticed him walking toward them with purpose. He leaned forward while taking long strides and bounced upright when he came to a halt.

"Ali told me you'd be the one holding a cake."

Artie set the cake box on the seat beside him. "Ali didn't want any, but you can have some if you'd like."

"And why didn't you offer any to me?" Gregory asked with a tone Artie couldn't quite read.

"I'm not allowed to serve it to members, only volunteers."

Gregory muttered something under his breath about dessert and waved Artie's explanation away with the flip of his wrist.

"I hate to cut your chat with Gregory short, but what I need now is for someone to hang up the decorations. Beautiful cake, by the way."

"Decorations?"

"We like hanging up these mini cameras and film reels and laminated Oscars before every movie night. The little things, you know."

"Got it. Atmosphere."

"Here's the box and a roll of masking tape. Just sort of scatter them around these two walls until the box is empty and find me. I think I'll need someone to do popcorn, if you're comfortable with that."

"I think I am."

"Great. I'm Howie, by the way. Welcome to GALS."

"Happy to be here," Artie said with a newfound softness after suddenly deciding that he found Howie attractive. "Thanks for the help."

Half an hour later, Artie was standing on the middle step of a ladder, hanging up the final decorative film reel, when he heard a newly familiar, disappointed tone.

"Artie, we need to talk," Ali said, holding on to a middle rung. "You sent two twinks into the orientation room."

"Oh, right, them," he said. "Is there a problem?"

"Orientation isn't today, it's next Monday. I walked in to grab something, turned on the light, and there they were, totally dazed and staring at the wall, like they would have been there all night had I not told them to head home. Told me some old guy said they should be in there. It scared the shit out of me."

"Sorry about that," Artie said, an echo of "old guy" rattling inside his head. "I just assumed it was tonight, since they asked where the room was."

"Just be more careful next time. I don't even want to imagine the shit show that would have happened if we'd locked them in."

"Oh please," Artie said, trying to add levity to the situation. "I think they would have figured it out before getting locked in."

"Ten seconds was enough to have me convinced they wouldn't have."

"Well, I'm sorry. It won't happen again," Artie said. "Are you staying for movie night?"

"No, heading home. Thank you for filling in, by the way," Ali said, their voice calmer and almost sympathetic. "It's appreciated."

"It's no problem. And again, sorry about the twinks," he said. He and Ali were just about the same age, Artie assumed, but had entirely different perspectives of work at GALS. To Artie, and most of the volunteers, it was as much (if not more) about the satisfaction they gained from providing a service. To Ali, it was rent. They shook their head at Artie one final time and told him to pay more attention.

The thing was, he usually got along wonderfully with femmes. The only time they hadn't seemed to love his presence was when he accompanied one of them to the Padded Pocket, a legendary lesbian bar the size of a walk-in pantry overlooking the Hudson River, just off the West Side Highway. Despite his being invited by a welcomed guest, the regulars stared daggers at him from the moment he stepped inside. Ali made him feel the same way—not just unwanted, but like a hostile invader.

But what was there to do? He couldn't be fired, and they didn't have to be friends. GALS was a walk in the park compared to his day job. *I am lucky*, he told himself. Constantly, in fact.

When the decorations were up, and the main room was marginally more celebratory than it had been half an hour earlier, Artie found Howie and asked for a new task. The chairs were filling up, and the members' booming conversations began making the vibe markedly less sterile and sad. "Know how to work a one-of-a-kind mid-century popcorn maker?"

Artie shook his head.

"Lucky for you there's an instruction card taped to the side. Head into the kitchen through that hall, then make a quick right and then another right and open the walk-in closet. The popcorn maker's on wheels, so just roll it out here and plug it in against the wall. Popcorn and oil's stored on the shelves behind it. You'll need that, too."

"Got it. By the way, any idea what we're watching tonight?"

"*Philadelphia*. Or *The Philadelphia Story*. I don't remember."

"Big difference, but I guess I wouldn't be surprised by either."

Howie shrugged and shuffled off, leaving Artie to his latest task. Artie found Howie's confidence in him to be sort of gratifying. He would be operating the popcorn machine all by himself! It was one of a kind, too! Probably breakable! He beamed with pride as he strutted off to retrieve all the pieces that would eventually come together in a fit of hot, splattering magic. He rolled it out, placed the tub of popcorn kernels and jug of canola oil on the top, and wheeled the antique into the main room, where it was greeted with a rapturous round of applause.

"Lizzie!" the chorus of voices exclaimed.

"Looking good."

Artie asked who Lizzie was, and a woman with bright yellow glasses stood up to give him a monologue she seemed to have given, or at least rehearsed, dozens of times before. "Lizzie, the popcorn machine you're holding at this very moment, is named after the late Elizabeth Showalter. She was a hell of a woman, loud and mean, loyal and generous. She was also a lifelong patron of the arts, just like her parents, who were filthy rich and founded the Showalter Cinema in Midtown, in case you haven't already put that together. When she died some five years ago, she bequeathed that fine popcorn machine to the center and asked that we use it during every movie night to keep it functioning."

"Hey, Annabelle, you forgot the part about how the two of you used to sleep together," the man seated to her left blurted out.

"She slept with everyone," Annabelle said. "And this isn't about me. It's about Lizzie."

"What those two are trying to say is that it reminds us of our friend," Gregory said calmly and sternly, like a grade school teacher.

Artie nodded, and the room returned to the state it had been in a few minutes earlier, back when no one acknowledged his presence. He consulted the instruction card, filled the popper, closed the panels, and plugged the machine in. To his surprise, the lights along the edges turned on and glowed a warm yellow, washing the entire side of the room in a tint that set the place back five decades. He gazed in awe at the machine, not just at its innocent vintage charm, but at the memory of Lizzie, whom he suddenly felt close to.

"She used to say that she took over the Showalter from her father because she wanted a place to eat as much popcorn as she pleased in the dark," Annabelle said upon noticing Artie's quiet bliss. Those who remembered Lizzie nodded, and so did Artie. He didn't need to have known Lizzie for her to quickly manifest as a fully formed person in his mind.

As the smell of hot oil began filling the room, the members began quieting down and moving to their desired seats.

"No one told me what we're watching tonight," said Ellis, looking particularly unkempt in faded jeans and an old tee from the 1994 NYC Marathon that had been too small for him since the aughts.

Jazmine, whose persistent fear of death betrayed her youthful style, shook her head and sank into her chair. "*Philadelphia*," she said. "If I'd have known, I wouldn't have come."

"Oh Jesus," Ellis said as he sat down and rubbed the bald crown of his head.

The first kernel popped inside the ancient metal bucket behind Artie, startling him. He stepped to the machine and listened to the mechanical churning as it was steadily overcome by a cacophony of pops. Before long the popcorn was tumbling out of the bucket and onto the glass below, eventually forming a pile large enough to scoop into bags. "Popcorn should be ready soon," he announced to the room. "Raise your hand if you'd like a bag!"

Artie filled the bags, and Howie handed them out to everyone who raised their hand, which was just about half of the thirty-some members in the audience. As his back was to the screen, Howie fiddled with the remote and clicked through the DVD menu, all the while gesturing to the crowd to keep their voices down. Artie filled the basket with the next round of oil and kernels. He jumped back as one of them shot oil in his direction, and dropped the lid so that it closed with a loud clang. He turned at the sound of a familiar orchestration and smiled at the old logo for TriStar Pictures slowly appearing onscreen. Once it faded to black, then there it was: the sound of Bruce Springsteen's voice, the only song of his that Artie had any affection for. *Philadelphia* it was, then.

"I never liked this damned movie," Ellis shouted at the title card. "It's for straight people."

"It's a movie for gay people that makes heterosexuals feel guilty," Jim said with the quiet condescension of someone who always thinks he's the smartest one in the room, which he typically was. The tallest, too. "There's a difference."

"Thank you, Roger Ebert."

Jazmine scoffed. "Will you two shut up?"

As the opening titles ended, Artie turned back to Lizzie and periodically refilled bags as members snuck up to him for the remainder of the movie, which was even harder to watch than he remembered. One hundred twenty minutes later, after muted applause, the members began discussing what they had watched, which was Artie's cue to roll Lizzie back to the kitchen and clean her out in private. He'd put in more than enough emotional work for the day simply by being in the same room as the movie, he thought, and couldn't bear the thought of participating in grumbling discourse about it. But as he emptied the machine and gently cleaned its parts with soapy water, he felt a low hum of pride over the constant laughter among the members. He even heard gentle inhales of weeping by the end. He could see this becoming a regular part of his schedule, not quite filling the void of his regular dinners with Halle, which he was already beginning to miss, but maybe, with any luck, approaching the brim.

As Artie emerged from the kitchen, Howie had just finished folding up all the chairs and putting them on the racks in the corner of the room. "Hey, Artie," he said. "I know you just cleaned up Lizzie, and thanks for that, by the way, but would you mind taking down the decorations before you head out?"

Artie nodded and began pushing the cart of AV equipment out of the room. Once all the members had left the space, Artie opened the stepladder and began pulling all the figures off the walls and ceilings, suddenly annoyed by their impermanence. Why had he put all these damned things up if they were only going to be unceremoniously ripped off a couple hours later? His pulls began getting more dramatic. Off came a film reel. Then another. And then the Oscars and the popcorn bags. He was getting angry. On his first day of this new experience—or was it more of an experiment?—he had been confronted with the very past he was trying to move away from. This enormous step forward, undermined by the Philadelphia story he wished he hadn't revisited. Goddamn that movie, he thought. Goddamn its legacy and goddamn himself. Goddamn these drawings, and goddamn the laminating machine used to make them stiff and ageless. Goddamn this film strip and the masking tape he'd use to attach it to the ceiling. "Goddamn it," he finally said as he slid off the ladder. And then, after he hit the floor and heard a whisper of a crack, he said nothing at all.

5

1992

THAT NONE OF them enjoyed celebrating the new year was an affinity that, once discovered, solidified their burgeoning friendship like fired clay. A shared preference for being far from the city when December 31 eased into January 1, away from the noise and excitement they otherwise craved, became a central commonality to their friendship. A shorthand to why they got along, like star signs or political affiliation. When asked what they would be doing for New Year's by other friends and acquaintances, Artie, Adam, Kimberly, and Waylon historically all took pride in saying they would be with their friends who also hated New Year's, a hundred miles from the dropping ball.

The question they never raised aloud, though, was whether their annual tradition of going away for the occasion would have become a tradition if they had ever been required to pay for it. Perhaps they would have found, via a friend of a friend who owned property, a home to rent in New Paltz or Woodstock or any of the myriad little towns north along the Hudson, but perhaps it happened only because Adam offered. His parents, they learned, spent the cold months in Florida, which meant their house in upstate New York sat empty for nearly half the year. In exchange for a monthly stipend, which he received regardless of the weather, Adam was tasked with regular visits to the home throughout the fall and winter, where he was to check for burst pipes and broken heaters and signs of intruders. (Once, he found a squatter inside who, thankfully, had no intention of sticking around once discovered.) But when he offered up the home the first year they were all friends, ritualized future visits became instantly clear, and as such, they treated the house with the reverence and care of guests who wanted nothing more than to be invited back.

"You almost had us fooled," Kim said as Adam pulled up to the massive house for the first time after their two-hour drive along the Hudson. It was late December 1988, frigid but not snowy, and the house was bathed in the cool, flat light of an early-winter afternoon. "Can this technically be called a cabin? Do we each get our own wing? When were you going to tell us your family was loaded?"

"Don't let looks deceive you. It's probably going to be freezing inside, so prepare to keep a few layers on. The boiler breaks all the time. Actually, everything breaks all the time."

"I think we'll manage," Artie said, slack-jawed in the backseat, where Way sat beside him, staring out the window facing the hills, as if he hadn't realized they arrived. "Way, wake up. We're here."

Waylon had been slightly more quiet than usual on the car ride there, which the others chalked up to exhaustion more than discomfort or wariness. They knew he'd been up late the night before covering a shift for a friend who'd called in sick, and that talking about it would only upset him further, so they let him sit in the back in relative peace during the drive. Every few minutes, Artie would turn to his right expecting to see Waylon asleep, but he just had his temple pressed to the glass with open eyes, ones Artie could tell weren't actually looking.

"Hey," Artie said, shaking Way's hand gently after the car had been in park long enough for him to notice. "We're here. You awake?"

"Yeah," Way said, unhooking his seat belt, opening the door, and stepping onto the gravel in a single, fluid motion. The slam behind him didn't feel pointed, exactly, but it felt like more than the mere slam of a tired person. These were the kinds of things you could learn about your friends when you went out of town: Some of them were grumpy after being in the car.

They had chosen rooms without fighting because there was nothing to fight about. Adam took the largest room, of course, and the others threw their bags into spaces in the order they brought their things inside. Kim was first, so she took the guest room on the first floor. Artie was next, so he took the room on the landing, across from Adam, and Way took what was left, the guest room on the third floor, which meant he had the entire floor to himself.

Artie opened his suitcase, the same one he'd moved to New York with only two years earlier. It was brand-new then, a graduation gift from his parents when they thought he'd use it to move somewhere more reasonable, like Cleveland or Chicago, even south to Atlanta. To them, New York existed only in movies and television. No one they knew actually aspired to live there, or even to visit—especially not their son, who'd never brought up his long-simmering fascination with the city. New York was where people went to die, whether through violence or incurable disease. It was the first thing his mother had said after he came out to them, which happened to be in the same sentence in which he told them he was moving to New York. "That's where AIDS is."

She was right, in a sense, but he refused to explore the nuance. "AIDS is everywhere," he snapped at her instead. "It's everywhere because Reagan decided he didn't give a single shit about us. You just think it's in New York City so you can convince yourself that bad stuff can never happen to you. Well, it can, OK? Bad stuff can happen to anyone anywhere. It can and it does. All the fucking time."

"Watch your mouth when you're talking to your mother," his father finally screamed with a brutality he typically reserved for drunken rants against his least favorite NFL team on game nights. He had no comments about his son coming out as gay, no comments about his son flying across the country to live in a den of iniquity, only about manners. Typical.

"I didn't mean for this to become a shouting match," Artie said, trying to calm his sobbing mother down with a softer tone of voice. "And I didn't mean for anyone to cry."

"Well, it looks like you failed," his father said, pointing at his mother as she stumbled down the hall toward their bedroom, still whimpering. "And it looks like we did, too. You said your flight's leaving tomorrow?"

Artie nodded.

"Make sure it isn't a round trip."

It wasn't until months later that they spoke again, when his mother called the number he'd left on their answering machine while his father was out running errands. She didn't apologize for the way they'd left things, but the love in her voice was impossible to miss. Even as she told him it would be the last time Artie would ever hear it.

After everyone unpacked, Way's sadness numbed, and he began to show an actual excitement for their first winter trip away together. Up until then, their only vacations as a group had been all-too-brief weekends on Fire Island or in Asbury Park, which were more like days-long parties than periods of rest and relaxation. Compared to the open air and allure of cool water and hidden corners, a cabin in the middle of nowhere felt practically claustrophobic. Would they make it through a holiday together when no one else was around? When no one had anywhere to escape?

The answer, quickly, proved to be yes.

The four of them spent the next few days cooking meals, playing board games in their chunkiest sweaters, and smoking cigarettes on the back deck in their winter coats, as Adam's parents banned smoking inside the house. The spell of the place was broken every time they stepped onto the creaky wood and shut the door behind them. The cold reminded them that they were only visitors, and that the weekend was always going to be a fantasy. *You know you don't really belong here,* Artie imagined a voice whispering as they blew puffs of smoke toward the Catskills. *You're just playing pretend.*

Despite those occasional confrontations with their lack of family money and anything resembling security, it became an escape they hoped to make every winter. For four nights a year, five if they were lucky with work, they would all pretend to be away from the miseries and disappointments in a place where pain and loss felt impossible because what surrounded them was an abundance of beauty. Without television reception or a working VCR, they felt cut off from reality in a way that could have become an addiction. How nice it was to be tucked away from the news, which provided a version of their city that always seem to downplay the crisis or ignore it entirely. The plague had been a brutal fact of their lives for as long as they'd known one another, and the world outside Manhattan felt blissfully, if horrifically, ignorant. It wasn't the real world, as so many people insisted; it was a rose-colored simulation in which everyone pretended the real world, their world, didn't exist. But there was no escaping the plague, and it was inevitable that one day it would follow the four of them to Adam's crumbling upstate familial mansion. By the time Way was positive, all of them were better equipped to be the kinds of friends he needed them to be. Helpful but not discomfiting. Affectionate but not suffocating. And when they knew the end was coming, they sat around him as he took those final, ugly gasps in his own bed, just as he requested.

·•◦●◦•·

MAYBE IT WAS Abe's presence that helped mask the pain, or maybe it was just that time had done a good job, but the trip during which 1992 turned into 1993 marked the first time since Way's death that the house didn't feel wholly miserable. They could still feel him, of course, that would never go away, but his name wasn't invoked in that tearful, aching way it had been throughout the previous two visits.

Way always managed to sleep through the whole drive.

Way used to say that was the most perfect tree he'd ever seen.

Way told me this was his favorite place in the world.

Remember when Way would just sit here and look out the window for a whole hour?

It's funny how you can't become immortal until you're dead.

Artie feared an uncomfortable conversation with Adam and Kim when he asked if Abe could join them at the house this year, but to his surprise they had both already discussed—and approved—the fourth guest. Since their fight at Adam's, Abe hadn't missed a single movie night, and the tensions never again simmered, let alone peaked as they had that first night. He proved a superior addition to their group, always arriving with a hosting gift for Adam—as any child with frigid, wealthy, God-fearing parents of a certain zip code is wont to do—and never displaying even a hint of discomfort while in their presence. Abe could be difficult and stiff, but Kim and Adam ultimately chose a generous read of his idiosyncrasies. He was, they decided, simply dealing with the fallout of his significant time in the closet, and who were they to begrudge him the opportunity to spend time with boring fruits like the three of them?

"You need more wine?" Kim shouted from the kitchen at Artie and Abe as they read in the living room, comfortably lounging on one of the many plush couches Adam's parents had paid someone to pick out decades before. When they both shouted back asking for more, Kimberly told them to come get it themselves. Once they were in the kitchen, she sighed, stirring something on the stove and looking utterly frazzled.

"I knew that was the only thing that could get you two back in here," she said. "Keep me company. I don't know when the hell Adam's getting back with more wood."

"It smells amazing as always," Artie said.

"The power of the allium," Kim said. "That's all it ever is."

"Where'd you learn to cook?" Abe said, leaning against the counter beside Kim with the casual yet intimidating physicality of a college professor you both feared and wanted to fuck.

Kim darted her eyes at him without turning her face from the sweating onions and garlic. "Oh, home, I guess," she said. "My parents loved to cook. We ate dinner every night together until I left."

"Where's home? Or where was home?"

Those introductory conversations always seemed to start with childhood—how you played it straight, what your parents were like, was anyone violent, was there a queer outcast in your family—then transitioned to the coming-out saga—who you told first—and then down a winding path of first kisses and awkward hookups. The bullet points were always going to be similar, but the friendships were forged by sharing the details.

"Texas," she said. "Houston, or just outside. My dad worked at an oil company, and my mom is a teacher. He's dead; she's still teaching."

"When did he die?"

"Right before I left. I told my mom I was gay at the funeral."

"Wow, what a choice."

"Yeah," she said, dumping cubes of beef into the pot and raising her voice just enough to overcome the sizzle. "I had to get out of there, but not without telling her the truth. And there's no way she didn't know, even if she claimed to have been blindsided. I got caught making out with one of the coaches at an away game once, and everyone knew."

"Do you two still talk?"

"Sometimes. Helps that I'm the only child and she's alone at home. She was basically forced into maintaining a relationship with me."

"That's good, or something."

"It is what it is, but it's not like we talk about who I'm fucking."

"More than *my* parents."

"Do they even know?"

"Know what?"

Kim turned from the browning meat and put a hand on her hip. "That you're . . . whatever you are. Artie hasn't mentioned a word yet, which is fine, I'm the last person to pressure someone into using a label. I just don't know what you call yourself."

"Well, I call myself Abraham, and no, they don't. But yeah, I guess I'm . . ." He shrugged before saying the word. "Bisexual.

It's as good a word as any. Before Artie, I'd dated only women. Actually, I'd only ever dated *a* woman."

"But you fuck men."

"Sometimes."

"Do those women know?"

"As I said before, there's only one."

"I don't care if there's one or a thousand. You're putting *her* at risk?"

"I use a condom no matter who I'm having sex with."

"I shouldn't have posed that as a question. You *are* putting her at risk."

"I'm not seeing anyone but Artie at the moment."

"'At the moment'? So that could change? What's this *one* woman going to say? What lie will you make up to save her heart from breaking?"

"That's frankly none of your business."

Kim looked at Artie, who just sucked his lips in and shook his head.

"I know I shouldn't interrogate you. I know you've proven yourself to me, but I'm just a little concerned for this woman, whatever her name is."

"Vanessa. We've known each other since high school. We dated in college, on and off since."

"She doesn't know you're not straight?"

"Not to my knowledge."

"Does she love you?"

"She's said it."

"Have you said it back?"

"Yes."

Kim scoffed. "When's the last time you and Vanessa had sex?"

Artie raised his hands. "Kim, come on. You're acting like there's a flickering light bulb dangling between the two of you."

"Fine, Vanessa's a low blow," she said. "But have you ever known anyone who had it? Someone you were actually close to?"

"Yes."

"And what did you do when you found out?"

"I told them I was there for them. Whatever they needed."

"And what did they tell you they needed?"

Abe shook his head. "They didn't."

"So you didn't offer anything? You didn't see them after finding out?"

Smoke began wafting off the meat, so Kimberly flicked off the burner with an unexpected force.

Abe's posture softened, and he leaned back against the counter behind him, adding more distance between himself and his interrogator. "I didn't. He died quickly."

"Did you go to the funeral?"

Abe rolled his eyes. "I get your point."

"Good," Kimberly said. "Then you get why I'm a little nervous about my friend getting involved with some kind of sexual tourist who treats being a fag like it's vacation."

Kim walked to the pantry and pulled out some beef stock, piercing the cans open with vigor while he continued talking.

"I have messed up a lot in my personal life, but I am trying *not* to fuck up here. With him," he said, pointing at Artie's cowering face. "You can all trust me."

"What can we trust you about?" Adam asked, holding a pile of wood in the doorway. "Did I miss a fight?"

Kim flipped the cans over and began pouring their contents into the pot. "Abe was just telling us that he's a bisexual who plans on treating Artie with respect, and I was about to tell him that I believe him. For now."

"Well, that's good, I thought I walked in on a fight," Adam said, beelining for the living room.

"It *is* good," Artie said, smiling.

"Anyway, I'd ask how you came out to your parents, but it's clear that never happened," Kim said.

"Once again, you're right," Abe said, moving over to Artie and rubbing the small of his back. "I see why you keep her around."

Adam walked back into the kitchen to a considerably less tense scene than the one he'd entered only a minute before. "Looks like everything's loosened up in here. What else did you boys do while I was chopping wood?"

"We just read in the living room and listened to Kim cook stew in here," Artie said, refilling everyone's long-empty glasses.

"Speaking of reading," Kim said after a generous sip of sauvignon blanc, "when do I get my paws on the book you allegedly finished, Arthur Anderson? I believe the first-reader privilege was promised to me—no offense, Abe."

"None taken," Abe said. "A promise is a promise."

"Soon," Artie said. "And I *don't* want to talk about it, so let's change the subject."

Adam grabbed Artie's shoulders. "Here's one: Why don't you two help me bring in the rest of the wood?"

As Kim finished dinner, the three men brought most of the wood to the shed and lugged a few stacks to the living room beside the fireplace. They would have offered to chip in for what they knew was an exorbitantly overpriced haul but knew Adam's parents footed the bill for all expenses related to home upkeep. Artie declared he'd be starting the fire and began arranging the logs in the stove as Abe and Adam looked on from the couch.

"Did you grab a newspaper from town for kindling?" Artie asked. Adam bolted from the couch and grabbed it from the kitchen table, where he dropped it earlier.

"They didn't have any *Posts*, so it'll have to be a little more sacrilegious. Does anyone want to read some of the *Times* before we set it on fire?"

No one did, so Artie ripped the first page off. But before he could ball it up, his eyes fell on the middle headline above the fold. "States Face Drop in Federal Backing for AIDS Prevention," it read, between stories about a Somali massacre and a five-month-old child's death. He pulled the page closer to his face and began reading, silently at first but then aloud, to the room. "'The Federal Government has notified states that it is cutting money for AIDS prevention programs, and as a result many states are reducing services even as they face a rising demand. State officials have protested to the Bush Administration. Federal health officials said that they were considering the protests but that there was little they could do because Congress had limited the amounts available,'" he read, finally balling the page up and shoving it under the pile of dry wood. "They're all liars, aren't they."

Artie continued crumpling up ripped pages from the *Times* and shoving them into the oven, eager to watch them burn. Kimberly announced the meal's completion with a melodramatic sigh as she sat down in a squeaky arm chair. Eyes still on the fire, Artie said, matter-of-factly but with a hint of melancholy, "Do you remember Derek's funeral? On Long Island?"

"Of course I do," Kimberly said. "It was six months ago."

"So you remember his mom did the typical thing, not mentioning him being a fag, not mentioning HIV or AIDS or even a generic illness, like he just suddenly died in his sleep in his childhood bed, never having lived a life outside their gaze. Even *she* told people to vote for Clinton. At the fucking funeral! Like she thought it was all she could do—tell people to vote. It pissed me off at the time, like this woman who went to college in the sixties couldn't *possibly* understand the act of protesting and fighting and still thinks the only way to make change is by voting. But then a few days later, when all the anger of the day finally subsided, I thought, *At least she tried!* You know? She tried more than most of them. Most of them act like nothing's wrong. Almost like they're glad their kid's dead because they don't have to be confronted by their reality anymore." Artie sighed heavily and struck a match, accepting the silence that followed as proof that he'd done nothing more than ramble off some stray, disconnected thoughts that didn't warrant a response.

"You know I haven't had sex since that whole inconclusive test disaster," Adam said.

"What? Why not?"

"I'm sick of having to work up the nerve. I'd rather just not try."

"I'm sorry," Artie said after sitting on the floor beside him.

He rubbed Adam's back as Abe twisted his mouth and bit his lip, unsure of how to say what he wanted to say.

"I am, too," Abe said. "But also fuck it. If it makes you nervous, then don't let anyone pressure you into thinking you should. The right time will come eventually, even if it takes a while."

Artie turned to give him an appreciative smile. Every time Abe revealed a bit of gentleness and humanity, Artie felt quietly relieved and, embarrassingly, vindicated.

"And now that the Holy Spirit is closing, I won't even have a place to go dance."

"What's the Holy Spirit?" Abe asked.

"What's the Holy Spirit? Why am I not surprised," Adam said with an attitude he quickly softened. "It's a members-only club in the East Village. We've been going for years. There's no better place to dance, no better place to meet people, no better place to forget about the entire fucking world. Only now that it's closing, you can't go without feeling like the world is closing in on it. After an hour there last weekend the MDMA hit and I just felt completely alone. Then I threw up in the bathroom, mostly in the bowl. I got my stuff, ran out, and stumbled home. Pathetic and humiliating."

"I've seen and done worse at the Holy Spirit," Artie said.

Adam didn't respond, so the two of them let him have the rest of the moment to himself. They were beside him, four shoulders to be leaned on, and Artie knew Adam would fall on them if he so chose. When Kimberly returned to the kitchen and began serving the meal, his tears were dry, and the fire was blazing hot.

···●●···

AFTER DINNER, THEY all put on their coats and sat on the deck for another cigarette. Between sips of wine, they talked about their work and politics and their latest crushes, how much they enjoyed *A Few Good Men* and *Erotica*, whether they believed Artie had actually finished a whole novel, and eventually which game they wanted to play after going back in. Trivial Pursuit beat Scrabble, so Kim and Adam set up the board as Artie and Abe cleaned up. After a few rounds, they smoked some more, then came back in for a final game and nightcap before heading to their respective bedrooms. This was how the nights always went: There was always food and wine, and there was always a game, and there was always at least one moment of emotional catharsis that was quickly brushed aside but made them all feel like the trip was fulfilling its duty. Even New Year's Eve was more of the same, with Kimberly cooking a meal of pork chops, cornbread, and black-eyed peas so good it might have actually made her parents proud.

But on the first night of 1993, and their last night in the house, the mood had shifted. There was a peculiar vibration to the house, one that made everyone feel both uneasy and excited for the future. It would be the first full year in which all of them would be in their thirties, and the shift they'd not considered even for a moment until they were hours into the new year suddenly felt momentous and huge.

"Doesn't this feel bigger than a new decade?" Adam had asked as they had their coffee that morning. "Such a random year,

1993, but I woke up actually feeling excited. I can't remember the last time that happened."

"I think I know what you mean," Kim said. "Maybe it's the thought of a new president?"

"No," Adam said in a piercing retort. "It's not that at all. I don't give a shit about him, or any president, not anymore. I'm talking about us. This is our year, I think. The four of us."

"I don't feel particularly enthusiastic or even all that different from yesterday morning, but I'd be happy to take your word for it," Abe said, turning to Artie. "What about you? Did you wake up feeling *excited* by 1993?"

"Now that you mention it," he said, "I kind of did."

Artie didn't elaborate on his feeling; he just took another sip from his mug and let the moment marinate. Maybe thinking New Year's resolutions were beneath him was the problem all along. Maybe the only way you can have a better year is to make the decision to.

6

2022

ARTIE WOKE UP laughing. But once he saw his surroundings—a white curtain on the right and a beige wall covered in an unnerving number of outlets to the left—he stopped. Worse, he forgot what had been so funny in his dream and wondered how his body could have conjured anything remotely pleasurable while lying on a slab of antimicrobial, industrial-grade foam with decaying plastic bowling alley bumpers on either side. He was still there in the hospital, eighteen hours after being admitted, though they would allegedly release him soon. He was still in pain, though there was less of it than there had been when he'd arrived. He was still alone.

He pushed the call button with his left hand, careful not to jiggle the needle jammed into his left arm. As he waited for the nurse, he scanned the room to see if it had changed at all since he had fallen asleep. It hadn't. Everything was exactly the same as it had been six hours before. The same beeps were beeping, the same fluorescent bulb was flickering, the same faceless cough was being coughed, and the TV in the corner still hung in front of him, broken as it was when he was wheeled in the day before. The newest thing in the room was the cast over his left foot, a bold, regal purple that made him grimace. Though he'd gone out of his way to avoid catching a glimpse of his injury immediately after the fall, the sound of the crack—which he learned later was a hairline fracture on his fifth metatarsal, right on the outer edge of his left foot—was enough to make him imagine the horrors that lay beneath the plaster and gauze.

"Eight weeks," either an impossibly tall rugby player or an orthopedic surgeon he knew only as Dr. Sanchez had told him yesterday, after the cast was constructed around his broken bone and left to harden. "Six if you're really lucky, and ten to twelve if you're not quite as lucky." Artie hadn't considered it at the time, but remembering the surgeon's words now, he realized that two months, the middle ground, was just plain lucky. Clever woman, he thought, trying his best to feel as fortunate as the doctor seemed to believe he was.

"How're you feeling, Mr. Anderson?" asked one of his nurses, Chani, as she glided through the doorway.

"Just wondering if I'll ever walk again."

"You're crazy, Mr. Anderson," she said, checking his chart and reading the numbers displayed on the monitors to his left. She reminded him of Kim, broad-shouldered with limbs that exuded strength, even through scrubs. "That foot is going to heal just fine. You'll be running the marathon next year, just wait."

"I've never been a runner, but I do love to walk."

She chuckled politely and replaced one of the empty IV bags with a plump one.

"You need to go to the restroom while I'm here?"

"No," Artie said. "But can I have some breakfast?"

"I'll let them know you're up, and it'll come around shortly."

"Thank you, Chani."

"You're very welcome. The doctor could be a while, so be patient."

"I'm good at waiting."

"Must be why I like you so much."

Artie found it funny how quickly he became used to life in a hospital and wondered if that's what had made him laugh in his sleep. He'd gone from being fearful of a brain bleed after hitting his head during the fall (he wasn't even concussed), to terrified he'd never walk again ("Don't be silly," said Dr. Sanchez), to friendly conversations with a nurse who was willing to escort him to a toilet, all in the span of a day. Maybe he should have been alarmed by his, and perhaps humanity's, ability to adapt to a sudden change of one's circumstances and surroundings, but in this moment it was only hilarious. Perhaps because he hadn't yet been forced to rehearse his new mobility outside the confines of a place where he was surrounded by people willing to help him. It would be a different story in his apartment, he realized. Who would be around to walk him to the bathroom in the middle of the night tomorrow and the next day? Where would he find a generous nurse to remind him that he'd suffered only a small fracture in one of his body's tinier bones? He picked up his phone, hoping for some kind of check-in from Halle or

Vanessa despite knowing there was no way they would have been told; he'd never set up the emergency-contact feature on his phone, and the only person he'd called since arriving in the hospital was his agent.

When Dr. Sanchez gave him the all-clear, reminding him to keep the foot elevated at night with a brutalist piece of foam and to take over-the-counter painkillers as needed since he'd rejected a hefty prescription for opiates, he was directed to the desk where he filled out the remainder of his insurance forms. He told Nikki to come whenever she was able and that he would be waiting for her in the lobby. She arrived within the hour and wheeled him to her passenger door. By six, nearly twenty-four hours after his body broke, Artie Anderson began the healing process at home.

····•◉•···

"I PUT A ziti in your freezer and some random groceries in your fridge. Executive decisions, but you have plenty of fresh food in there to last you for a week, not that I don't have faith in your cooking abilities. Is there anything else you need before I go? Or do you need me to stay the night? I can let Nick know."

"No, no, it's a broken foot, not a broken back. I'll be fine," he said, appearing to mean it. "And if I'm not, I'm sorry to say you'll be the one who finds my decomposing body."

Nikki looked up from her phone. "What was that?"

"Nothing."

He looked at his kitchen, spotless and actually sparkling in some places, and the thought of making it dirty by hobbling around attempting to cook and then eat made him shake his head. When he did, an envelope on the island caught his eye. He hopped toward it, his arms shaking slightly as his body got used to the crutches.

"Who's this from?"

"No idea. Someone brought it to the front desk yesterday. Dennis sent me up with it when I brought the food over earlier."

Artie wiggled his way into one of the bar stools and rested the crutches on the island, moaning slightly with every move. He ripped the envelope open and pulled out a gift card for a meal-delivery service. Inside the flap, someone had scribbled "ARTHUR" on the TO: field, and beside FROM:, just "The GALS."

"Huh," he said, considering a smile.

"Seamless gift card? Who's it from?"

He held up the card so Nikki could read it, but after squinting and leaning in, she still maintained a puzzled look. "The GALS?"

"Gay and Lesbian Seniors," he said.

"Oh, right, where it all went down."

"So to speak."

"That was nice of them."

"It was," Artie said, a smile finally glazing across his face. "God, what a disaster this is."

"It's six weeks. Six weeks is nothing."

"Six to eight. Maybe more if my body sucks."

"Your body doesn't *suck*."

"Can you get me something to work on? Any projects floating around the office looking for a housebound writer? Even something you'd never consider me for, something you'd say was beneath me. Isn't there always some child star who hates their parents?"

"If I hear of something, I will let you know," Nikki said. "But have you considered actually listening to my advice from before and taking some time off? I know exactly how much money you make, and I have enough of an idea about your expenses to know you can afford it. You could probably afford to retire."

"My brain turns against me when I'm not working." He looked back down at the gift card, which he was now holding tightly enough that the paper started to bend. "It really was so nice of them to send this."

"Isn't that the point of that place? Coming together, companionship, chosen family, et cetera?"

"Et cetera."

They both lingered around the obvious solution to Artie's boredom and newly cleared schedule, but neither took the silence's discomfiting bait.

"So you're good?"

"I'm good. Thank you for everything."

"You're very welcome. As your agent, if something comes up, I'll let you know. But as your *friend*, I think you should just consider . . . healing." Artie offered her an unconvincing nod. "Question, though. How's the, uh, dressing situation going to work? What happens when you can't just slide parachute pants from the hospital over that thing," she said, pointing at the purple cast on his foot.

"I ordered a few pairs of these pants that zip up on the sides that my nurse recommended. They're not exactly fashionable, but neither am I, so it's fine."

"You're fashionable. At least you dress better than Nick."

"That's not the compliment you think it is."

"Ha ha," she said, leaning down to hug Artie as he sat on the stool. "Call me whenever," she said before making all the sounds he recognized as a definitive exit.

"Love you dearly," he whispered, unclear who he was directing it to.

· ·•◉•· ·

AFTER MAKING IT though his first of at least forty-two nighttime routines without incident, he pulled his phone from the nightstand and tapped Halle's name.

> No need to call or worry, but I broke my
> foot a few days ago and will be Colin
> Craven in my apartment for the foreseeable
> future. Just wanted you to know to keep
> you in the loop, but again, all's well!

She didn't respond in the forty-five minutes it took him to fall asleep in such an uncomfortable position, on his back with his left leg propped up on the cushion from the armchair in the corner, but notifications for a missed FaceTime call and follow-up text message were the first things he saw on his phone in the morning.

> I tried calling but you must be asleep. I'm so
> sorry about the fall! No head injury, right?
> They better not have given you opioids. If
> they did, toss them, but not in the toilet. I'm
> serious. Call me back whenever, and let me
> know if there's anything I can do from here.

He sighed with a smile. It was too early on the West Coast for a call, so he drafted a quick text.

> I'll be here. (Literally. I'll be here for the next
> two months.) Ha. Talk soon.

He twisted his body, moved his legs to the floor, and reached for the glistening pair of crutches he'd propped between his nightstand and the bed. With a grunt and a groan, he was up, and his morning routine had begun. After brushing his teeth, he gave the shower a worried stare, then sniffed his armpits. Feeling the burden of putting a garbage bag over his foot once a day, he decided that he might become one of those every-other-day bathers. It's not like he would be working up a sweat, he thought.

The rest of his day was a steady hum of quiet angst: solitary time with a book or his thoughts punctuated by eating, no part of any activity even remotely enjoyable. When his foot finally began to hurt, the result of waning intravenously delivered painkillers, he sat and elevated it, as directed, and popped a Tylenol. He briefly wondered how fentanyl would feel, whether he'd ever experience that kind of euphoria, then shoved the idea out of his mind. His addictive personality—which he chalked up to his father, a gambling addict with a drinking problem, or maybe the other way around—was best left to things like caffeine and work. Around midday, he wanted nothing more than to go on a long walk outside. Through the window Artie could see fall approaching from the north, as if the leaves of the Hudson Valley were sending a message to him that all would soon be different—cooler and more comfortable. Then he remembered his medicinal ball and chain, that hideous cast, and the wiggling of his arms as he got used to the crutches and realized it would be a few more days until he'd be comfortable enough to venture off without fear of falling and breaking something else. He turned on a movie and did laps around the apartment, as suggested by the recovery plan he'd taken home from the hospital. By the time it was over, he felt slightly better. It wasn't much, but it was an accomplishment. And that was enough for now.

In bed, trying and failing to start his second book of the day, a soon-to-be-published likely bestseller Nikki had left him on the kitchen counter, he spoke for the first time since waking: "This sucks." It was 10:05 p.m. One day down.

It took a week of walking around his block—first once, then twice, and ultimately on a loop for an hour—for Artie to feel comfortable out in the world, but once he crossed the street, the new fear of a crosswalk-related disaster entered his mind. *Picture it,* he thought, *me writhing around on the bed of thick white lines like a cockroach stuck on its back, crutches strewn at my sides as a delivery truck barrels through the intersection because the driver is looking at their phone.* The city had opened back up to him—there it was, just across the street—and now it shrank down to the size of his block once again.

In his aftercare documentation he found a recommendation for a knee scooter, a tricycle for the elderly and infirm—or, in his case, both. It arrived fully assembled and ready for motoring from a mobility store downtown the next day. Though wary of the device initially, and the way it made him unable to mask his fragility to the world, all it took was a single spin around his apartment for Artie to fall in love. The city was once again his to conquer by foot, only this time there would be just one of them, plus three wheels to keep it company.

Dennis beamed as Artie returned from his first journey into the great beyond and pulled the door open with an eagerness Artie found warm and infectious. "Welcome back, world traveler! The scooter treating you well, I see?"

"I feel like I could walk five hundred miles."

"And you look like you could walk five hundred more. Go anywhere special?"

"Nowhere in particular, just a stroll. But a few blocks is better than nothing."

"Glad to hear it," Dennis said, and Artie believed him.

⋅⋅•●•⋅⋅

ARTIE RODE THE high of the excursion all the way up the elevator, but the excitement faded the moment he was home alone, in the brutal quiet, without a thing to do or deadline to make. He found it frustrating that a feeling could come and go so quickly, like a seed washed away before sprouting its roots.

He sat at his kitchen island, where his laptop and charger had been sitting for days, and turned on the television. NY1, news as white noise, blared as he scrolled through recent headlines and checked his emails. As the traffic report was delivered—surprise, there were slowdowns in every borough—he clicked on an email from GALS. A weekly update for volunteers: new events to sign up for, recaps of the last week's happenings, birthday announcements—the sort of thing you open and instantly begin to scroll through, picking up just enough words from enough paragraphs to feel like you've gotten the gist. Less a message than a prod, reminding you of an association you once made and, with any luck, still have and respect. So, in a sense, it did its job, as it reminded Artie to check the schedule and sign up for his first volunteer opportunity since the fall—one he could do while sitting down.

When he rolled off the elevator the next afternoon at the GALS center, he was greeted by silence. No one lingering in the banks. No one at the front desk. It wasn't until his wheels crossed the threshold of the darkened cafeteria that someone noticed him. "Can I help you?" Howie said. "Oh! It's you! You're alive!"

Artie laughed. "Alive *and* well. I'm here to work the front desk for the dinner service. Saw there was a cancellation yesterday and I've got time to kill."

"Oh," Howie said with a subtle reserve. "I think that may be, actually . . . just hold on. Let me talk to Ali."

Artie deflated at the mere mention of their name. "OK. I'll be over at one of the tables, so just tell me what you need when you're ready." Once seated, he spread his hands across the wrinkled, light blue tablecloth, then flipped through the pages on the clipboard in the center, reading the list like it was a handwritten poem. Some members were on every page. Some just twice a week. Some came at random. Some seemed to have come just once. The variety of routines filled him with a sense of calm, and he felt a whisper of relief about his impending old age. Or was it already here? Either way, here was proof that there was more than one way to do it. More than one way to go about life, especially life as an old single childless queer in the city. Just as he'd settled into a routine when he could no longer walk as he once did, he would eventually settle into a routine when he could no longer cook as he once did. Maybe he would simply lose the passion for it! Whatever the case, he saw the clipboard as proof that all was not lost. That is, until he heard Ali clear their throat.

"Arthur," they said, sternly but with a hint of begrudged compassion. "I appreciate you signing up today, and I do take pleasure in seeing that you're going to recover from your incident, but we can't have you volunteering today."

"Oh, no worries. You should have seen me three weeks ago, but now I'm a pro on this thing," he said, tapping his scooter with a performative pride. "Better on it than a ladder, I mean."

"That is," Ali said, scratching the side of their neck, "nice to hear, but unfortunately you're an insurance risk in your current state."

"A what?"

"If, god forbid, something else were to happen to you while

you're in this condition, it would be hell for the center. Not to mention you. We just can't risk you working for us while you're unwell."

"But I told you, I'm fine!"

"It's not a question of how you feel, Artie. It's how you are."

"Don't you think that's a little ableist?" Artie asked, smugly. But Ali did not waver; they didn't even consider taking the bait.

"I don't," they said, as calm as ever. "But if you'd like to stay for dinner service, you should. You came all this way."

All this way, Artie thought, his silent grimace leading Ali to explain the rules. *Sixty years and one nasty fall.* Though he wasn't yet at the age for automatic admittance (that didn't happen until sixty-five), he was eligible for admission by administrative review. According to the bylaws, Ali explained, queer-identifying people could apply to join the center once they were sixty. All they had to do was explain why their circumstances required the center's assistance. What he didn't know, not at the time and not ever, was that not once in the history of GALS had an application for early admittance of a sixty-to-sixty-five-year-old queer person been rejected. Who would have told him?

Artie's eye twitched, and he squinted as he nodded. "I guess that makes sense, and I wouldn't want to be a burden to the center. It's just that I have an abundance of time and a willingness to help. I'd rather be a volunteer."

He watched Ali carefully as they formed a response, rolling eyes visible through their closed lids. "*I* understand that," they said. "But I need *you* to understand why I can't allow you to.

GALS is bigger than each of its members. It's everyone. It's a community."

He grabbed the handles of his scooter and stood, rejecting both Ali's and Howie's offers to assist him, and once he was firmly upright, a pair of gay right angles on wheels, he took a deep breath, swallowed his ever-dwindling pride, and rolled to the elevator bank. When the door finally opened, he waited for a man—tall and white, like him, but hunched over a walker— to scoot out. Upon noticing the tears welling in Artie's eyelids, the old man offered a gentle chin raise.

"You got off lucky," he said. "Have a good one."

The walk home was direct. No zigzags or thoughtless meanders, as was once typical, just the path of least resistance and fewest steps, from embarrassing point A to miserable point B. But when he returned to his apartment, all 1,100 empty square feet of it, he bristled at the clock in the kitchen upon realizing the amount of day there was left to fill. But no, he thought, he couldn't have stayed. This feeling, the one he was experiencing so deeply right then, did not mean he had made a mistake back at the center. He pulled his phone from his pocket and tapped Halle's name. With his finger hovering over the call button, he considered the consequences. Now that their relationship was largely text-based, he knew a call would compel her to answer, thinking something was up. Assuming someone was dead, or at least en route toward it, she'd answer, not hiding the worry in her voice. He'd respond brightly, too brightly perhaps, and begin by assuring her that nothing was the matter; he just wanted to check in. See how she was doing. Maybe he'd say he was missing her, perhaps even add that he was feeling "blue," to squeeze out as much empathy as he could without actually explaining the cause and extent of his misery. They'd have a pleasant conversation about her plans for the day, how she was liking the new house, and he'd give her a truncated version of his afternoon at the center. And when she'd say it was time for her to get ready for a doctor's appointment, one of those regular pregnancy checkups, he'd wish her luck. Once they both hung up, he'd feel slightly better, and she'd feel ill at ease, maybe even annoyed. He moved his finger from the screen to the button on the phone's edge and pressed harder than he needed to, shutting off the screen and shutting down his plans. She was a crutch, and he had a newfound disdain for those. With his elbows propped on the counter, he rested his head in his hands, palms touching eyelids, and wept. He wept more than he'd wept since the injury, despite feeling less physical pain than he had in weeks. And when he was finished, he didn't feel any better. No, he felt worse. Because he felt hungry. So he scanned his barren fridge and swallowed the only thing left to consume: his pride.

·•◦●◦•·

ALI WASN'T EXACTLY kind on the phone with Artie the next day, but they weren't exactly mean. They responded to his barrage of questions with the distant specificity of an automated customer service robot: filled with answers to all of Artie's questions but precisely no humanity. Yes, Artie was technically allowed to join GALS as a sixty-year-old. No, he wasn't the first. Yes, he was eligible for the same events as everyone over sixty-five. No, it didn't prevent him from abandoning his membership and volunteering once his foot was fully healed. They didn't editorialize in the affirmative or the negative, which made Artie feel stuck. He wanted to be swayed, one way or another, but Ali seemed happy to let him dangle between the two options, feeling nothing but the harsh pull of gravity thanks to his inability to swing toward an edge on either side.

"Is there anything else I can answer for you before I get back to work?" they asked, expertly nudging him to bring the call to a close.

"No," he said. "I suppose I'm ready to join."

"OK," they said, exhaling with a force Artie assumed they intended to be noticed. "I suspect you already know how to apply?"

"I do."

"Then I'm sure I'll be seeing you soon."

"I'm sure you will be. Thank you for the help."

"Of course," Ali said just before they hung up.

Artie looked at the CALL ENDED screen with a hint of disgust, then, with a few quick taps, ordered dinner.

·· • ● ● ··

LATER THAT WEEK, Artie arrived at the GALS center at 4:30, a full half hour before the meal service began. Fearful of entering a room where he wasn't allowed, he loitered in the lobby, slowly rolling along the perimeter as he read every bit of signage plastered all over the walls, before finally taking a seat at around 4:45. As other folks began to file in, Artie felt a kind of anxiety he hadn't experienced in decades: the fear of rejection. Alone at one of the dozen or so circular tables scattered throughout the enormous, multipurpose space, he had the nerves of a child worried he'd be picked last before a kickball game. But the first GALS member to sign in put a stop to that line of thinking the moment he bypassed the empty tables and chose a chair directly beside Artie. "You must be new," he said, extending his hand. "Nobody's ever here before me."

"I had a, uh, a bit of a mix-up," Artie said, taking the man's hand, which he found pleasingly and surprisingly soft, and shaking it. "I'm sure you'll return to being the first from here on out. I'm Artie Anderson."

"Jim Thornton," he said. "Glad to see a fresh face spicing this place up."

"I'm not sure another white guy's all that spicy," Artie said.

"Oh, that depends," Jim said. "What happened to the foot?" he asked, gesturing at the cast with his chin.

"I fell. Right over there, actually," Artie said, pointing toward the wall of windows on the south side of the room.

"Oh, that was you! I was there that night, must have been one of the last people to see your foot in its pristine state," Jim said. "You were the talk of the town for a couple of days."

"And then what, did something more interesting happen?"

"Someone passed, and I'm sorry, sweetie, but a broken foot can't compete with death."

"Oh, I'm sorry. Who died?"

"Woman named Vera. Heart attack. In her sleep, thank the lord. Didn't need to die in a hospital."

"Still, how awful."

"That's what happens," Jim said, scanning the empty room as if looking for signs of Vera. "People don't stop coming to

GALS because they don't like it. It seems like I've been losing friends for as long as I've been making them."

Artie felt tears approaching, and patted Jim on the knee as if trying to knock them back into their ducts. "Well, I'll try my best not to drop dead on you anytime soon."

"Easy for one of the youngest members to say."

Artie laughed. "I'm not technically a member, anyway. They just let me eat here tonight."

"Oh, sweetie, that's how it always starts. You just come to check things out, then it's dinner once a week, then three times a week, then five times a week, then you know everyone's business, even if they didn't tell it to you. You've got a lot to catch up on."

Artie took a shallow breath. He knew that if he tried to cut the conversation short, tried to express less interest in the center, that Jim would get the message. It was clear he was quite astute at reading the way a person holds themself in silence. Artie also knew that if he acknowledged his actual interest in the space, which was admittedly growing by the minute, he would find himself caught. Jim would cast a lure, Artie would take the bait, and before long he'd be flopping around in GALS like exactly the thing he always feared he would be: old and dependent. He recalled what Jim had just said, or what he didn't say: that people don't stop coming to GALS unless they die. But when he thought about the past few days of his life, not to mention the preceding months and years, he felt like he hadn't changed in ages. He'd stayed the same. And what's death if not one's final evolution? Was he already there? Not yet. So he took another breath, deeper this time, and responded to his new friend. "Such as?"

Jim delighted at the question, and sat up straight in his seat before scooting it even closer to the table. He gave Artie the rundown of the most prominent members as quickly as he could, pointing them out as they walked in and painting them with stunning and vivid splotches of color. Artie recognized many of them from his fateful movie night. There was Brian, the bossy old queen who always barged in on conversations to steer them in whatever direction he saw fit. Then Annabelle, a tremendously wealthy lesbian who hadn't had sex since the Reagan administration because "that was the last time she was truly happy." But most of the descriptions came in one-to-three-word-grunts. Gregory? Loved by all. Gene? Loud but harmless. Terrence? Loud and harmful. Helen? Always crying. Jazmine? Secretly dying. Fred? Hilarious and asexual. Hazel? On wheels. Miguel? Nonbinary, successful painter. Harold? Gay and potentially a TERF. Ellis? Jim's best friend. It's not that Artie felt like he was in high school, because Artie hated making friends in high school—he avoided the cafeteria and ate a lunch he always packed himself in the courtyard, at a bench beside the oak tree with the most shade. Instead, it was what he always imagined high school could be, if only he were a different kind of person. But he wasn't a different kind of person now. He was still himself, just older.

Artie's laughter caught the attention of a few other members, some of whom quickly caught on to what was happening and laughed, while others looked over, angered by Jim's obvious delivery of reductive dossiers. But a new face looked over with neither enjoyment nor disdain. The only thing it communicated was interest. Whether it was interest in the conversation or Jim or himself, Artie couldn't deduce, but he could sense a kind of intrigue from far away. The face was rough and round, with a bushy beard that seemed to be antagonizing the bare scalp above it, and sullen eyes covered by thick glasses in clear frames.

"Who's that?" Artie asked.

"Don't know him at all," Jim said. "I've never seen him before. But by the looks of it, I'm guessing . . . white?"

"Yeah."

"Cis male?"

"Likely."

"Gay?"

"Let's hope."

"Whatever he is, I'm sure plenty of people here are happy to take a look."

"Looks like it."

"You gonna leave me and make a move?"

Artie laughed. "Of course not. I haven't made a move in . . . what's today?"

"Monday."

"Monday? Yeah, OK, so then it's been about, let's see, twenty-nine years."

It wasn't entirely the truth, but it got a laugh out of Jim, and that was all that mattered in the moment. And as dinner was served to the table, now almost filled with new people for him to meet, Artie excused himself to the bathroom, where he could sit in the comforting confines of a stall, processing the evening's first information overload before beginning round two.

When he returned to the table, the white cis male with the oval face and clear glasses was sitting in one of the previously empty seats. "You glide on that thing like an old pro," he said, pointing at Artie's scooter.

"Thanks," Artie said. "It wasn't as hard to get used to as I expected."

"This is Carson," Jim said. "He's new to the center. Can't remember the last time we had two newbies in one night."

Carson was shorter and heavier than Artie. He smelled like Listerine and a full ounce of cologne, and though he was in a crisp white oxford shirt, Artie had the sudden urge to see him in flannel, maybe even holding an axe. No, he wanted to see him in nothing at all, and he introduced himself with a tighter handshake than was his norm. He briefly considered giving Carson the long version of his membership story but settled on something more concise. "I'm new, too."

"Carson was just telling me that he thought dinner was 'surprisingly good,'" Jim said. "What exactly were you expecting, young man?"

Carson laughed with an open mouth, showing off his frustratingly perfect teeth. "I didn't expect it to be bad, I just didn't expect it to be this good. I guess I was expecting something more like hospital food."

"As someone with recent experience, hospital food's gotten a little better."

"How'd you end up in that thing?" Carson asked, leaning in a little closer and pointing at Artie's cast.

"It's a long story, but I'm on the mend."

Jim turned to Artie. "Well, I need to go to the bathroom.

This bladder's not going to empty itself. I take pills to prevent that."

Carson laughed heartily, earnestly. Artie just smiled.

"So," Carson said once they were alone at the table. "What do you do?"

"How lovely that you assume I'm still young enough to still be doing it."

"Does anyone actually retire these days?"

"Oodles of people."

"So you're retired?"

"God, no, I'm a writer."

"A writer! That's cool," Carson said, completely satisfied with the answer. As if no follow-up questions could possibly exist.

"What about you?" Artie asked.

"Oh, I'm retired."

Artie considered telling him how long it had been since he'd laughed as hard as he was right then, but stopped himself before letting it out. Not out of the fear of being too vulnerable in front of a new friend, exactly—though maybe that was part of it; rather, he wanted to respect the moment for what it was, a good one. One that didn't need explanation or qualification. Free from the burden of context and memory. It was a good moment, a happy and funny one, and that was all he—and, Artie assumed, Carson—needed it to be. He had been so overwhelmed by the thought of making a friend when Nikki assigned him the task, and now here he was, laughing with one.

An hour later, after they all said their goodbyes and made plans in front of the center to see one another at the next dinner,

Artie gripped the handle of his scooter more tightly than ever before, and his stride was the longest it had been since he could walk without aid. On 8th Avenue, just around the corner from his apartment, a couple moved to the right so he could whir right past, ignoring him otherwise and continuing their conversation as though he and his scooter were just another fact of the city.

7

1994

ARTIE SHOOK THE snow off his coat under the awning of the shop and watched it fall in a circle on the awning-shaped bare spot of the sidewalk. A soft and friendly bell rang as he pushed the door open with his foot, but no one seemed to acknowledge its clanging chord. He crept through the store holding the heavy box tight, like a thief holding his stash, and craned his neck around corners, searching for signs of life until a voice behind him said in a grizzled baritone, "Are you tonight's author?"

Artie flinched, then turned around to see a gaunt man about his age, suspenders holding up his thick corduroy pants and covering a gray sweatshirt, squinting at him aggressively.

"Yes," Artie said. "I'm the author. A little early, but I was antsy and in the area and thought it would be nice to come in out of the snow."

"No problem," the man said. "I'm Emmett. Let me show you where you'll be reading."

He led Artie around the tables of featured releases, mostly novels, through nonfiction and memoir, and into the back room, where roughly twenty folding chairs were set up facing a podium, surrounded by shelves of old books with brown and red spines.

"This is the antique books room, where we do readings. Feel free to hang out here until it starts. I'll be in the front if you need something."

"Thank you," Artie said. As he worked up the nerve to ask if Emmett had read *Four Squares*, the question was suddenly answered.

"What's your book called again?"

"*Four Squares*," Artie said.

"Right. That one. We've got a couple readings this week, wasn't sure which one you were. I see you brought books, good. You can pile them on that table in the front," Emmett said, disappearing around the corner and into the claustrophobic stacks.

Artie removed his scarf and coat and draped them over one of the chairs in the front row, then took a few deep breaths to warm himself up with the room's surprising heat. He unpacked the books and built them into a few different shapes before settling on four horizontal stacks of six upon which he placed one upright and fanned open. Of the remaining two, he put one on the podium for reading, and the second on a chair in the front row. Maybe, he thought, he'd give it to Emmett upon leaving. Or maybe he'd sell it. It wasn't an impossibility!

Beyond Abe, Adam, and Kim, he'd invited his agent and

editor, a bar full of people in Julius', his old RKS partner Annette, the attendees of his Monday ACT UP meetings, and his parents.

They hadn't spoken in years, but they must have received his letter. Since moving to New York City, he had written them once a week, despite never having gotten a response. If they wouldn't return his letters, if they would hang up the phone if he was on the other line, they would at least have to suffer his presence through the consistent arrival of a return address. Even if they never opened his notes, they would be reminded of his decisions and autonomy once a week. It was easy to imagine his father tossing them into the trash rather than showing them to his mother—that kind of hatred felt so primal and clear. More difficult was imagining them being read. Sometimes he'd picture his mother pulling one out from under a mess of food and used tissues, where it had been shoved far and away by his father, reading it in secret, and then choosing not to answer. He could understand a pure and fiery hatred, but silent, aching curiosity? A glimmer of residual love? It made him resent them even more. And it made him keep sending the letters.

"The book I told you about comes out in January," he wrote to them a few months prior in a note tucked into a padded envelope that also contained an advance copy of *Four Squares*. "I asked a bookshop in my neighborhood if they could host a signing for me on the day it's published, and they agreed." He gave them the address. The dates. The nearest train station. A list of cheap hotels in the neighborhood. He even offered to let them stay in his apartment while he crashed with a friend. But he never heard back, not even to say congratulations for doing something real with his life. He wondered if they even opened up the copy to see its handwritten inscription on the cover page, which was, though far from poetry, entirely pure. "For Mom and Dad."

Adam and Kim barged into the store with such force that they stripped the bells on the door of their capacity for melody, causing them to crash instead of ring. "We're here for the reading," he heard Kim say to Emmett, who told them to head into the back room.

"Congratulations, Arthur the author," they screamed upon entering the sacred little room. Artie covered his ears and laughed. They were holding balloons and flowers, both things Artie had begged them not to bring, but they looked so happy, so proud, so buoyant with love, that he forgave them their indiscretion and spread out his arms, inviting a group hug that they accepted without hesitation.

"You're the first ones here, so take the best seats in the house," Artie said, offering the front row with a wave of his hand.

"Where's Abe?" Kim asked.

"He told me he'd probably be here right before it started. Work's extra crazy, apparently."

"I feel like it's been crazy for months," Kim said, instantly regretting the tone and reverting to the chipper mood she entered with. "Where's your agent, what's-her-name? The straight one?"

"Nikki. I don't know, but she and my editor are the only two other people who have actually confirmed they're coming."

"Oh, whatever, it's still early," Adam said.

Artie noticed his eyes bulging, checking the time, and was

grateful that he didn't comment on the fact that it was mere minutes from showtime. Once they were seated and Artie stood uncomfortably at the podium, the front door swung open again, this time with less force, and Artie heard two voices he recognized chattering with Emmett. In seconds, in walked Nikki and Rebecca, Artie's editor, red-faced and stripping themselves of their coats as they coasted through the door.

"We made it!" Nikki shouted. "And I ran into this one on the train." She looked around at her surroundings and scoffed with surprise. "Wow, it's so nice in here. I've never been before."

Rebecca smiled politely and gave Artie a hug. "Congratulations," she said. "Big day." She spoke, as she always did, in a monotone, with the same cadence and volume for every mood and situation. When she'd offered to buy the book, when she told him what he needed to change, when she told him the first printing would be smaller than she'd anticipated, when she told him they wouldn't be providing any money for him to promote it around the country, everything was delivered with the same formal apathy, as if she were delivering a eulogy right after learning she had just two months left to live.

"Saved you some spots up front. Actually, I saved you the whole room," Artie said, trying to lighten his own mood. As Artie shuffled back to the front to find Emmett, his friends exchanged pleasantries with the two straight women, answering horrible questions like "How do you know each other?" and "What do you do?" in high-pitched half-truths, ones that deliberately precluded follow-up questions and masked the dreary origins of their collective friendship.

Artie found Emmett reading a small paperback of poetry at

the front desk and tapped on the corner delicately to get the man's attention, as though he would have otherwise been invisible.

"Everything OK back there?" Emmett asked.

"Actually, I was wondering if we could push the start to 7:30. Just want to make sure no one else shows up."

"Fine by me," he said. "As long as you're all out of here by eight. We close at eight." He never looked up from his book, a collection of poems by Mary Oliver that Artie had heard of but never read, but Artie was fixated on his face. Through the sparse tufts of hair falling over his forehead Artie could see a purple lesion and instantly felt a pang of sorrow and pity.

"Fine," Artie said with a newfound performative politeness. "We'll be out by eight for sure. Thank you again for hosting us. It's a perfect space. My favorite bookstore."

Emmett nodded and Artie heard the front door swing open. Abe burst in holding his briefcase and a bottle of champagne. "Author! Author!"

Artie beamed, then, afraid of Emmett's judgment, gestured for him to quiet down. He kissed Abe with less passion than both of them wanted, and pulled apart at the sound of Kim's clearing throat.

"We thought you'd never make it," she said.

"Busy day, but I'm here," Abe responded coolly.

"Is this stupid?" Artie asked the space between them, unsure of whom he wanted to respond. "It's practically empty."

"No," Kim finally said, breaking an uncomfortable few seconds of silence. "It's not stupid."

"Absolutely not," Abe said, overlapping her. "Now, get in there."

"Everyone in that room has already read it. It's not like I'm going to make any sales."

"We'll all buy second copies."

"And maybe even a third and a fourth and a fifth," Abe said.

"I appreciate that," Emmett said softly, eyes not leaving his book.

No one else came to hear Artie read the first chapter of *Four Squares*, or to hear Artie's friends each ask a question they already knew the answer to during the overly giggly Q&A portion, but Artie still found the evening successful. Even after offering the box of unsold books to Emmett, free of charge, to sell in the store, which were declined because they already had a single copy on the shelf, Artie was satisfied by the two hours he spent hiding from the cold and the snow outside. It was enough to see Abe and Kim and Adam there, cheering him on in a room surrounded by the voices of history, their history. It was enough to write "I couldn't have done this without you" in all their books and mean it with all of himself.

He gave Nikki and Rebecca a hug and thanked them for all their help, slightly worried they'd inquire as to where the celebration would be migrating, but to his relief (and mild offense) they waved goodbye without so much as alluding to an afterparty. Once they were on the other side of the door, out where the snow had finally stopped falling, he turned to his friends and asked with a wink, "Julius'?"

As they put on their coats in the cramped stacks, where not a single customer had come to browse during the reading, Artie approached Emmett, who was nearing the end of his book of poems. "Emmett? I wanted to thank you again for everything tonight. And if you don't have plans, you're more than welcome to come with me and my friends for some drinks over at Julius'."

Emmett looked up from the book and squinted at Artie. He tightened his jaw and then bit the inside of his cheek. "That's quite kind of you, but I think I'll just be heading home tonight."

Artie nodded. "Sure. Well, thanks again. And here," he said, dropping a copy of *Four Squares* on the desk. "For you, not the store. I'm sure you have plenty to read, but if you feel like giving it a go, maybe you'll enjoy it."

Emmett looked down at the book and turned the cover to face him. Artie felt he was looking at it for the first time, reading the cover like it was its own piece of art.

FOUR

SQUARES

A novel

Arthur Anderson

For the first time Artie noticed a kind of poetry to the cover design, and he was moved by all that it communicated about him and the novel in just six words.

"Thank you," Emmett said. "I'm looking forward to it. Congratulations, by the way."

Artie nodded and tapped on the desk twice as a kind of goodbye. What more was there for the two of them to say?

"Hey," Adam said, grabbing Artie by the shoulder, breaking the spell of the moment. "Just grab a table and we'll meet you there. Kim and I have to run back to the apartment real quick."

"Why?" Artie said, smiling coyly.

"You'll have to wait and see, bitch!"

And off they went, leaving Abe and Artie alone at the door. The two of them walked a block in silence before Abe finally told Artie how proud he was, but Artie was too distracted by his own anxieties to accept the compliment.

"Why were you so late?" he asked, stopping in front of a beautiful brownstone on Gay Street.

"I told you, work's crazy."

"Don't turn me into someone ridiculous, Abe. Don't turn me into the person my friends already think I am."

"What do you mean?"

"Vanessa. If you were with her, you need to tell me. If all these 'crazy' work nights have been her, you *need to tell me*." Abe shut his eyes and took a deep breath. "Don't lie to me."

"I didn't want to do this here."

"Jesus Christ, Abe," Artie said, burying his face in his shivering hands.

"What we have is so complicated, Artie. You wouldn't understand the way we grew—"

"Life is fucking complicated, Abe. Everyone's life. Not just yours. Not just Vanessa's. So you don't get a free pass to lie to me over and over and over again. Goddamn it, so you *were* with her. I knew it!"

"But I came!"

"Only because I delayed it."

"I'm here now!"

"Were you late because you were fucking her?"

Abe turned his gaze from Artie, took two deep breaths, and

looked back. Artie's eyes hadn't moved in the slightest from the direction of their skepticism.

"No. Not tonight."

"But you have. Recently. Since you said you'd stop."

"Yes."

Artie gritted his teeth and squeezed his eyes shut, activating every muscle in his face. "I knew it! I knew it and I didn't say anything because I didn't want to be *that* person," he said, opening his eyes, now red and watering. "Does she even know about me? Does she know about *you*?"

"No."

"Great, so you're lying to two people. Does she think you want to marry her? Do you want to marry her?"

"I don't know what I want, Artie, that's the whole fucking problem. It's been the whole fucking problem for my entire fucking life! I didn't think I wanted to be in a relationship with anyone until I met you."

Artie nearly succumbed to the beautiful weight of Abe's admission but shook himself out from under it. "I know you think of *this place* as where you come when you want to get off, but people live their whole lives here. They die here. They can't just take the 2 train uptown and play house. I can't. You think you're the only one who doesn't know what they want? You think you're the only one who met someone at a bar one night who changed everything they thought they knew about themselves? Fuck you for being so selfish."

"Artie, can we talk about this at your place?"

"No! My *friends* are throwing me a party. God," Artie said, almost laughing. "Do you know how many conversations I have had with them about this? Do you know how many times I've told them they're cruel for expecting the worst from you? Do you know how completely fucking ridiculous I feel right now?"

Abe shook his head.

"Of course you don't, you don't have any friends. All you have is a handful of people who have no idea who you really are because you've never told anyone the truth. Anyway, thanks for choosing to do this to me on this particular night. Great timing, as usual."

When Abe grabbed Artie's shoulder to keep him from walking away, Artie brushed it off like it was a mere dusting of snow, something that didn't even require a glance. "Please don't follow me," he said before starting off to Julius' without turning around. He thought it sounded like Abe was crying, though he'd never actually seen him do so, but knowing that empathy would get the best of him prevented him from checking.

After rounding the corner, unable to stop imagining Abe's own tears, Artie collapsed on the first available stoop and poured out some of his own. He stared blankly across the street and just sobbed, unbothered by the number of people passing by and pretending not to notice his misery. He cried until the crying stopped, and then, after a few deep breaths he hoped would close up his tear ducts, used his scarf to wipe all evidence of pain from his face. Once inside Julius', he made a beeline for the bathroom and splashed his face with cold water, hoping the redness in his eyes would subside at least a little, before his friends arrived. A short while later Kim arrived on her own, claiming that Adam got held up with something at the apartment. They sat in the back of the bar, where it was quieter and more conducive to conversation.

Artie told her Abe had to run back to the office for what would certainly be an all-nighter, and that an hour away from work was the best he could do. Simply making it to the reading was a huge sacrifice, Artie assured her, and there's no way he could have spent the night drinking in Julius' while the other associates were trapped in Midtown. His explanation was met without too much concern, and after they jointly recapped the event—specifically the strange allure of Emmett—Artie demanded the subject be changed to anything but himself and his stupid book. Kim told him about the first half of their evening, how she and Adam had an early dinner at Shanghai Lee followed by a quick drink at the Henrietta Hudson, where Kim was asked to make an appearance by someone named Billie whom she'd gone on a date with the night before.

"Drop by Henrietta's tomorrow night or I'll die," the gorgeous redhead told her in bed some eighteen hours before. "Even if you can only stay for ninety seconds, let me inhale you for as long as I can."

Kim told Artie that Adam stood across from her at the bar, sucking down his drink as quickly as he could before stares from the other women began melting his skin, as Kimberly did as she was told. She told Artie that it was sort of thrilling to be worshipped so openly and passionately in front of them.

"Well, she seems nice," Artie said when the story was over.

"'He,' actually. Billie prefers to go by 'he.'"

"OK, well, *he* seems nice. And you seem very happy. But I appreciate you choosing me over him tonight."

"It was tough, believe me. It was extremely tough."

"Let me get us a drink first," Artie said. "The drunker I get, the less I'll be able to resist all my friends paying for my *celebratory drinks*," he said with a slathering of sass. "What do you want? Gin and tonic?"

"Whatever you're having," Kim said.

After ordering, he scanned the bar and saw Brian and Todd and a bunch of other weeknight regulars, no one cute enough to ignore his best friends over, and then, right beside him, grazing his shoulder, a man in all black with his face in a book. Artie shivered and felt the blood pumping in his neck with intention. For half a second, he was certain it was Abraham, but upon further examination, he saw it was just a normal person. Someone he didn't hope to see atop every stool in every bar in the neighborhood. Someone he didn't love. The man—he was quite handsome now that Artie had a moment to consider him as someone new—caught Artie's staring and cleared his throat.

"Can I help you?" he said, shutting the book and holding the page with his pointer finger.

"Oh, no, sorry," Artie said. "I thought you were someone else for a second. But you're not! You're you."

"I am me," the man said. "And who are you?"

Artie grabbed his gin and tonics, dropped cash on the bar, and said, as gently as he could muster, "I'm so sorry for interrupting you."

The man rolled his eyes and opened the book back up. Artie almost wished him luck but thought it best not to push his own.

Artie and Kim weren't halfway through their drinks when they heard a familiar voice screaming through the bar noise.

"Everyone give my friend Artie Anderson a round of applause," he shouted, stealing the attention of everyone in the bar, all of whom did as they were told while Adam marched toward his friends in the back. Artie erupted in tears and laughter as he watched Adam, delicately holding both sides of a sheet-pan-sized cake, approaching him as every patron applauded with their whole heart despite not knowing why.

Once the cake was set down and filling more than half the table, Artie was finally able to read what had been written in icing: "To our favorite author, Our Favorite Arthur."

"If you're gonna bring in cake, you'd better offer me a slice," the bartender screamed at Adam.

"I'll give you anything you want, Orlando. You know that," Adam fired back.

"This is so beautiful," Artie said after hugging his friends. "I want a slice right now. But what will we do about plates?"

Adam pulled out a stack of paper plates from the tote on his shoulder, then a box of plastic forks. "I always come prepared," he said. "Let me get us another round of drinks and we'll dig in."

Artie watched Adam order at the bar, and noticed his laser focus on the task at hand. Adam didn't give the meat market around him a once-over as he usually did, and didn't so much as count the number of people seated on the stools at the bar. To him, Artie thought, the man to his right, the anonymous non-Abe reading man, was as good as a ghost. And he felt a sudden warmth for his friend as he returned with drinks for the three of them. He had come for his friends and no one else. The affection only grew as he watched Adam slice the perfect cake into perfect squares, revealing a yellow cake with perfect crumble beneath the chocolate frosting. It was Artie's favorite combination, something he couldn't remember telling Adam but knew that he must have. Something Adam remembered and Artie didn't. He wondered how many of those memories existed between them, the ones that only one side took the time to file away, and felt a nebulous pang of guilt.

A couple of hours into their revelry, after all the cake had been doled out to various queers around them, the misery hit. He knew it would eventually; it was a misery that never missed—or made—an appointment, but it arrived later than normal, which was the sign of a good night—and one the misery had to come ruin.

In the middle of a conversation about Nikki's and Rebecca's "hysterical heterosexuality," as Kimberly put it, Artie put his head in his hands and pulled at his hair for a few silent moments before sitting back upright. "It's always so strange to realize I'm actually having a nice night. Remember when it was all we could talk about?"

The others shut up and turned to their friend, his hair suddenly a mess. They all knew "it" wasn't just one thing. They knew it was the plague. They knew it was death. They knew it was misery. Koch and Reagan. ACT UP and Larry. Waylon. They knew it was the entirety of their anxieties since arriving in New York City at a moment when people in their community began dying of a plague that no one outside seemed to care about.

"Now it's just there. Still buzzing, but it's sort of like we've stopped swatting at it. It's just this white noise we've gotten used to. Remember Derek and J.C. and Miguel and Kevin and

Kyle and Dominic and Marcus and Rob? Marissa? Yvonne? How do we just watch movies and get drunk and eat fried rice and go to work every day when it's still going on?"

"What's the alternative?" Adam asked with a bold, drunken authority. "You want us to just stay angry all the time?"

"Yes! Stay angry *all the time*! Fight *all the time*! Quit all of our bullshit jobs and go back to organizing and protesting 24/7, like we used to. We may as well quit fucking each other, too."

"I mean, we absolutely could," Adam said, shrugging. "Plenty of people do. They stop fucking. They make the cause their full-time job. A combination of the two. Are you saying that's what you want?"

Artie laughed at the words about to come out of his mouth, thinking again of the argument with Abe. "I don't know what I want. But I'm done, really. I'm not going to cause a scene, I'm just tired. I know you all are, too. And I know we're all dealing with everything differently. It's just, having a party for a book I wrote about the four of us that only three of us will ever be able to read feels so fucking unfair. The memorial services have slowed down but haven't stopped. It's just unfair to be celebrating in the back of Julius'. It's unfair to feel happy at all. None of us deserve it."

"That's exactly what we deserve," Adam said. "That's exactly what everyone deserved. They deserved to be happy and healthy and not shit on by this bullshit world."

"I know you're right," Artie said, his body falling more limp and more unwilling to keep itself upright. "But it still feels like we're disrespecting everyone we lost. Everyone we're still losing."

"So are you going to take that vow of chastity and charity?"

"Honestly? Maybe."

"OK, so if you do, what then? You're going to stop seeing Abe? You forgo any kind of pleasure until when exactly? Until people stop getting it? Until there's a cure?"

"No. Until I feel like I've done enough."

Enough. They all privately considered what it meant. If there was a universal answer. Something objective. Or if it meant something different to each of them, and if that was OK. Enough. Was it allowed to change as they did? As the city around them did? Was it allowed to change as their attempts to make change were rejected or whittled down? Was it allowed to change because so many people refused to? Their relationship with "enough" was not something they'd ever spoken about until now, though it was a thought that came to them in their darkest, quietest hours. They'd all done enough to survive— their literal survival was proof of that—but had they done enough to make sure survival was a guarantee? Since their lives had incrementally begun to improve, since their careers had started sprouting roots, and their sex lives had returned to some degree, they found themselves wondering more often. But only Waylon had answered that definitively. No. He had not done enough.

It wasn't how the night was supposed to end, but it's how the night ended anyway. They lived in a world filled with people equally accustomed to disappointment and sudden left turns. And when Adam and Artie hugged on the corner they shared, both of them were surprised by how long their bodies remained stuck together, how quickly their heartbeats synced up.

"I'm sorry for how I've been," Artie said, still tucked snugly in the crook of Adam's neck. "I'm so lucky to have you in my life."

"Ditto," Adam said, a tear falling down his cheek. "So don't apologize. Please. You have nothing to apologize for."

Artie pulled away from Adam's grip.

"How many years has it been since the last time?"

Adam sighed. "I don't know. A few."

"So do you want to come up?"

"Artie," Adam said, taking a step back. "I think you should get some sleep. You've had a wild day."

"OK, fine," Artie said. "Whatever you say. I just miss you sometimes."

"I'm always right down the street," Adam said, stuffing his hands in his pockets. "Love you dearly."

"Love you dearly."

Artie collapsed on his bed after brushing his teeth and woke up nine full hours later. The next morning, he spent his time in the shower regretting his behavior and unpacking his feelings about Adam. Did he actually want to sleep with him, or was he just directing his anger at Abe toward a nearby source of potential pleasure? He picked up the phone and dialed his friend, and started speaking the moment he heard Adam answer.

"Morning, it's me."

"Feeling better?"

"Feeling fine," Artie said. "I just wanted to apologize for how I ended the night."

"I was wondering if you'd remember that."

"I do, and I'm embarrassed. Thanks for taking care of me despite my ridiculous behavior."

"Don't be embarrassed, babe," Adam said. "Life's too short."

"For the record, and I say this in the kindest way possible, I don't want to sleep with you again. I was just angry at Abe."

"For the record, I don't want to sleep with you, either, and I'm angry at Abe, too. More importantly, I need to get a bite to eat."

"Me too."

"Just buzz me whenever, I'll come down."

His life was, from some angles, in total shambles, with the rubble of recent romantic and career disappointments still steaming front and center. Wasn't it wonderful, he thought then, that he had at least two people who always seemed to make everything so damned easy?

8

2022

THE FIRST TIME Artie entered the GALS center, he had contorted his body in a way that's all too familiar to residents and
employees of old folks' homes, one that's not dissimilar from
the way a person sinks into themselves when entering a hospital.
Some may chalk it up to a fear of death, or an unwillingness to
confront one's mortality, but the ugly truth is that it's more to
do with shame. Artie, like any child visiting their dying grandmother in a stale-smelling hospital wing, felt as though he
shouldn't be seeing these people, these pitiful older people, as
they went on with what was left of their lives in their crumbling
little bodies. His shoulders fell. His head collapsed an inch or so
toward the ground. His whole body seemed narrower.

But when he walked into the dining hall on the first Monday
of November, he stood more erect. He took up more space. He
overcompensated for his brokenness—that obvious physical

brokenness—by assuming the personality of someone who had no idea that they were broken. The sadness in his eyes began to disappear and was replaced with the barely visible existential worry that was always there. He wasn't put off by the larger-than-normal crowd. If he had to explain who he was to another member, he'd use a well-rehearsed introduction. If he had to make small talk, he would do so with a smile. And if he had to answer a question about his injury, he would tell them the full truth. He was briefly a volunteer, but then he fell, and now he's here. By the time he made it through the trenches of the drinks station to Jim's table, one of two with an open seat—and the only with Carson—he had done all three.

"Hello, hello," Jim said as Artie set his plate down at the seat beside him. "Wasn't sure if we'd ever see you again."

"Why's that?" Artie said, unwrapping a pat of butter for his slice of bread.

"You're a baby! Babies get nervous their first time. They feel like they don't belong. Plus, you didn't come to the Halloween party. Second best party of the year."

"What's first? VE Day?"

"Jim's talking about New Year's Eve, but I personally prefer the Oscar party."

Artie snapped his head toward the new voice. Short and round, with a head of untamable, unkempt hair, he reminded Artie of a frightening English literature professor he hadn't thought about in decades.

"Ellis," he said. "I know you're Artie. New guy. Fell off a damned ladder."

"We met before it all went black. I remember."

169

Ellis nodded once, a brash, almost military-like snap of the neck. "Nice to see you, too."

"So I looked nervous? I thought I was hiding it pretty well."

"You weren't hiding shit," Ellis said. "But I'm glad you're over it now because we're all in the same boat here. Sooner you recognize that, the better."

"Listen to Ellis," Jim said. "He's the wisest one here."

"Bullshit. I'm just old. And none of us are wise."

Artie glanced at Ellis and tried to guess his age—over seventy, maybe even eighty, though, Christ, what if he were only sixty-eight or sixty-nine? Artie had always had such a hard time guessing the ages of his elders, as if all of them were exactly the same kind of old. When he was a child, adults of all ages blurred together into a single amorphous version of grown up. A therapist had once suggested this was likely due to his being an only child, with no one in the house close to him in age to help him figure out what it means to be a little older or a little younger. Artie shook his head and said, "I don't think that sounds right." He never liked Dr. Beichmann.

Artie spent the bulk of his meal listening and smiling, trying not to seem too eager for attention. He nodded and laughed, did as much active listening as possible, and when asked questions about his own life, he responded succinctly and without flourish. Was he single? Yes. Ever married? No. Live alone? Yes. What does he do? Writer, books. Boring stuff, nothing you've read. He decided to ease into the reveals. Besides, he was more interested in everyone else's stories, and when Jim mentioned their regular movie night, he couldn't contain his excitement. Perhaps too much.

"Wait, it's not the GALS one?"

Ellis scowled at him. "We exist outside this place, kid. Just like you."

"Of course you do," Artie said, trying to mask his discomfort with a laugh. "I just thought it sounded fun. My friends and I used to have a standing movie night, but that was forever ago."

"Well, then, you should come to our next one."

Carson raised his hand. "Am I invited, too?"

"Why not, we could use more fresh meat."

"That would be great. What are we watching?"

"Oh, we don't decide until the night of, so I hope you enjoy a little mystery."

"A little is exactly how much mystery I enjoy."

Ellis smiled and turned to Artie. "So what happened to yours?"

"My movie nights?" Artie's eyes darted around the space in front of him as he considered how to respond. "It's a long story. And not exactly the most pleasant one."

"Ah," Ellis said. "Well, we've all got plenty of those."

Artie nodded. "Saturday nights?"

"Not all, but most. We usually decide by midweek. I miss the days when planning ahead could be done with a little more confidence," Ellis said with a sigh. "Let me write down the address. Six p.m. Movie starts at seven p.m. sharp. Actually, I'm lying. Movie starts eventually."

"Can't wait."

"Surprised a young man like you doesn't already have plans on a Saturday night."

"Oh, I'm sure you all live more exciting lives than I do, believe me. I haven't been on a proper date in years," he said, suddenly worried he was revealing too much about himself to his new friends.

Jim cleared his throat and cocked his head. "'Proper' meaning what, dinner? A movie? Foreplay? Sex party?"

Artie shrugged and gave Carson a nervous glance he hoped would not be noticed. "All of the above. I'll use the apps every once in a while, when I work up the courage, have an awkward encounter, and then another few months will pass before I'm ready to try again."

"Do they ever want to see you again?"

"Sometimes."

"And you tell them no?"

"Yes. But lately I sort of feel like I'm more open to the idea."

Ellis couldn't help but chime in. "Why's that?"

Artie almost guffawed. *Why?* What kind of question was that? How was he supposed to articulate the irrational inner workings of his clearly messed-up brain to near strangers over salmon, mixed vegetables that leaned too heavily on corn kernels, and a hunk of French bread?

"Why? Well. I don't know."

"Guess."

"OK, well, when my partner died, I didn't feel like getting attached to anyone else. Then time passed, and I got comfortable with being on my own. Then it just stuck."

Jim took back the reins. "That sounds incomplete."

"Oh, does it?"

"It's either incomplete or it's a total lie. You mentioned a niece earlier. Or niece figure. Whatever. When did she come into the picture?"

"Eighteen years ago, when she was six."

"And when did she leave it?"

"Just before this," he said, pointing at his healing foot.

Jim held his hands up in a kind of triumphant shrug. "So there you have it. How often did you see this niece?"

"Halle."

"How often did you see Halle?"

"When she was growing up, every Sunday. Once she went to college, in the city, every few months or so. Birthdays. Holidays."

"So you two were close?"

"I think we still are. We text now that she's gone. It's always been hard to get her on the phone."

"And you wanted to keep her there."

Artie squinted. He wanted to hear Jim take his theory all the way through to the end.

"If you're seeing someone, bringing them home, talking about them, answering calls from them, thinking about them, she'd have noticed. And you would have worried that she'd think she was no longer your number one priority."

Artie shrugged. "I guess that's not far off."

"So how'd you know this girl, if she wasn't family? Something to do with your ex, the one who died?" Ellis asked with a casual tone that made Artie feel a little crazy.

"Abraham. She was his daughter."

"And when he died, she had you."

"She also had—*has*—a stepfather."

"A mother, a late father, a stepfather, and you."

"Exactly," Artie said. "How do you know my life story before I got any of yours?"

Jim laughed. "What do you want to know? He's an open book."

"Where were you born?"

"Long Island." Ellis said.

"Where on Long Island?"

"Hicksville. Grew up in Patchogue."

"When did you move to the city?"

"I moved after high school. For college. City University."

"What'd you study?"

"I feel like I'm on a first date."

Artie laughed. "OK, no more biographical bullet points. You can print me out a résumé later. What made you decide to join GALS?"

"I was bored."

"What made you bored?"

"What do you mean, what made me bored? I was bored."

"Were you always bored, or did you become bored?"

"I became bored."

Artie nodded, hoping Ellis would continue.

"My best friend died."

"And then you joined GALS."

"And then I did nothing for a whole year."

"Nothing?"

"Literally nothing. I didn't leave my house."

Artie tried to imagine Ellis, the most taciturn, no-nonsense person he'd met in years—not just at GALS—alone in an apartment, with no one around to amuse or bemoan. He was a man who seemed to need other people like other people needed sunlight. He was powered by their presence, by their stories, to the extent that Artie assumed he'd power down and die if left alone for more than a few days, like a house cat trapped in a room without food and water.

"A year," Carson said, finally joining the conversation. "How awful."

"It was and it wasn't," Ellis said. "Rent control. Running water. Meal deliveries. Eventually I got Netflix, thanks to the kid who moved in next door. He was a student, checked on me sometimes, offered to pick up anything I needed, connected my television to his internet and his Netflix account."

"Nice of him."

"It was, until he moved out."

"Young people don't know how to stay put. It's exhausting."

"He said he'd keep in touch. Left his phone number. I gave him mine," Ellis said, shaking his head.

"But he never did," Artie said declaratively, as though he knew the young man himself.

"They love to drop in, don't they," Jim said. "They love to say, 'I'm here for you. I can get you groceries. I can run your errand. I can take you somewhere.' And they do! And when they do, it's nice! But you know what else they love to do? They love to disappear."

"Eh, I don't have it in for them. Not really," Ellis said. "Plenty of people don't even want to pretend to give a damn. It was just embarrassing to know that when Kevin left—that was his name, Kevin—I was helpless."

"You weren't helpless."

"I was pretty damned close!"

"Because you lost your independence?"

"No, because I didn't have any goddamned Netflix anymore! Didn't have no goddamned internet at all! The television was stuck on NY1! Still is."

"So that's why you came to GALS. Because you lost Netflix."

"It's as good a reason as any, right?"

"I guess so."

"What about you, Jim?" Artie asked.

"Oh, you want another sob story after that one? I didn't know you were such a masochist, Mr. Anderson."

"I just want to get your full stories! You know mine."

"I don't even think we've cracked the *surface* with you."

"Well, you know more about me than I know about you."

"Fine, I've been coming here for twenty years."

Jim watched as Artie quickly did the math in his head.

"And yes," he said. "That means I'm eighty-five years old. I know I don't look a day over fifty."

"It's true."

"Now ask how long it's been since I've gotten laid."

"How long has it been since you've gotten lai—"

"Twenty years."

"Oh, I don't believe that."

"Laid badly? Seven or eight. Laid *well*? A full twenty. But it still works, I check every damn day! Why don't people seem to believe that it still works?"

"So what was it that happened twenty years ago?"

"My mother had a stroke. She lived with me back then. Had to put her in an assisted living home. And not a good one, either."

"How long did she live there?"

"She didn't make it a year. But once she was gone, when it was just me, the house felt empty. I didn't have anyone to cook for anymore. No one to talk to about who was getting on my nerves. So I came here."

"You needed somewhere to gossip?"

"Basically."

Artie raised his glass of water up to the group. "Well, I'm always here to receive what you're willing to give."

Jim shrugged. "I was never much of a top," he said.

"You've been awfully silent throughout all of this," Artie said, turning to Carson.

"There was so much to take in, that's all," he said, his face turning a dull shade of pink.

"What's your story?"

"Where do you want me to start?"

"Wherever works."

"I was a teacher," Carson said. "I was a teacher for a long time. At a private school, then a public school, then a private school again. Then my partner, Roger—we never married—died."

"Cancer?" Artie asked.

"Brain. Sudden. There was nothing they could do once they found it, but I don't think there's any conceivable world where they would have found it earlier."

"I'm sorry."

"Thank you. But he didn't suffer much, and he had just enough time to say goodbye to everyone he loved. And he loved and loved. He loved more than I ever could."

"That's all you can ask for, isn't it?"

"I guess," Carson said, staring down at his long-empty plate. "We had this big life together. People everywhere, friends all over the country, all over the world, stuff to do every weekend and most weeknights. But when Roger died, I realized they were all his."

"The friends?"

"Yeah. They kept in touch for a little bit. Brought me food and paid for a house-cleaning service and gave me gift cards for delivery stuff. Sometimes they asked how I was, but I could tell they didn't really want to know. None of them were the same. I didn't recognize them anymore. Then I realized Roger was this kind of interpreter throughout our entire relationship, and now that he's gone I don't know the language well enough to get back in their circle. And I don't really know that I want to."

"That's a good metaphor."

"I know, stole it from my therapist."

Jim cleared his throat. "So that's why you decided to go to GALS?"

"Oh, no, I didn't decide to go to GALS. My therapist decided that for me. Embarrassing, I know."

"It's not," Artie said, resisting the urge to give him a friendly pat on the knee. "I should probably start seeing one again."

"You don't have a therapist?"

Artie shook his head. "Therapy and I didn't really get along. You think I should give it another shot?"

"I'm pretty sure everyone who goes to therapy thinks everyone needs to go to therapy, so yes. I don't know where I'd be without mine. He suggested GALS a month or so after Roger died. I didn't want to go at first. I thought it would make me feel old, which I am, but he told me to give it a shot. It was my *homework*. Said having platonic relationships with new queer men could be helpful. Maybe even healing."

"We're more like old queer men," Artie quipped, and when Carson laughed, he smiled. "Did you even try with the old friends? Roger's?"

Carson straightened his back and clenched his jaw. "What do you mean?"

"I mean, did you really want to be friends with them? Did you try to speak their language after Roger died? Or did you kind of, maybe deep down, want to start all over?"

Carson relaxed and became overcome with an exhilarating uncertainty. "That's a good question. That's a really good question. Maybe. Either way, I think coming to GALS was the right move."

"Can I ask when he died?"

"In June. Now you can ask if I think that's long enough to properly mourn."

"Believe me, I would never ask that."

"Thank you."

"Well, I'll be damned if this wasn't the most emotional dinner conversation we've had since Martin was alive," Ellis said.

"Who was Martin?"

"Martin Magnussen. Maybe you know the name. Broadway actor. Loved attention, loved to get people fired up, and made these big emotional speeches."

"I must have seen him in something once."

"I'm sure you did. We lost him last year. Natural causes, can you believe it? That's all the doctors said. 'Natural causes.' Sort of like dying of a miracle."

As the others sank in their chairs, accessing memories of their late friend, a click-clack of heels grew louder and eventually stopped when the noise felt as though it were right behind Artie.

"All right, who died?"

"Martin," Jim said.

"That was months ago, and he'd hate to see you all choked up over him when you should all be telling jokes about poppers," Annabelle sneered before shoving a chair into the space between Artie and Carson.

Artie scanned her outfit as she adjusted herself beside him, marveling at the volume of every item, from the shimmering black pumps on her feet to the four scrunchies holding her halo of curly gray hair out of her face and behind her head like a salt-and-pepper shrub. Her style was loud, louder than anyone else's at GALS, but never to the point of wanting to turn her down. She brought a much-needed aesthetic intensity to the room and, Artie assumed, to the center itself. While so many people, himself included, tended to lower their sartorial saturation as they aged, sinking into either black and white or full-on sepia, Annabelle seemed like she must have a walk-in closet filled with a representative of every possible shade—an infinite supply of tops and bottoms and overs and underneaths—not to mention all the chunky jewelry and accessories to finish off every look. She claimed to have been photographed by Bill Cunningham over a thousand times, and a quick search of her name in the *New York Times* archives made it clear that her exaggeration probably wasn't too far from the truth. The only constant in her wardrobe, beyond its ability to stop traffic—or at least a gentle photographer on a bicycle, oh, how she wished Bill were still alive—were her glasses: a pair of glossy yellow pentagons connected at the bridge by a blue arch.

"I love your glasses," Artie said. "But I'm sure you get that all the time."

"You assume right," she said in a near shout, as if a boom mic only she could see was hovering in the space just above them. "When I die, I'm being cremated, but I'm also getting a coffin made just for these."

Artie laughed.

"You think I'm joking."

Artie actually gulped. "You're going to bury your glasses? Not even a full outfit?"

"Darling, my clothes will be archived. Maybe even put on display in a gallery. I've had calls with the Met."

"You have not," Jim said.

"Everyone wants a piece of my closet. *Architectural Digest* did a tour of it some years ago, just Google it. You'll see. But what everyone wants most of all are the glasses."

"And you don't want to give them away?"

"It's either burn them or bury them, and I'd much rather my own flesh and bone turn to ash than these glasses."

"Where'd you get them?"

Annabelle's gasp was loud, but Jim's and Ellis's were even louder. "Arthur!"

"I prefer Artie."

"I prefer Arthur. Arthur! I know we haven't known each other long, but that is one secret that I'll take to the grave."

"Or the kiln."

"Ha! Yes, exactly! The kiln! You're funny. You should be a writer."

"I am one."

"Of course you are, darling. I have a way with guessing that sort of thing—what people do, I mean. How they live. How they work. But I'm afraid I cannot tell you where I got these glasses. I cannot tell that to anyone. My life is a matter of public record, darling, for better or worse. Has been for eighty-two years. But I believe one should keep at least one secret just for oneself. A secret you don't tell your partner, your priest, or your therapist. Drove my first husband mad. Didn't seem to matter to my second, which is part of the reason we divorced."

Artie laughed. There was something about the booming mid-Atlantic theatricality of Annabelle's affect that made chatting with her feel like you were watching a talking head in a documentary. There was no way she could be in a room without being the main character in every story, and she spoke as if providing narration to all of them at the same time.

"I'm sorry for interrupting all of you, but I'm here to extend an invitation. I'm going to have a little party in a few weeks and thought it would be such a delight if all of you came."

"Isn't it rude to invite us within earshot of everyone else?"

"But I'm inviting everyone else! It's been too long since I've had a proper party for the center, and this seems like the perfect time. Knee-deep into fall but not quite Thanksgiving."

"Since we missed Halloween, I assume it's not a costume party."

"Everything I've ever worn is a costume, daaarling."

With that, she stomped away and back toward her table, which she typically shared with Gene, Helen, and Jazmine, Jim had explained earlier that evening, arguably the three most timid dinner regulars.

"How big is her apartment?" Artie asked, still vibrating from Annabelle's presence.

"Let me put it this way," Ellis said. "When you ask how to get to the bathroom, take notes."

"Her apartment could hold everyone who comes to GALS, but not that many people ever actually come, they're too intimidated," Jim said. "It's why she invites the whole damn place, because three-quarters of them have no interest in showing up."

Artie turned to Carson. "Do you have any interest?"

"Oodles," Carson said.

"I'll go if all of you go," Jim said. "Ellis?"

"I'll go if all of you go. Artie?"

Artie turned back to Jim and Ellis, both of them leaning toward him in anticipation of an affirmative, then back at Carson. "I'm in," he said.

Jim offered Artie an approving nod that felt like a jolt of caffeine.

· · ● · ·

THE FOUR OF them rode the elevator down together after dinner service and stood outside, a few steps from the building's entrance, huddled on a part of the sidewalk covered in cigarette butts. "Well, that was nice," Carson said.

"You boys coming over for movie night on Saturday, or was that just a bunch of hot air?" Ellis said.

"I'll be there with bells on," Artie said.

"Me too, but I lost my bells," Carson said, stone-faced.

Jim gestured his head toward the subway entrance up the block. "Everyone taking the train home?"

Nervous to let them see the precarious way he hobbled down and out of the subway station with his scooter and unwilling to suffer the embarrassment of the assistance Carson would certainly offer—an air of politeness was a central part of his musk—Artie told them he would be rolling home. "I could use a walk," he said. For a moment he worried Carson would ask to join him, as they were both headed south. "And a think."

"Part of your creative process?" Carson asked.

"Ha. I don't know. Maybe. See you all this weekend?"

Ellis and Jim saluted and turned toward the subway, but Carson lingered for a few seconds, his face contorting into something between a skeptical smile and wanton stare. "See you Saturday," he finally said. "Get home safe."

Artie zigzagged toward home, thinking about his new friends and the sudden appearance of two social events on his calendar, until his broken foot began to throb. Upstairs, he took a seated shower with his entombed leg dangling out of the bathtub and, for the first time, didn't take note of its awkwardness. There was too much else for him to think about, and this once difficult and clumsy way of bathing had become routine.

A text from Halle littered with questions was waiting for him when he sat down on the edge of his bed.

> How's the foot? Thanksgiving plans? Will
> you be in the city?

Artie hoped she was still at her phone and started typing out a response.

> Foot's good! Healing nicely, I think. No
> plans for Thanksgiving yet and no reason to
> travel, but I'm looking forward to it.

He stared at the phone, hoping for a bubble indicating Halle was typing out a response would soon appear, but his message seemed to go unseen. Maybe she and Nolan were eating dinner. Maybe they were watching TV. Maybe she was looking out the window of her new home and rubbing her growing belly, thinking about how long it would take for her to stop being struck dumb by the view.

He placed the phone on his nightstand and plugged it in, screen side down, stood up, and hopped to his desk in the corner of the room. With his computer tucked into his armpit, he hopped 180 degrees and returned to his bed, where he propped himself up—back against the headboard and broken foot on the medical pillow—and flipped open the screen. In bed but not tired, content in his silence but also craving a story, Artie began catching up with Peter and George and Patricia and David as the next chapter of their lives appeared onscreen, word by word. How nice it was to see them again.

9

―・。◉。・―

1994

IT DIDN'T TAKE long for Artie to realize *Four Squares* was a disappointment. He never saw it displayed on a table at the Strand, and was certain the copy propped up in the window at Oscar Wilde Memorial Bookshop was the only one they'd had in stock for half a year.

"How could you possibly know that for sure?" Kimberly asked him one mopey Friday evening as they smoked on his fire escape.

"Because I marked the inside cover with a red dot six months ago, when I started to suspect no one was buying it."

"So you vandalized your favorite bookstore."

Artie tried to explain that it's not technically vandalism if it's done to your own work of art, but Kimberly pointed out

each of the flaws in his argument in the span of a single cigarette.

"I love you, Artie, I love you dearly, but you have to move
on. Not every book can be a bestseller, which is precisely why
people care about that list. Think about that. You wrote a
book that people can buy, if they choose to. Fuck, man. That's
incredible."

"I never wanted it to be a bestseller," Artie shouted, embarrassing himself in the process. He quieted down, took another
drag. "I never wanted it to be a bestseller. Hand to god, I knew
it wouldn't be. It's about us, it's about some fucking faggots.
Regular people aren't going to break down doors to get a copy,
I just wanted more of—this is so dumb—I just wanted more of
my people to read it."

He was rambling, but Kimberly could cut through his buzz
to hear the ache and passion behind it. "Your people did read it.
I read it. All of us did."

"You know what I mean."

"I'm not sure I do," Kimberly said, rubbing Artie's knee.
"You did something amazing. Full stop."

"I understand that. I do. I am genuinely in awe every time I
see it on my shelf or in the window of Oscar Wilde, even if it's
just collecting dust." Artie gripped the rusty rail to his left and
adjusted his stance. "How's what's-his-name?"

Kimberly held the lighter to her mouth. "His name is Billie.
And that's over. But it's fine. Fine as always."

"What happened?"

A spark, a flame, a drag. Kimberly shook her head as she let
the smoke fumble out of her mouth and back into her nose. "He

said he's not ready for a relationship right now, which is essentially saying nothing."

Artie was only a casual smoker, but privately hoped Kimberly, who had smoked a pack a day since well before they met, would never quit simply because he took such pleasure in watching her do it. He looked at her and saw the Marlboro Man's more alluring sister—the embodiment of everything that made tobacco companies salivate and surgeons general quiver—and wondered how anyone could ever find a reason to break up with her.

"Idiot."

"Yeah, whatever. I really thought . . ." Kimberly said, her voice trailing off and hiding in the sounds of the city.

"You thought what?"

"I thought we'd make it work. I didn't think forever, I'm not an idiot, but I thought . . . a while? I don't know . . . a year? Maybe we could have moved in together? I thought we could give something else a try, something I've never tried before." Kimberly sighed.

"Sorry."

With her left pinky, Kimberly wiped her eyes, getting the glowing embers of her Marlboro Light dangerously close to her hair in the process. "Dumb to want what breeders have, but sometimes peace and quiet sounds really nice."

Artie nodded and fought back a tear. In the silence that followed, the two of them looked down at their neighborhood, more pulsating and alive than it had been when they'd sat down half an hour before. It was late summer, a time of effortless sexiness—especially when temperatures dropped slightly at night—and everyone below them was dressed like they'd cobbled together half an outfit after realizing they'd kept putting off laundry day. He wondered how many of them knew where they were going, or if they were just walking with nowhere to go but anywhere. If he and his friends had never wavered in life and had always known where and who and why they wanted to be, it's unlikely that any of them would have ended up in a place that attracted generations of wanderers, some of whom were intent on wandering forever, while others hoped for a destination. But which kind of wanderer was he? More important: Which kind did he want to be? He couldn't decide for sure, and as he exhaled a drag toward the street, he wondered how many people poking through the cloud of smoke did.

"Let's go," Kimberly finally said as she flicked her cigarette butt so far Artie couldn't see it land. "Adam is probably there already."

When they stepped inside Julius' a few minutes later, they discovered how right she was. Abe was seated beside Adam, their thighs touching amicably. Artie stopped for a moment, first out of shock, but then, as he took in the totality of the room, where his three favorite people were surrounded by a room of his favorite strangers, out of gratefulness. He had to memorize this moment, this messy, wonderful feeling of forgiveness and love, of family and friendship, of coming in out of the darkness and into a faint, flickering, and inarguably welcoming light.

"You," Abe said to him later that night. "What I want is you."

··•●•··

A MONTH LATER, and eight after *Four Squares* was published, Artie arrived home from his not-so-new-anymore job at an advertising agency in SoHo, which he had despised from the moment he stepped inside for an interview and accepted only because he needed the money after his modest book advance ran out, and because he could walk to the office in under twenty minutes. On his answering machine was a message from his agent, Nikki, making a vague offer regarding a ghostwriting assignment that required Artie to sign an NDA before receiving further details, but might he be interested anyway? The next afternoon, Artie lied to his indifferent boss about a dentist appointment and took the train to Nikki's office, where, after signing a stack of papers, he learned that Sterling Bismarck, a hairy blond mountain man of a hunk who starred in an hourlong drama about an undercover police officer in the '70s called *Upton Undercover*, wanted to publish a memoir in which he finally came out as gay. It was the kind of news that wouldn't surprise his most dedicated fans—gay men who trafficked in Hollywood gossip—but to the general public—the ones who bought the image crafted for him by publicity departments hook, line, and sinker—it would be a bombshell.

"The man has stories, but he doesn't have the desire or, more importantly, the energy to write it himself," Nikki said to Artie seconds after he signed the documents on her desk. "Plus, he picked you."

"He what?"

"He said he read your book."

"One of the fifty people who read my book was Detective Bruce Upton?"

"Apparently. When *his* agent asked if he had any names in mind, yours is the only one he mentioned."

"Huh. Is he dying?"

"Not officially, but I assume there's some less-than-stellar prognosis in his rearview mirror."

"Does he live here? In the city?"

"Upper West Side."

"Will my name be on it?"

"That's up to Sterling and the publisher, but I'm going to go out on a limb and say probably not," Nikki said. "Is that OK with you? Because we need to get them an answer quick if this is going to work."

He couldn't tell Nikki that he was remembering the many times he jerked off to an image he'd seen of Sterling on the cover of *People* magazine in 1978, the one where his flannel shirt was open, revealing a tuft of blond chest hair that didn't quite match the shade of his giant mustache, so he just nodded and said, "Great." He was thrilled to not have to think about boring ad copy again, thrilled to have a new story, even if it was someone else's.

·· • ● ● •·

ARTIE WIPED HIS sweaty hands on his pants every time the northbound B train stopped, disgusting both himself and the young child beside their mother in the seat across from him. He felt the way he typically did before a first date, when every insecurity became magnified to the extent that his sense of self morphed into something so hideous and undesirable that he wondered why he ever bothered stepping outside. While he stood there, trembling with the subway cars as they picked up speed between Columbus Circle and 72nd Street, he was Artie with the sweaty hands, Artie with the love handles, Artie with the cowlick, Artie who always had some mysterious stain on his pants, Artie whose laugh sounded like honking if he really found something funny, Artie who was called a terrible fuck in 1989 by some asshole named Sam, Artie who was called a fake writer in 1992 by some asshole named Abe.

He needed to fixate on something else, so he tried to remember the movie. What was it called? He'd seen it only once, in middle school, when it played on TV late at night. Sterling was young, and hadn't yet grown out the mustache that made him famous in his forties, but he was still handsome. Still cast for his desirability. In the movie (the name still hadn't come to him), Sterling fell in love with a married woman, older than him but not actually old. They spent the whole movie talking about everything except the obvious passion they had for each other, and the movie went out of its way to find opportunities for Sterling to take his shirt off. It was unlike anything Artie had ever seen at the time, and though the ending was sad—the woman didn't leave her marriage to be with Sterling, and he didn't even seem to want her to—he'd never forgotten the way it made him feel: enraptured and curious and something both nebulous and all-encompassing that he didn't necessarily understand at the time.

A crackling metallic voice overhead said, "This is 81st Street, Museum of Natural History. Transfer is available to the C line," and Artie returned to his surroundings just in time to escape through a pair of closing doors.

What the fuck, he thought, out of breath and newly horny. *What the fuck is wrong with me.* As he made his way to the exit, Artie stared at the playful dinosaur mosaics on the wall and felt jealous of them for dying in the flaming, wretched aftermath of a meteor strike.

·· •●•· ·

STERLING LENARD BISMARCK lived in an apartment on Central Park West, one block north of the natural history museum and miles away from the excitement of the Village. The building was just over twenty stories tall and stretched its yellow facade all the way from 81st to 82nd Street. Its imposing breadth and sinister pointy towers reminded many passersby, Artie included, of the setting for the film *Rosemary's Baby*, even though that building, the Dakota, was several blocks south. Still, there was something unnerving about the place, and Artie grew nervous as he walked north from the train station toward one of its entrances.

To his surprise, there was no dapper doorman lingering beneath the awning letting people in, so he pulled the heavy glass pane himself and stepped onto the checkered white-and-black tile leading him toward the reception desk.

"May I help you?" asked the forty-something man behind the desk without looking up, as if Artie's unworthiness emanated from him like a stench.

"Yes, I hope," Artie said. "I'm here to see Sterling Bismarck, in 21D."

The man, whose name tag Artie now saw read STANLEY, turned his head upward and then gave Artie a once-over. Artie squinted at Stanley's closely cropped beard and wondered if he was gay, too.

"Is he expecting you?"

"I believe so," Artie said, clicking his tongue. "Stanley."

Stanley's jaw tightened. "Name?"

"Arthur Anderson. Or Artie Anderson. Maybe A. Anderson or just Artie. I'm not sure what you were told, but I'm whichever one of those is on the list. Or at least I should be."

Stanley narrowed his eyes and sucked on his teeth before repeating his name with more than a bit of skepticism. He picked up the phone to his left, dialed a few numbers, and waited for someone to answer without breaking eye contact with this man whose name he didn't quite believe was real.

"Good morning, Mr. Bismarck, a visitor is here for you," Stanley said. "Arthur Anderson. Goes by Artie. Says you're expecting him."

Stanley hung up the phone and offered one final stinging glance that made Artie flinch. "He says to head on up. Elevator's down the hall in front of you to the right."

Artie nodded and thanked the man as kindly as he could, given his nerves. Stanley stopped him before he got too far. "He sounds, well, tired, by the way. So don't be loud. He doesn't like loud when he's tired."

"Got it," Artie said. "Thanks again."

Artie fixed his hair in the decaying mirrored walls lining the elevator and took a few deep breaths while feeling himself rise higher and higher. He checked the bag slung around his shoulders for the notepad, pen, and recorder, three items he knew were inside but just wanted to confirm once more out of sheer anxiety. There they were, and with a ding, there he was. He stepped outside and saw the door to 21D just in front of him.

He knocked twice, then waited a minute. Another knock, another minute. *Maybe he's hard of hearing*, Artie thought, and, deciding to risk a noise complaint, banged even harder. A voice grumbled in the distance, behind the wooden door and perhaps around a corner covered in framed paintings and photographs; then, after the deafening sound of latches being undone, the voice had a face: Sterling Bismarck's. On it was the same mustache that Artie had once found so confusing, but the sex appeal had been lost—drowned out by alcohol and cigarettes and, it seemed, a total lack of care. There was no joking that he was "seventy years young." No, he was an old man who answered the door in his old robe. All that living, with the joys and miseries of every year carved onto his face like it was made of brass.

"You're the writer," he said with a threatening certainty.

"Yes, Mr. Bismarck. Artie Anderson. Arthur Anderson. Whichever." He held out his hand, but Sterling never seemed to notice it.

"Which is it? Said Arthur on the book."

"I prefer Artie."

"Then why the hell didn't you put that on the book?" Confident he wasn't about to receive an answer, Sterling kept talking. "All that banging on my goddamned door's made my bitch of a headache even worse."

"Sorry about that, I wasn't sure you could hear," Artie said, stepping inside and closing the door behind him, hoping

Sterling wouldn't take offense at a stranger's comment on his hearing. "Beautiful apartment."

"What?" Sterling asked. "Oh, yeah, been here for forty years, can you believe that? Forty goddamned years in this place and I'm still the only one in it."

"Present company not included," Artie said with a smile.

"Don't tell me you're some kind of comedian. I thought you were a writer."

"I am! My agent said you read *Four Squares*, by the way. As an admirer of your work, it means so much to know you enjoyed it. Honestly, the fact that you read it at all," Artie said before Sterling turned around and slapped him on the shoulder.

"If we're going to work together, you're gonna need to cut the shit."

"Sorry?"

"None of that humility bullshit. None of those counterfeit manners. I can't stand any of that fake stuff out there, it's why I stay in here to begin with. They're all a bunch of goddamned liars."

Artie was speechless, but Sterling didn't seem to want a response. He just turned back around and kept walking through the hallways, which were exactly as Artie pictured, covered in framed photographs and paintings, until the walls opened up to reveal his sitting room.

It wasn't exactly a mess, nor was it particularly clean—there were no piles of clothes or plates or newspapers, no flies or bugs or even traps—but it was dark and dusty and filled with stale air. Sterling seemed to be the kind of person who put things away when finished with them, but not the kind who spent time doing actual cleaning beyond that. The apartment was covered in a layer of not filth but time.

When Artie sat on the armchair, as directed by Sterling's hairy left hand, a cloud of dust puffed up around him.

"So," Artie said. "You're writing a memoir."

"I'm not writing a thing with my arthritis. That's why you're here."

"What made you decide that now was the time?"

Sterling cocked his head and grabbed the big brown mug on the wooden table beside his sofa.

"You're queer, aren't you? You'd better be, or I've really lost my mind."

"I am," Artie said, swallowing nervously. "I'm gay, yes."

"Figured. I read your book, knew it had to have been written by a fag."

"Well, you sussed me out, I guess."

"Always was one of my talents. You knew that, right?"

"Knew what?"

"That it was all bullshit, the women and the dates and the love scenes and the goddamned *Upton Undercover*. All of it was for show."

"Oh, yeah. I mean, I heard rumors."

"The fags always knew, but that never seemed to matter back then. Most people bought what I was selling, and that was the important part. I did go to bed with most of them, though. The women, I mean. Why not."

"So that's why you want to release the book? You want to come out of the closet?"

"I don't like that phrase, 'come out of the closet.' Like I'm stuck there, suffocating. I'm not stuck inside anything at my age. Can't remember the last time I screwed anyone. I want to release the book because I'm dying and that's what you do when you're a guy like me. You put your face on a book while you're still clinging to what's left of your dump of a god-damned life so you can take control of the story before you're in the ground. Or, if those jokers actually read my will, floating in the wind."

"I think I understand."

"You know what I liked about your book?" Artie didn't have a chance to answer before Sterling started spouting off the an-swer to his own question. "It reminded me of the friends I used to have, in the early days. Before it all got too out of hand, when I could balance the truth and the bullshit. Back when I could shoot a movie and then go to Fire Island. Before *Upton*. That was ten years, that show."

"I remember it well."

"How old are you?"

"Thirty-two."

"What a goddamned year I had at thirty-two."

"I'm looking forward to learning about it," Artie said, and Sterling could see he meant it.

"When's the last time you got laid?"

"Sorry?"

"Before I open up to you about the whole of my pathetic and wonderful and occasionally revolting life, I want to know a little bit about the person who's going to write it all out."

"Sure," Artie said, feeling a tinge of confidence for the first time since waking up.

"Tell me about the last time you got laid. Not that hard, I imagine. Man like yourself."

"Oh, um," Artie said, closing his notepad even though he hadn't written a word. He was starting to wonder why he'd brought it at all.

"It was a guy," he said.

"Well, that part I guessed. Who was he?"

"My friend. My boyfriend, actually."

"Boyfriend, well, I'll be damned."

"It's a long story."

"Yeah, well, you're young, so it's only getting longer," Sterling said, refusing to hide how irritated he was by the descriptor. "Tell me about him."

"His name was, or is, Abe. Abraham. We've kind of had an off-and-on thing for a while, but now it's officially on. For good, I think. I hope, actually."

"So you want to screw this guy for the rest of your life?"

Artie laughed. "I guess. Yeah."

"What's he look like? Describe him to me."

"Um, well, he's a year older than me. Slightly taller than I am. Short, wavy brown hair that looks effortless and never messy. Fit, I guess. Or more fit than me."

"White? Black? I've nearly got him pictured."

"He's white."

"What's he do for a living?"

"He's a lawyer. Kind of a fancy one."

"Other aspirations?"

Artie squinted. "He doesn't talk about those much, but I

think he would want to be a writer if he weren't so busy with work. Nonfiction probably. He'd write about the past."

"So you have good instincts."

"I'd like to think so."

"Abe, the handsome, tall, white lawyer with beautiful hair who maybe secretly wants to be a writer. Sounds lovely. Even sexy, if you don't mind me saying."

"Right on both counts."

"You two are using rubbers, I hope?"

"Yeah. Maybe foolish since we're not seeing any other people, but—"

"Never foolish," Sterling interrupted. "Will you see him tonight?"

"We see each other most nights. We might even move in together soon. His apartment is huge."

"Ahh, so nice when you don't have to travel for a roll in the hay. You know when I last had sex?"

"I don't."

"Guess."

Artie opened his mouth but couldn't begin to speak. He shrugged and held his hands up in a pathetic surrender.

"Fine. 1989."

Artie nodded, certain of why it had been that long without Sterling explaining it himself. He'd suspected it, of course, but now it was plain as the day outside his dusty curtains. "And what did *he* look like?"

"You calling me queer?"

Artie laughed. "Sorry, what did *this person* look like."

"He was big. Enormous, actually, in every possible way," Sterling said, a smile forming, then fading fast. "But now he's dead, like all the others, and I'm not far behind. I suppose it won't be a shock to your system to know that I've got it."

"At this point, nothing about it shocks me anymore. Except maybe the fact that I don't," Artie said, expecting a response from Sterling that never came. "But I'm sorry. How long have you known?"

"A few years. The doctors have me on a cocktail of pills they told me Magic Johnson is using. Can you believe that? Magic Johnson. He's not even a fag. And you don't want to know how expensive it is."

"I've heard about that. It's the miracle, right?"

"I think it might be. Maybe that's why I feel like shit every time I pop 'em. How would you feel if you made it to the surface and gasped for air a second or two after your friends drowned on their way up?"

"Sorry, I just—" Artie said, cowering a bit in his seat, which suddenly felt so comfortable, as though it was molding to his backside. "After all this time I guess I still don't know how to ask. It seems like there's no sensitive way in. You talk to people and they're fine and then they're dead. You talk to people and they're miserable, but they hang on for dear life. They keep hanging on."

"They call that survivor's guilt, what you're feeling now."

"I know what they call it," Artie said with a snap he quickly regretted. Then, softening, "And I hate it."

"The feeling or the name?"

"Both, now that you mention it," Artie said. "But mostly the feeling. I'm sick of it. Horrible thing to say, horrible thing to be sick of, given everything, but I am. I'm sick and tired of it. I'm sorry, but it's true."

Sterling raised his hands up in protest, refusing Artie's apology with a downturned mouth and shake of the head. "Don't bother. Feel whatever you want to feel, I couldn't care less, but know that I feel jealous."

"Of me?"

"Yes, you, damn it. You and everyone else who gets to see what we become now that this has all happened. When did you move here? When you were twenty? Twenty-one?"

"Twenty-four. In '86."

"So you have no idea what it was like, this city. The way it was. The way it sounded and the way it looked, the way it felt," he said, clasping the air in front of him. "My god, the way it felt. The way they all felt. Los Angeles? Pfft. That whole city felt like work. You leave the set, people scream at you on the street. You go home, you get calls from your agent or the producer or the network. You get up early to do interviews with magazines you don't subscribe to or TV shows you don't watch because you'd rather be asleep. But when I came here, oh, it was a sweet release. It was like coming home after months trapped in an office building, not that I've ever worked in one."

Artie laughed. Both because he felt like it and because he felt like it would make Sterling more comfortable, he propped his elbow on the arm of the chair and rested his head in his hand. *Go on*, he seemed to say. *Never stop speaking.*

"I could hide. I could be myself. Isn't that funny? I was only myself when I was in hiding. Sounds wrong when you say it out loud, but it's the truth. The parties I'd go to, the men, the nights, the mornings. You know I own a house on Fire Island?"

Artie shook his head.

"Haven't been in years, but that was just . . ." he said, trailing off, as if there were no word big enough to finish his thought. "And then like that. Gone. Or at least that's what it felt like. The happiest days of my life, and the happiest places of my life, became death."

A silence filled the room and hung there for a moment as Artie bit his lip, deciding whether or not to speak. "I can't imagine how many people you lost."

"You should," Sterling said, a newfound sternness in his voice. "Don't be like me. Don't let the fear of it make you ignore it. Don't run off to the other side of the country because you can't deal with the agony. Don't abandon us."

The "us" made Artie flinch. "I could never. It was the whole of my first years here. All the marches and the anger and the dying. I didn't have as much fun as I wanted to, maybe I was overly cautious, maybe I still am, but I never thought about leaving. I wouldn't."

"But you still have people left, don't you? You've got to have people."

"I did." Artie thinks quickly of Waylon. "I mean, I do. Thankfully."

"That's good. All mine are dead," Sterling said, glancing at his glistening wristwatch. "And I'm running late, as usual."

Artie offered the old man a smile he didn't mean.

Sterling shook out his robe and crossed his legs, their pale, sparsely haired frailness suddenly becoming visible to Artie. "Why do you think *you* should write this? I know you're capable, I read your novel twice. But why did you say, 'Yeah, I'll have a meeting with that old fart and try this out.' This would be your first memoir, am I right?"

"It would."

"So before I hand you the reins for the increasingly rickety carriage that is my life, answer my question: Why you?"

"Because I think your story should be told."

"Cut the bullshit. You're a writer. Give me a better line than that."

Artie scratched the back of his head and scanned the room to take his eyes off Sterling's piercing stare, but even as he looked up and down and to the left, at the bookshelves, at the hallway walls covered in memories, he felt it stabbing him through the cheeks. Then, slowly and with intention, "I think it's my responsibility."

Unprepared for the answer, Sterling readjusted himself on the couch and gave Artie a confused, almost skeptical glare. "You'll have to explain what you mean."

"My own family doesn't know my whole story, and I've tried to tell them, many times. They don't know what it's like for people like us right now, even though it finally started getting on the six o'clock news. They don't know what everyone's been fighting for the past decade, and they probably never will. But— and I haven't even told my best friends this—I still write to them. Every week I write my parents a letter. I tell them about my life. I don't spare any details, either. Give them the full mess of a picture in glorious Technicolor. They don't write back, though, not even once. Not a call. Not a telegram. Not a postcard. To be honest, I think they throw them straight in the trash. I guess what I'm saying is, I can't make people listen, and I can't make people care, but what I'm good at is telling the story *anyway*. It doesn't matter if they like it or not, I just think it's a story that needs to be told. Otherwise, you know . . ."

"Who else is going to tell it," Sterling said, nodding as he looked out the window. "Good. That's good. And what would you call it?"

Artie squinted and bit his upper lip. "Call what?"

"The unwritten book about my life. The one I think I'm ready to ask you to write. What would you call it if you had to give it a name right now?"

The words came to his lips instantly, as though he'd had the idea before stepping inside the apartment and being totally surrounded by the old man's life and words. "I'd call it *The Outcome*."

Sterling scoffed, then pursed his lips in an exaggerated way that suggested he was making some kind of decision. "*The Outcome*, by Sterling Bismarck. I like it. Clever. A little much, but clever. I hope someone describes me like that one day."

"Then I'll make sure you say that in your book."

"Good. You're hired, by the way."

"I figured."

"I knew you were smart. I could tell. I'm not convinced *you* believed half of what you said about not giving a shit if people like your stories, but I'll be damned if you made me believe it anyway."

"You clocked me, but all that counts is that you did."

Sterling laughed that booming laugh of his that Artie remembered emanating from his parents' heavy brown console TV. Artie inhaled and memorized the feeling so that he could recall it the next time he was depressed. For the rest of his life, whether that amounted to one year or seventy, there would be no denying that when Artie Anderson was thirty-two years old, he sat in the sitting room of Sterling Bismarck's apartment on Central Park West and felt deliriously, maddeningly happy.

He felt excited for the future. He felt alive. He couldn't wait to tell Abe everything.

10

2022

IT HAD BEEN only a few months since his last project officially ended, a memoir by an actor known for an iconic movie role in the '80s, a battle with bulimia, and little else, but in that time he felt everything he knew about writing had dried up inside him. His morning routine, adjusted for the injury, had gone off without a single misstep: from the ever-easier act of getting out of bed, to showering, to putting on clothes, to grinding the coffee beans, to forming a perfect leaf out of foam and espresso crema in his warmed cup. On paper it was the prologue to what anyone could turn into a productive day, but as he sat in front of his computer, the solid white screen of the Word document taunted him with its emptiness. It dared him to type, but all he could do was take another sip from his coffee cup. Then another. Then another. And when he was finished, but still inadequately caffeinated, the screen of his laptop dimmed and then turned off. Apple called this a power-saving feature. Artie called it a personal attack.

What Artie loved most about writing for someone else was the becoming. He spoke to them in person. He spoke to them on the phone. He read their diaries and rough manuscripts. He spoke to their friends and family. He watched their old films and shows. Without fail he began to dream as them, knowing them so well that he could sometimes manifest versions of events that had actually happened to the person while unconscious, somehow finding truth and clarity in the silence of a REM cycle.

After *Four Squares*, his name no longer appeared on the covers of the books he wrote, and if he was credited at all, it was never in a way the average reader would notice. Usually he'd find himself mentioned in an unspecific acknowledgment in the back. He was an "assistant." A "researcher." An "editor." Once, a "writer friend." Sometimes he would be name-checked in an interview between the star and a journalist, but those interviews typically featured far more titillating details than the name of a ghostwriter. But none of this bothered Artie. In fact, all of it fueled him.

He believed he couldn't commit to the act of pretending if his name were on the cover, and privately considered his lack of egotism a little bit brave, maybe even noble. His agent simply and openly found it relieving, as there would never be a fight over accreditation or a cowriting credit. The celebrities he wrote for did, too, because it made the pretending mutual. If Artie pretended to be famous, they could pretend to be writers, and no one, not even Oprah, would be able to squeeze out the truth.

But this new novel, the one he'd begun pecking at the night before, couldn't be written by anyone else. It needed Arthur Anderson on the cover. Arthur Anderson on the title page. Arthur Anderson on the top left of every spread. He'd spent so long writing in the voices of others that he forgot how to find his own. But now, with a broken routine and foot, Artie was compelled to turn inward. For the first time in years, he was kicked off autopilot and forced to imagine his future instead of just drift passively toward it. Suddenly reminded of his life's potential, he felt a renewed interest in fiction, and with a tap, his laptop lit back up, and he gave the three messy pages he'd written another look. Yes. He would write a sequel to *Four Squares*. The only snag now was remembering how the first one ended. So he did something he hadn't done in over twenty years. Something he'd sworn he would never do again, and had taken nearly every possible measure to ensure that he didn't. He decided to read it again.

Sometimes Artie would search online secondhand booksellers for copies, just to see how much other people decided his art was now worth. They were usually expensive, between ninety and a hundred dollars, but only because there were never very many of them. For a while he'd order them, and immediately throw the unopened packages into the garbage chute. The book was never given a second printing, so the hardcovers that were printed in 1994, with their tearing jackets and warped edges and occasional dog-ears, were the only ones left to sell. The last few times he searched, one of the few available copies was in a New Jersey bookstore. He imagined an older straight woman picking up the cover and examining its spine. *Never heard of this guy,* she'd think. *Isn't that sad.* This woman he'd created, he'd named her Corinna, his grandmother's name. The straightest woman he'd ever met. The kind of straight person who was so straight she couldn't even bring herself to be disgusted by queer people, as if the very idea of a man not marrying a woman, and vice versa, was the sort of fact her brain was incapable of computing.

There it was. The same copy in Bayonne, listed as "LIKE NEW" for $85.99. At least shipping was included. He considered ordering it for a moment, to give this new Corinna a jolt, but stopped after adding the item to his cart. If he bought it, the listing would disappear. There would be almost no proof that a single copy of his book still existed. It wasn't even in a branch of the New York Public Library. Hell, it wasn't even in Brooklyn—he'd checked. So he let it stay, and then clicked on the storefront and spent eighty-five dollars on other books from authors whose books were in plentiful supply.

If he was going to write a sequel well, he would need to return to the source material. Not just reread it, but study it. The problem was that he didn't keep a single copy—not even the original manuscript—in the apartment. All of it was in his storage unit downtown, which he hadn't visited in over a year. So he grabbed his scooter and he went there.

Artie rented the unit six months after Abe's death, when he realized living among all of his things would be just as painful as having them all thrown out or given away. Though he donated some of Abe's possessions—warm-weather clothes and books and electronic devices, things that could be used by others—the modest collection of sentimental stuff went into a five-by-five-foot space between Chambers and Reade Street. Inside were three Rubbermaid bins filled with notebooks and photographs and artwork and clothes. The sorts of things that were so intwined with Artie's perception of Abe that he couldn't bear to have them connected to anyone else. They were fragments of him, even more valuable than the crushed bone and burnt ash he kept in a box inside his closet. All of those things greeted him when he unlocked the padlock in the chilly, solid white space, where every noise he made seemed to create a sound that wanted to echo for infinity. Those things, and, of course, a dozen or so copies of *Four Squares*.

As he pulled the bins out to sift through them—he didn't remember which was which—he briefly regretted not accepting the young employee's offer for assistance when he'd rolled through the lobby, but when he ripped off the first lid and swore he smelled Abe, he was glad to not have an audience. There on top, the clothes he was wearing when he had his heart attack, unlaundered and trapped in a terrible time. Artie resisted lifting them up and inhaling, instead trying box number two. Another loser, he sighed. Just photos and small paintings and tchotchkes Abe kept on his bookshelves. The two of them outside a restaurant after a birthday dinner. A photo of Abe's father. Another of his sister. A brass giraffe Vanessa bought him on a vacation. It was the only thing he'd kept from their marriage, that giraffe. Artie considered it now, and had a thought that had never come to him in the decades of their relationship. Abe had thrown out the ring. Sold or donated everything they'd bought together. He'd tossed all the photos. And, to the best of his knowledge, shredded all the legal documents documenting their marriage.

Every memory of her was gone except for that giraffe. Well, that and Halle.

Maybe the giraffe represented something more than the mere sentimentality Artie always privately assumed it did. Maybe it was the height. Their perspective. The rare ability for a flightless animal to see the forest for the trees. Abe was not a sentimental person, nor was he superstitious, but he did always seem to be on the hunt for poetry, for meaning, and grasped at it when it arrived. Maybe he thought the fact that Vanessa gave him this small statue of an animal looking beyond the muck at its feet and toward the horizon, something brighter or at least farther away, was an act of poetry on her part. A message she was sending him without words. But then again, Artie thought as he shoved the lid back on, maybe it was just a giraffe.

The books were just as he left them years ago, spine up, like an accordion of disappointments at the top of the pile. He grabbed a few and fanned them out, imagining them everywhere as he once used to, then chose the shiniest of them and put the rest back. He flipped it around and smiled at the spare rear jacket cover. Just a silhouette of Manhattan, the whole of the island, and a square around the West Village from which a zoomed-in square detailed the setting of the novel: "Inside this square are four smaller ones, inside which people smaller than those squares live and love." He'd always found it elegant and alluring, better than a blurb or photo of him or a more detailed synopsis. He'd always hoped to catch someone in a bookstore picking up a copy and turning it around, but despite his frequent wanderings through various bookstores in Manhattan in the month after its publication, he never saw a person so much as push it aside to grab the title beside it. But there was comfort in looking at it now and still feeling a modicum of pride. He'd written the book, and here it still was. Even better, it was serving a new purpose. A more noble one than ever before.

Artie smiled and stood, so excited for an afternoon of work that he almost forgot to squeeze the lock back on the door of the storage unit.

He started reading in the back of the cab home, and had zipped through twelve pages, thrilled by the feeling that they were both familiar and brand-new, by the time the driver pulled up to the awning of his building.

"Need help getting out?" the driver asked, a pair of kind eyes staring back at him in the rearview mirror, not mentioning his foot.

"I'm fine," Artie said. "But thank you." He yanked the scooter out of the car, and it fell to the street with a crash, but he propped it back up on his own and waved to the driver after sliding the door shut.

It wasn't as constant as he'd expected, the concern from strangers and second-guessing when he denied their kind offers, but Artie did still find a comfort in it when it happened, that reminder that people are actually quite kind and empathetic as a general rule. It's just a shame that they only reveal it when someone's in obvious need, and not all of the time. He counted himself in that latter group, though he hoped this experience would push him more firmly into the former camp.

He finished the book in a single sitting that afternoon, diagonal on his sofa, both feet propped up on the coffee table. When he laughed, it was at the memories he would have never dared to put in the novel. When he cried, it was at his friends' endings, not his characters'. But when he closed the book, he knew how the characters' story could continue, because he knew what his friends deserved.

Back at his desk he returned to the foreboding glow of his laptop. *Four Squares* was a story about four queer people: Peter and David and George and Patricia. Their friendship was complicated by sex and solidified through shared trauma. It was about HIV/AIDS and activism and sex and love and survival. The sequel would follow all of them thirty years later. An easy concept. And he could call it . . . what would he call it? He would get to that later.

The sight of the blank page excited him, and he began to write. No need for an outline at this point, he thought. He would just put his hands to the keyboard and see what happened. Two hours later, he had two thousand words and an idea of where about eighty thousand more could potentially go. It was the most productive writing day he'd had in years.

For the next three weeks, Artie developed what he'd been craving since his injury: a routine. In the morning he did his stretches and little exercises assigned to him when he was discharged, showered, had coffee, and wrote for two hours. Then came lunch, which he was able to prepare on his own thanks to the mobility and good mood afforded to him by the scooter and the stretches and the productivity. After lunch, more writing. On days he went to GALS for dinner, he wrote until leaving; on others, he called it quits at six. Revisiting his friends for hours a day, imagining where their lives could have gone had they not been cut short, was as cathartic as it was traumatizing, and the satisfaction he felt while writing was instantly replaced by a rush of longing as soon as he stopped at night. The jubilance of their potential futures snuffed out each time he shut his screen. To ease himself back into the painful reality, he'd take a ride around the neighborhood, come home, order dinner (he considered daily takeout as a luxury he deserved thanks to being A. injured and B. at work again), and watch one movie before bed. Always one from at least thirty years before, one he'd once shared with them.

As the temperature dropped, his word count increased, and by the day of Annabelle's party, he'd written over thirty thousand of them. They weren't all winners, and they wouldn't all make it past his first edit—whenever that came—but they were all words that hadn't been put together in that particular way ever before. Not by him. Not by anyone.

When it was time for lunch, he slammed the laptop lid shut and picked up his phone. In the hours since flicking it to silent mode and turning it upside down on his desk in anticipation of a productive few hours of work, he'd missed two texts, both from Carson.

Do you really plan on going to Annabelle's pre-Thanksgiving thing tonight?

I was more than a little overwhelmed by our first interaction, but simply must see that apartment.

Artie laughed and typed out a response.

Agree. Think we should show up together?
As allies?

The bubbles indicating Carson was typing appeared, and Artie felt himself begin to sweat at the brow.

Great idea. Shall I come to you? I don't want
to make you roll any farther than you have
to. (Am I allowed to joke about your injury?)

Ha ha, of course you are. How's my
apartment at 7:00?

Perfect. Address?

Since Abe's death, there had been no sex—or even the potential for it—inside Artie's apartment. All his handful of hookups were at the homes of others, most of them gracious, few
asking questions about his reluctance to have them over. It
wasn't a fear of disrespecting Abe or his memory—Artie was
certain that if he'd been the one who died suddenly, Abe would
have had invited someone over before his own body was cold.
Artie simply wanted to be sure the apartment was always a
place he could escape to. A place of which he had total control,
untainted by the potential discomfort or awkwardness that
comes from getting to know another person. To Artie, avoiding
the worst case was preferable to risking the best. But with Carson he felt like it was time to let someone else in, and for the first
time in almost two decades, his space—all of it, if he was

lucky—would be explored by someone new. He'd give a tour, explain knickknacks and paintings, photographs and pieces of furniture. He'd wash the sheets, even though he washed them two nights before. He'd even buy flowers for a rarely used vase in the kitchen and hope it would seem like the vessel's normal state, as if it were something he did all the time. But Carson wasn't coming over to fuck—at least that wasn't what Artie wanted then. He was just coming over to see him. The thought of a platonic guest was somehow more debilitating than the alternative, and made Artie shiver in his chair. What's more mortifying than being seen so clearly, without the certainty of sex clouding one's vision? He typed out his address, hit SEND, and slammed the phone face down on his desk.

Lunch. Cleanup. More work. At six, the end-of-workday alarm on Artie's phone went off and he lifted it up to stop the noise. Below the alarm was a text from Carson. Artie read it and banged his fist on his desk. "Fuck!"

The message was short: "En route! Be at your place at 6:30!"

Had he not gotten swept up in his own words and thoughts, getting dressed for a social event would have taken Artie well over an hour. There was the scanning of the closet and pulling out three or four potential outfits, then trying them on and evaluating the attributes of each in the full-length mirror on his closet door, and then there was the choosing of one, following by a quick steam for a final bit of polish. With half an hour to spare, Artie had to move briskly through just a few of those steps, but which ones to cut? There certainly wasn't time to try more than one outfit on, so which would it be? What made him most comfortable and confident? Nothing in his closet made him feel sexy, but certain fits felt flattering. He riffled through the oxfords and thumbed the sweaters and tapped his nose at the thought of a suit, then decided on something simple yet reliable: blue slacks, white shirt, gray blazer. Wait, no. Not a blazer, he realized. Vaguely chic zip-up slacks he'd found online, white shirt, blue sweater. That would work, he thought, nodding at his wobbly reflection before stripping off his clothes and pulling everything on at record speed.

He was running a brush through his hair when Carson's buzz came through. "Send him up," Artie said breathlessly after a clumsy crutch-aided sprint to the kitchen, where he waited until Carson knocked at the door.

"Welcome, welcome," Artie said, gesturing for his guest to come inside. Once the door was shut, Carson gave Artie a hug, the surprise of his warmth knocking him off-balance.

"Oh, sorry," Carson said, steadying Artie with both hands on his shoulders. "I shouldn't have grabbed on to someone in a foot brace."

"No, no, it's fine," Artie said. "Come on in and have a seat anywhere. I'm nearly finished getting ready, if you don't mind waiting a few minutes."

"Not at all," Carson said. "You look nice, by the way."

Artie blushed. "So do you, of course. Great blazer," he said, pointing at the bright red velvet draped over his body. "I wish I had the courage to wear colors that don't appear in nature."

"Red appears in nature."

"I guess I meant in nature, in the dark, to color-blind people."

"Ha," Carson said. "Thanks."

"I'm just a bore is all," Artie said, realizing he was talking too much. "But like I said, I just need a minute to finish getting ready."

While Artie fixed his hair and applied a little cologne from a bottle he hadn't touched since Halle's graduation, Carson wandered through the living room with his hands in his pockets, craning his neck to find every possible piece of himself that Artie put on display. When Artie returned to the living room, hands smoothing his pants, he noticed Carson hovering over his desk.

He pointed at the once pristine copy of *Four Squares*, now dog-eared and filled with colorful flags, sitting behind his laptop.

"And here's the famous novel."

"Ha, it's the decidedly *un*famous one."

"You know, I tried to buy a copy, but it's not the easiest book to find."

"Yeah, I think I probably have most of the copies. Humiliating."

"You should display them. Or give them away."

"Eh, no one wants to read it."

"I do."

"Well, then, I'll be sure to pull one out next time I'm in my storage unit."

"Oh, I don't need one."

"Ha ha, see? No one wants to read it."

"I didn't say I don't want to read it, I just said I don't need it."

Artie took his hands off the handles of his scooter and put them on his hips. "Are you telling me you bought a copy?"

"Like I said, it's not the easiest book to find. But it's findable."

"Don't tell me how much you spent. I know how much they sell for these days."

"Doing a little self-Googling?"

Artie blushed. "Maybe."

"So are you going to ask me what I thought about it?"

Artie squinted and put his hands back on the scooter. "I'm not sure I'm ready for that just yet," he said, rolling to the front door. "Isn't that third base?"

"I think it might be," Carson said.

"That takes time," Artie said. "Well, time or a drink."

"Lucky for you, I make an incredible martini."

"Then why don't you go ahead and make two?"

Artie sat at the island and watched Carson make his way around the kitchen with a chef's ease, charmed by his lack of questions or requests for permission. Carson was making drinks, not asking for help, and Artie was happy to watch it happen without having to lift a finger or a foot. "Were you ever a bartender?" he asked as Carson rinsed both glasses in a splash of dry vermouth.

"I was, actually," Carson said, pulling ice out of the freezer. "In college. But that was mostly just opening bottles and pouring whiskey. The most complicated order was usually a vodka tonic. I don't know if I could stand it these days, with everyone ordering espresso martinis and Aperol spritzes, Negronis with things that shouldn't be in Negronis."

"Seems like you'd be good at it, though."

"Oh, I'd be incredible at it. No doubt about that."

Artie laughed, or no, he giggled, and covered his mouth at

the surprise of the noise he heard escaping it. "I admire your confidence."

Carson held the shaker over his right shoulder and did what the vessel was designed for, starting slowly, then picking up speed, all the while keeping his eyes on Artie as the ice and vodka sloshed back and forth, forming condensation on the metal. "I think that's good," he finally said when the kitchen fell silent, dumping ice from the coupes and filling each with five ounces of a perfect martini.

"A little twist," he said, peeling two strips from a lemon with a paring knife and squeezing them both over the glasses before dropping them in. "And now we're done."

Artie took a few seconds to marvel at the drink and the expertise with which it had been made, right in front of him, then picked it up and clinked his glass against Carson's. "To a fabulous night."

Carson grinned. "It certainly is."

· · • ● • · ·

ARTIE USED TO be good at parties. Charming any random roaming body inside an apartment he'd never been in before, flirting with people he wanted to fuck, making banal conversation with people he didn't, typically going home alone but somehow satisfied regardless—these used to be his talents. It was everything that came after—the solidifying of the casual acquaintances into actual friendships, and navigating from flirting to sex, especially—that he found difficult to master. When he was a young man, that was a compromise he was happy to make. As long as he was socializing regularly, he was in a good place. It was a kind of stasis, but at least it was an enjoyable one. When he and Kim, Way, and Adam came to a party together, Artie's skills increased tenfold. The four of them always brought a kind of celestial energy to parties, even if they were at the home of someone they'd never met. People orbited them as though their gravitational fields were inescapable, or at least too comfortable to leave. But now, out of practice thanks to decades of solitude, he felt like a piece of space junk hurtling into infinity.

"I should tell you now, I'm not very good at parties," he told Carson with his eyes on his scooter while hopping up the steps to Annabelle's door. "So I may attach myself to your hip."

"I didn't think that was in the cards tonight," Carson said with a wink.

"I'm serious. GALS is different. It's seated. I'm worried about how I'll navigate a bunch of conversations and rooms and groups of people when I have free rein of some big open space."

"Feel free to attach yourself right here, then," Carson said, sliding a finger through one of his belt loops. "I don't mind."

"Thanks."

It was when Carson rang the doorbell that the extravagance of Annabelle's apartment suddenly hit him. "Hell of a sign when there's just one buzzer for the whole damn building."

"I mean, everyone said she was rich rich. I wonder how long she's owned the place."

"Since 1977," Carson said with authority. "I Googled it."

They were both surprised when a person who was not Annabelle or a member of GALS opened the door. The person was seemingly in their twenties and quite short, but stood with a militant rigidity that made them feel as aggressive as someone twice their height. "May I help you?" they said with a distant coolness that caused Artie to lean back as far as he could without tipping over his scooter to double-check the building number.

"I'm not sure if we have the right address, actually. We're here for Annabelle Adams's party?"

"Of course," they said, stepping to the side to allow the two guests inside. "Shall I help you inside, or are you OK?"

Artie navigated his scooter around the peculiar man and onto the slippery marble of the vestibule. "No, no. I'm fine. Just a little awkward going through crowded doorways."

"Let me take your coats and then you can follow me into the sitting room."

"What's your name?" Carson said as they pulled the coat off his back.

"Edgar," they said after a brief delay, as if they weren't quite sure.

"And you work for Annabelle?"

"I do," Edgar said curtly, as though that was the end of their job description. They hung the coats in the wardrobe in the foyer, whose floor comprised a slightly different pattern than that in the vestibule, and led Artie and Carson down the entryway and into the only open door in sight. As Artie squeaked his way onto the parquet floors of the sitting room, he glanced at the massive wooden doors Edgar clearly hoped they'd disregard and wondered what treasures lay behind them. But before he could make any guesses, he heard her voice.

"Darlings! You made it!" Annabelle cooed. Her "*daaaarlings*" should have been grating—so should have everything about her—but listening to her stretch the word to its absolute limit felt like something specific and natural to her, an earnest expression of herself, and that was precisely where her true power lay. She was over-the-top, but anything under that would have been a lie, a facade, a disappointment. "You both look smashing. And fashionably late, too! Just divine."

"Thanks for having us," Carson said. They hugged, and Annabelle moved toward Artie. After looking him up and down, she clasped her hands together and smiled like someone who believed they were in an extreme close-up, lit in chiaroscuro.

"If it weren't for the cast and the scooter, I'd hardly know you were injured. Can I hug, or will you simply collapse if I apply some friendly pressure?"

"You can hug," Artie said, widening his eyes at Carson as Annabelle's tight squeeze forced his chin to latch itself onto her shoulder. When their bodies disjoined, he gave the room a performative scan. "Your home is stunning."

"Isn't it? Some days I feel like it's due for a renovation. Rip the whole thing up, right down to the studs. Fill it with new furniture. New paint. New *everything*. Spend two fortunes— I've got at least five to go." She sighed and put her hand on her hip. Then, with a musical pop: "But! Certain things never go out of style, I suppose. Even if they're ancient. Perhaps I'll always keep it just like this."

"I think that's a fine idea," Artie said, meaning it.

"Do you? Wonderful. We're so in sync, you and I. Now, feel free to mingle with the others and grab a drink at the bar. I'll give everyone a grand tour in half an hour or so."

A glass shattered in another room—Artie couldn't deduce

which—and she glided away in the general direction of the noise, announcing to the room more than once that none of them need worry. When she was out of view, Artie tapped Carson on the shoulder and lightly slapped himself on the cheek. "Does she know the Gilded Age ended before she was born?"

"I'm not sure we know for certain *when* she was born."

The tension Artie had felt before arriving was assuaged in that moment as he observed all the people he knew from GALS in a different context. None of them, himself included, seemed to blend into their extravagant surroundings. He watched their nervous glances, the delicate grips with which they held their drinks, and found comfort in the realization that they were all uncomfortable together.

After ordering two martinis at the bar, he and Carson walked toward a rousing conversation between Jim, Jazmine, and Helen. All three of them were laughing as Artie's legs trembled into a seated bend. Though a pain shot up through his body, his smile didn't fade. How strange and lovely it was to see Helen laugh, he thought.

"Looks like we found the party within the party," Artie said.

"Did you know these two used to fuck?" Jim asked, making Helen and Jazmine laugh even more. Both of them were in sparkling gowns, Helen's a form-fitting silver that exposed her arms and most of her legs, and Jazmine's a looser gold with full sleeves.

Helen buried her face in her hands. "Don't say it like that! We were in a relationship!"

"'A relationship' could mean anything these days. What I said's the truth. You two were fucking!"

Jazmine slapped Jim on the shoulder and took a sip from her glass of seltzer—or was it a highball? Artie couldn't decide. "Jim! Stop it! It was years ago and didn't last long. I'm surprised you didn't know already."

"No one tells me anything. I have to make educated guesses, then I tell everyone else what I assume."

"I've never heard gossip defined in such elevated terms," Jazmine said, a playful condescension in her voice. "Why is it that women just go out and say it, but men feel like they have to call it something else? I'd just say, 'Oh, we're gossiping.' Jim has to say, 'I'm making an educated guess.' Call a spade a spade, you old fool."

"Fine, I love to gossip. There, happy?"

"I am, now would you mind gossiping about someone other than me?"

There was an exhilarating discordancy to the room—all these playful, ordinary, borderline-crass conversations being had against a backdrop of excess and privilege and polished formality. The sheer absurdity of his presence here made the conversations feel easier than Artie had ever expected. Because it was deeply apparent that none of them belonged, there seemed to be an unspoken agreement that all of them did.

Just as Carson brought Artie their second round of drinks—Artie found it kind of him to get them without even asking—Annabelle appeared in the room as if summoned by an unspoken spell and announced the tour would soon begin.

Through their conversations in the first half hour there, Artie learned that plenty of the guests had been to Annabelle's home for parties in the past. Ellis had been no fewer than five times, Jazmine and Helen, too. It was Bill's second and Jim's third. Some of them, though, whether because they'd never worked up the courage or because they were new to GALS, had never stepped foot in her manor before. But everyone looked forward to the chance to see it for the first time or be reminded of how Annabelle Adams lived her fabulous life. The old, cherished things with which she surrounded herself. The ornately framed photographs of her with Bill Clinton and Judy Garland and Jean-Michel Basquiat. The art she had purchased from Andy Warhol's studio, from Andy Warhol himself.

"We're going to skip the kitchen, my marvelous kitchen with a giant gas range and breakfast table and cabinets for days, because it's crammed at the moment with the brilliant caterers, and I wouldn't dare intrude on their space," she said, gesturing toward the closed swinging door, behind which Artie imagined caterers rolling their eyes at their current boss's eccentricities while feeling a palpable relief at her refusal to make them unwitting props on her tour.

"How are my differently abled friends doing in the back? Artie? Hazel? Are we moving at a suitable place?"

"All good," Artie said.

"Me too," echoed Hazel, pushing the wheels forward alongside him. It was the first time he considered her wheelchair, what it would mean for the rest of the tour, but then he decided a home like this simply must have an elevator.

"Through that panel is the elevator," Annabelle said as the thought finished forming inside his mind. "Disguised it well, didn't we? My legs are just dandy at the moment, but piece by piece they'll start to crumble, I'm sure of it. If anyone needs to take it up later, feel free and I'll be your Shirley MacLaine."

Carson whispered, "What does she mean by that?"

"*The Apartment*," Artie said. "Haven't you seen it? Jack Lemmon?"

"No."

"You need to rectify that immediately."

"You'll have to show it to me sometime," Carson said, correctly predicting that Artie would ignore the hint.

The formal dining room contained a table so long Artie wondered if it had been constructed inside. Too often dining tables can seem unused and bought for the sole purpose of filling a room. But this one looked beloved and inviting, the sort of table that seems to ache when it's empty, one that can't bear to gather dust.

From there, Annabelle doubled back through the butler's pantry and into the entryway, again past the elevator, which Artie entered with Hazel once Carson followed the others up the stairs. The elevator was just big enough for the two of them and their wheeled contraptions, and so slow Artie wondered if it was powered by Edgar alone, pulling at ropes behind a wall.

"Incredible place, isn't it?" Artie said as they creaked upward.

"It is," Hazel said, with something uncertain behind the words. "It's maybe too much, though. Almost offensive to know people live like this. But here I am, in my best dress, enjoying it. How much longer in the cast?" She pointed at his bent leg resting on the scooter and looked up at him with an apathetic gaze.

"A few more weeks. Then I'll move on to a cane, which I'm looking forward to. How long have you been using a wheelchair?"

"Most of my life. Since I was fourteen."

"Was it a specific incident or something else?"

"Specific incident," Hazel said. "Fell off the roof of my house."

"Oh no, I'm sorry."

"Eh," Hazel said. "I used to climb up there with a telescope because our sky was so dark. This was the New Jersey suburbs."

"What were you looking at?"

Hazel cocked her head.

"The night you fell. What were you looking at in the telescope?"

A smile filled her face as she plucked the memory.

"Saturn. I always looked at Saturn. I could never believe the rings. Have you ever looked at Saturn in a telescope?"

"I don't believe I have."

"Oh, you have to. Light pollution ruins everything around here, but if you drive not too far out of the city, you can point any old telescope up into the sky and there it is. Rings and all."

Artie looked up, briefly expecting to see something other than a dull yellow light in the elevator's ceiling.

"It's amazing what you can see up there," Hazel said, adding with a final wistful whisper, "'Radio waves of the first explosion.'"

"Radio waves of the first explosion?"

"From a poem."

"Who's the poet?"

"I don't remember, actually. But I can probably recite the whole thing." She inhaled, shut her eyes, and recited a few lines.

"'Through the telescope. Crater of the moon. The rings around Saturn. A light floating in. Radio waves of the first explosion. As I stepped back, an image. Quick constellation of a figure. I knew—'"

The elevator dinged, finally arriving after an ascent so slow it felt like the two of them weren't moving, and the doors scraped open. Artie wasn't sure whether they'd hit the top floor or if it kept going up, but enjoyed the punctuation of tinny mechanical noise.

"How was the ride?" Carson asked as he squeezed through the others to grab Artie's hand.

"Impressive. Beautiful, even," he said, smiling at Hazel, who smiled right back.

A buzz from his pocket broke the spell of the moment, and he pulled his phone out with a grunt. A text from Halle, responding to a weeks-old text from him.

> Artie! Sorry I forgot to respond! But that
> sounds great. I may be in town for
> Thanksgiving, but nothing's set in stone.
> Hope you're feeling better every day! I have
> to run out in a bit but could FaceTime now if
> you want?

Artie considered breaking away from the tour, not to videochat but to confirm the message's receipt, but decided to wait. The second floor of Annabelle's home was a force he couldn't

resist, and he wanted to enjoy it in all its splendor. He shut off
the screen, shoved the phone back into his pocket, and rolled
toward the others. Halle, he thought with only a sliver of annoyance, would have to wait.

Annabelle's bedroom was a studio apartment, complete with
wet bar and en suite bathroom. It was the kind of room he
could imagine himself never leaving, plush and cozy and
brimming with inspiration thanks to the wall of books that
doubled as a shelf of knickknacks across from the wall of photographs that doubled as a largely chronological record of Annabelle's life.

As the host explained the history of the bed frame and the
difficulty in finding just the right drapes, Artie perused the photos, starting at the top left and then across and down, reading
her story like a wall-sized page in a book. Somewhere in the
middle, between a solo photograph of Annabelle and one of her
sunbathing beside a woman who appeared to be Lily Tomlin,
was a man he hadn't thought about in years: Sterling Bismarck.

He was handsome as ever, and provided a sense of timing
and context that old photographs of Annabelle tended to require. Her loud style had been consistent since she'd first been
able to dress herself, and like so many people tormented in their
youth for looking older than their age, she grew into an older
person who tended to look younger than it. A photograph of
Annabelle in a bright boxy red cover-up with chunky yellow
glasses popping beneath a sheath of gray atop her head could
have been taken anywhere from 1975 to 2022, but when a
youthful Sterling Bismarck, sturdy and strong but clearly past
his prime, sat beside her in a beach chair on what looked like

Fire Island, Artie realized that it must have been taken in the early '80s. 1983, he guessed.

"Which one are you eyeing there, darling? Me and old Bizzy?"

"Fabulous picture," he said. "All of them are, really."

"Feels like bragging in a way, but they are my friends. It's why I keep them in the bedroom. They're my fondest memories, but they're also quite, I don't know, showy. A little obscene in their way."

"You know I knew him, too."

"Who, Bizzy?"

"I did. But never as Bizzy. He was always Sterling to me."

"Oh, did you two screw?" Annabelle said, totally rapt and ready to hear a story. "I heard he was a fabulous lay. From him, of course, but still."

Artie laughed. "No, no, I wrote his memoir. It was my first big job."

"Darling, that's astonishing! I read it myself, though didn't everyone," Annabelle said, giggling at a memory. "It's just like Bizzy to pay someone to do something for him. To think someone with those biceps could be so lazy."

"Oh, he did the work, told me all his stories. I just wrote them down, really."

"Were you at the funeral?"

"I was."

"Can you believe it? We were in the same room and we didn't even know it."

"Small world," Artie said, looking back at the photographs.

"Oh, no, it isn't, darling. It's enormous. One day you'll

realize that. Maybe when you're older," she said with a wink that Artie turned back just in time to see.

"Well, in any case, I think these photos are just marvelous," Artie said. "Must be so lovely and warm to wake up every morning and see them all around you."

"When I wake up, the world's all a blur, darling," she said. "I don't see them until I put my glasses on. But I quite like my failing eyesight, don't you?"

"How do you mean?"

"A day can be magical, but isn't being alive a little horrific? When you wake up and see nothing but colorful smudge, you have the time to get your mind in order before you decide to start really looking. Before you get assaulted by the thought of living another day. Poor eyesight's a kind of gift."

"I'd never thought about it like that before."

"Well, it's time you started!"

Carson stepped in when he could see Annabelle about to drift into another story. "It's funny that you say assaulted by the thought of living another day. You seem to find such joy in it."

"Those two things are far from mutually exclusive, darling," she cooed.

And then off she went, toward the next conversation with the next person in the room. Artie watched her with a visible awe, struck by the practiced informality of her hosting skills. That she could strike up a conversation with any of her guests at any time, making them feel like the only person in her home for a glorious ninety seconds, was a skill in and of itself. But her ability to end the conversation and move on down the line without leaving behind a feeling of abandonment was her true gift. She knew how to make a moment more than enough, and as Artie turned once more to the wall of photos, he realized that of course she did. She knew more than any of them the value of a moment, and how a life could be remembered as little more than a series of them.

To people like Artie, developing the arc of one's life was a preoccupation. Constantly thinking of the past and the future in such a way that the present became a mere consequence of memory and preparation. If only he could be a little more like Annabelle, for whom nothing had ever been more important or meaningful than right now. Even when she looked to the past, she reveled in the act of remembering without resentment over it being from another time. The act of remembering was a new moment, a new experience in itself.

Artie and Carson poked their heads in her en suite bathroom but didn't dare walk in, though Annabelle had already made it explicit that no room was off-limits for their perusing. Maybe before their conversation they would have considered it, peering into her shower and reading the labels on all the bottles she kept out in view, but after that moment of vulnerability, the two of them felt like a tour of the place where she kept all the pills and creams and devices that helped her become the physical being they knew her to be felt like an overstep, as if they'd be asking too much from someone who had already given so much of themself in such a short amount of time.

The tour moved on, through the guest rooms and the library, then back down to the main floor, where the dining table had been transformed into a buffet fit for triple the number of people

at the party. After browsing the selections, Carson asked what
Artie wanted to eat and insisted on serving him. "Go sit and
keep mingling," he said. "I'll bring you a plate." When he returned to a spot in the den, at the end of one couch, saving the
adjacent armchair for Carson, he took a deep breath. Others
might have identified it as the exhaustion of someone uncomfortable on their feet, but it had nothing to do with his foot.
He'd just forgotten how nice it could be to have company. Not
just Carson and his affectionate—if nurse-like—assistance, but
also the people and stories found in other places, other rooms.
GALS, he realized then, was only the beginning of his journey
toward new relationships, a brief prologue to chapters that
could only exist outside its walls. The key to socializing more,
he remembered with a sudden wistfulness, is to socialize a little.
Invitations beget invitations. Parties beget parties. Friendships
beget friendships.

"Should we split a car home?" Artie whispered to Carson at
around eleven, once only about half the attendees remained. "I
can request it if you give me your address."

"Sure," Carson said, grabbing the phone from Artie and adding his apartment as the second stop after Artie's. "I can get the
next one."

"The next car home from Annabelle's?"

"Just the next one," he said, his face stern and eyes fixed on
Artie's.

"OK, thanks."

In the foyer, Annabelle gave them both big, burly hugs that
conflicted with her petite frame. "Do come back soon, OK,
dear?" she said, holding Artie's hands tightly. "We can talk

more about Bizzy and see if there's anywhere else we may have crossed paths back in the old days."

"I'd love that," he said, about to end it there but then deciding to keep speaking. "Why don't you give me your number, and I can give you a call."

"Oh, darling, that would be delightful!" she said, shuffling back to a room down the hall and returning in seconds with a business card. "We'll talk soon. Thank you for the lovely company."

Easy, he thought. *All it ever takes is a sentence.*

11

1996

THAT THE FOUR of them were so comfortable with everything that had changed over the past three years was entirely
due to everything that had stayed the same. Artie moved into
Abe's apartment in the Village and began ghostwriting full
time. Kimberly's photography was being published in a new
magazine every month, to the point that she was running out of
business cards to pass out at the Cubby Hole. Adam decided to
embrace his generational wealth and began making plans to
open a club in the East Village, in the same spot the Holy Spirit
had occupied years before. But they always made time for one
another—for movie nights and takeout and Julius'. Had they
not, they all privately acknowledged, everything else would
have crumbled. Artie considered their good fortune after finishing his work that brisk December night, delighting in the fact
that their upstate trips were still his favorite part of every year

and hoping that they would be until no years were left. When the phone rang, his smile grew. Perfect timing, he thought. As usual.

"I think I'm in love," Kim said as soon as Artie answered the phone.

"What's her name?"

"No. You always ask for their names and then you conveniently forget. Or you pretend to forget, which is worse. Either way, I'm not letting you do that again. It'll make me feel silly when all I want to feel is good about this."

"Jesus. Not sure why it's unfair of me to ask the name of a person you're *in love* with."

"I didn't say I'm in love, I said *I think* I am."

"How?" Artie asked, all humor drained from his voice. He hoped she would provide an answer that could change his own life.

"Because I've never felt this before. Not with anyone."

"So it must be love," Artie said, realizing it wasn't a question.

Kim shrugged. "Why shouldn't it be?"

Artie switched the receiver into his other hand and smiled into the mouthpiece, hoping Kimberly could somehow picture it on the other end. "You're right," he said. "Why shouldn't it be? I'm really happy, and I hope you introduce me as soon as possible."

"After the trip?"

"I'd be honored to be your third wheel. But will you give me something? A little nugget?"

Kim groaned.

"Tell me one word about the person you may or may not be but probably are in love with."

Kim was silent on the other end for so long that Artie checked to see if she was still there.

"Vegan," Kim said.

"Interesting."

"That's all you're allowed to say."

"Fine. Then I'll say it again. *Interesting*."

Kim sighed with so much force that Artie flinched. "Listen, I know it's late notice, but can we do something? Please? I need to not think about her. A movie? Food? Both? Julius'?"

"Absolutely," Artie said, mindlessly flipping through the drawer of takeout menus next to the phone, the only remotely messy space of his and Abe's palatial apartment. "Come over now, Abe is already on his way, and I can call Adam." He realized their restlessness was more than mutual, it was telepathic, and they had all convened at his building within the hour.

"What time do we have to leave on Tuesday?" Artie asked as they began walking toward Cinema Village. "I'd leave earlier than usual, if we're all up for it. I have so little work to do this week."

"Yeah, I'd love to be out of the city as quickly as possible," Kimberly said. "But I guess it all depends on the driver."

Adam, who drove every year, shrugged. "Why don't we just leave on Monday night? I'll be finished with work at five. Traffic will be awful that late, and I'm pretty sure it's supposed to snow, but it'll be nice to wake up there on Tuesday morning instead of rushing out. Plus we get another full day out of it."

Abe rubbed the top of his head. "Shit, I don't know if I can make it that early. I have to run into the office on Tuesday morning."

Artie couldn't hide his frustration. "You said you were to-tally free next week, that you wouldn't have to think about work at all."

"It's barely work—a client needs to come in and complete some paperwork in person before they head out for their own vacation. I drew the short stick."

"Do you mind if I go with them?"

Abe rolled his eyes. "You know the directions better than I do. I don't want to get lost up there."

Artie looked at his friends, who were stifling their laughter about this minor domestic quarrel. "Can you hold down the fort before we show up?"

"I'd prefer if we were all there the first night," Kim said, a glimmer of irritation at the edges of her voice. "But sure. Just come when you can."

At the box office, the movies they had hoped for, *Evita* and *Scream*, were sold out, leaving only *The Evening Star*. Thirty minutes into the movie, Kim leaned into the center of their group and whispered, "Can we leave?"

Artie and Abe nodded and began to stand before Adam swatted them back down. "No, stop! We do not walk out on Shirley MacLaine in this family!" After being shushed by a face-less patron who seemed to agree, they all returned to their seats and waited impatiently for the end credits.

"Well," Kim said to Adam as they walked out onto the street some two hours later. "What did you think?"

"What I thought doesn't change what I said. We don't. Walk out. On Shirley. MacLaine."

Two blocks later, they grabbed slices of pizza, less out of

hunger than the fear of drinking on an empty stomach. The slices weren't good, but they finished them anyway. In the years since, Artie often remembered the way the pizza had tasted that night and felt a peculiar, overwhelming sadness. The slices were undercooked and discomfortingly wet, with overly sweet sauce and cheese that fell off the top in room-temperature clumps instead of stretching.

And when he thought of time spent in his youth at Julius', he tried to remember it as it was that final night they were all together: a warm, welcoming reprieve from the cold, filled with the loves of his present and the possibility for love in the future.

··•◉•··

ARTIE WAS PACKED and ready to go that Tuesday morning, his foot tapping nervously on the gorgeous red Persian rug beneath him while he waited for Abe to return home from the office. The two of them had decided to move in together a month before, but Artie hadn't begun packing—let alone broken the news to his landlord. The thought of bringing even one box over the threshold seemed to him like a decision that could never be undone. More than the predictable anxieties over cohabitation, Artie worried the intermingling of their possessions would exacerbate all the differences between them. Abe's apartment was filled with inherited items holding a kind of aesthetic and monetary value Artie felt unable to compete with. Like the rug, Abe's dining room table, dresser, credenza, and half the art on the walls were taken from the Fords' many homes simply because they were free. That they also happened to be timeless and well-made was merely another thoughtless bonus afforded to those with generational wealth. It's not just money that trickles down; it's ease and comfort. Artie was staring at the rug, imagining the life of the person who made it, when the front door burst open with Abe sighing behind it.

"Finally," Artie said, jumping up from the couch. "I thought you said it would only take an hour?"

Abe threw his coat on the hook beside the door and yanked off his boots. His hair was wet from melted snow, and his nose was red, the winter giving his face a kind of youthfulness it typically lacked. "Yeah, well, they were fucking late. I was fucking early, and they were fucking late. It's so disrespectful, but there's fucking nothing I could have done. God, rich people are insufferable."

"I hate to break it to you, but you're technically rich people."

"No, no," Abe said, wagging his finger at Artie as he ran into the bedroom to grab his things. "There's comfortable and then there's rich. Comfortable people are the ones I work *with*, and rich people are the ones I work *for*, and they're the fucking worst."

"Nothing screams rich to me like comfort, so we'll just have to disagree on this one. You're all packed, right?"

"Yes, just want to change and then we can head out. The snow is really coming down, so we'll have to take it slow."

"They're going to be so pissed."

"Did you call them? Let them know we're running late?"

"No one's answering—I bet the snow took out a phone line or something. Adam said it could happen. Or maybe they're just pissed and not answering."

"Don't make me feel worse about this," Abe said, swapping out his dripping business casual for sweatpants and a long-sleeved tee.

"Fine, fine, but can we go?"

"Right now. I parked the car right outside, too," Abe said, pulling his keys out of the bowl beside the front door and pulling it open with a graceful swing. "After you, sir."

"Why, thank you," Artie said, throwing a scarf around his neck.

The doorman jumped when he saw the two of them approaching with their bags, opened the door with a nervous urgency. "Can I help you take those to your car, Mr. Ford?"

"We've got it, Dennis, but thank you."

"Headed someplace warm, I hope," Dennis said, letting go of the door and watching as the two of them loaded their weekend bags into the trunk of Abe's BMW.

"It's not always warm, but it's definitely more comfortable than it is out here. You staying warm?"

"Oh, sure," Dennis said. "The uniform's great in the winter. I'm worried about being too hot in the summer, though."

"See you in 1997," Abe said, waving as he stepped into the driver seat.

"Oh, right! 1997! See you then, Mr. Ford."

Artie waved through the passenger-side window and turned to his left. "What happened to the other guy? The old one?"

"Oh, Roman? He finally retired."

"This guy seems nice. Think he's a friend? I've got a feeling."

"You always get a feeling. But maybe. I don't know."

And off they went, snaking through Manhattan until hitting

the Lincoln Tunnel, where they rolled at a glacial pace before emerging, like magic, in New Jersey.

"How long do you think it'll take?" Artie asked.

"At this rate? Another three hours. If we're lucky."

"I don't know that I can listen to NPR that whole time," Artie said, reaching below his seat and pulling out a book of CDs. He laughed while flipping through them. "How much of this collection is *The Path to Power*, by Robert Caro?"

"About 30 percent. Another 30 percent is *Means of Ascent*."

"Is there any music in here?"

"There should be."

Artie flipped and flipped and flipped until, finally, he gasped.

"Abraham fucking Ford," he said. "You bought the *Romeo + Juliet* soundtrack?"

"What? It's good!"

"I know it's good! I'm just surprised that you bought it."

"Everyone bought it."

"Do you mind if I slide it in?"

"I never mind when you slide it in."

Thom Yorke was crooning something indecipherable when Artie interrupted, "You were really at the office this morning, right?"

Abe's head jolted to his right, the car swerving slightly in the process. "What do you mean? Of course I was at the office."

"OK, good."

Abe's gaze slowly returned to the road ahead, snowy but not as treacherous as they'd both feared. After a dozen or so barely discernible white lines zipped past, he spoke up again. "Why would you ask that?"

"You know why I would ask that."

"You don't trust me." It wasn't a question, because he knew, right then, that he was stating a fact.

"I usually do," Artie said.

"You either do or you don't."

"Then I guess I don't."

"Do you think I was with someone?"

"Not 'someone,' I think you were with her."

"Vanessa?"

"Who else?"

"I haven't seen her in two years."

"OK."

"OK? Do you always think I'm with her?"

"No, not at all," Artie said, lifting his head from the glass and facing Abe's anxious-seeming profile. "But something about this morning felt off."

"It was hectic. Stressful. But I wasn't with her. I was at work, making sure a presumably dying and certainly miserable man named Wendell completed the sale of his company before the new year."

Artie nodded. "I'm sorry, I get nervous sometimes. Especially when I'm happy."

"So you're saying you're happy," Abe said coyly, feeling like he'd won their little argument.

Artie felt a sudden pinch of shame for even bringing it up, especially when the drive had been, until that point, so pleasant and, to his surprise, beautiful. Snow was falling gently, enough to give the outdoors a coating of wintry beauty but not so much that the surrounding landscapes—the rolling hills of the encroaching Catskills—were obscured. And here he was, ruining the moment with baseless allegations. "I shouldn't have said anything. I'm waiting for the other shoe to drop. Forget I said anything."

"The other shoe is not going to drop. At least not with me. I'm not fucking Vanessa again. I'm not even speaking to her. Which isn't exactly difficult because she finds me repulsive and despicable now. Anyway, I heard she has a new boyfriend. Some doctor."

"Who told you that?"

"Who do you think? My mother." Abe flicked on the turn signal and veered off next to a small shack of an empty gas station. He pulled up to the outside pump and stopped the car. "She said she finally read *The Outcome*."

"Your mom read my book?"

"She doesn't really understand *how* it's your book, but yes. I think the idea of a ghostwriter feels too foreign to her. She muttered something about it being dishonest. Not of you, of Sterling."

"Well, it was nice of her to read it."

"It was. People can grow up, you know. Even when they're that age."

"My parents can't."

"I think everyone deserves the benefit of the doubt. To a point."

"You're right."

"So do I have yours? For now?"

Artie reached across the center console and clutched Abe's right thigh. "Yes." He kissed Abe with intention, and gracefully yanked at the pull between the seat and the door to recline the seat. They were out in the open, windows foggy but far from opaque, but no passersby paid attention to a parked car in the lot of an abandoned service station. The snow was getting too heavy, the air too cold. Everyone had somewhere they needed to be.

When they arrived at the house some four hours later, Artie didn't notice the missing car until his knocks at the door went unanswered.

··•••··

IN THE DECADE he'd lived in New York City, Artie had been to more than enough funerals and memorial services for a dozen lifetimes, but it was rare for him to attend one in a church. An AIDS death was an affront to God, but death by car accident was a tragedy worthy of being lit through stained glass.

Artie convinced an old poet friend of his, Grace Oriel, to speak at the memorial service. They had met at an ACT UP meeting not long after Artie moved to New York, and were friendly at events, but most people who knew Grace knew her from funerals. For years, she must have been the busiest person in Manhattan, and the one with the most important job. In those days she attended multiple funerals a week, sometimes two in one day, speaking to mourners and offering them the gift of beauty. She didn't arrive in black, always in Technicolor. Her fashion was bright and hopeful, impossible to ignore; not a costume, but armor to protect her from the misery that surrounded her. She found it her duty to accept everyone who requested her presence, and Artie couldn't recall a single funeral where she had not said a few words, sometimes a poem she'd recited many times before, sometimes—if she knew the dead—something more personal, and sometimes a complete improvisation. Most memorials took place in nonreligious places, which made Grace's presence all the more valuable. She brought light with her, light and hope, and when she spoke, it was impossible not to feel like the dead person was somewhere better, even if you were otherwise certain no such place could possibly exist.

"Hi, Grace, I don't know if you remember me, but this is Artie Anderson," Artie said when Grace answered his call. He had hoped it would go to her machine, as being confronted with her booming, perpetually theatrical voice made him feel all but voiceless. "Two dear friends of mine died. Kimberly and Adam."

"I'm very sorry, Arthur," she said, which was enough to make his eyes well up.

"They weren't sick, it was a car accident. But I know they would have wanted you to say some words at their memorial. If you can. If you want to. I don't mean to pressure you at all, I just wanted to ask."

"Just tell me when and where."

"Thank you, Grace."

"And, Arthur, I remember them. And of course I remember you."

He sighed and gave her the details. "I'll see you soon. Thank you again."

When she hung up the phone, Artie cried as hard as he had after confirming the accident with the police, when he realized he and Abe must have passed the crash site on their way to the house. The ghosts totally ignored, not even a day after their deaths.

At the funeral, Adam's parents were kinder than he'd expected, but he didn't say a word to Kim's mother, who was as cold and unpleasant as she had been when Artie called her after it happened. "Thank you for telling me. I'll find a way to be there," her mother said. "But please don't call here again." Once the priest finished his blessing, he called for Grace, who stepped down the aisle in a form-fitting yellow dress with precision, a cloud of crowd whispers and the echoes of her heel clacks filling the nave.

"Good afternoon," she said, adjusting the blue fascinator atop her head before reciting a poem from memory, one Artie had never heard before. Before he could thank her for coming, she was gone.

· · • ◉ • · ·

ABE WAS BY his side in that first month, but they both knew it was over the moment they walked into that house. They just didn't acknowledge it until later, when the view of snow falling gently in the night outside their windows was too much for Artie to bear.

"I can't be here anymore, Abe," he said, his eyes following a single flake as it danced downward. Abe's sigh was all it took for Artie to know he wouldn't put up a fight. "When I look outside, it feels like they're missing. When I look in here, it feels like it's all my fault."

"Artie, it's not your fault. It's no one's fault. I'll keep saying that for as long as it takes you to realize you did nothing wrong."

"I don't know if that'll ever happen," Artie said, his forehead now on the glass, the rising heat from his body fogging the window around it. "I can't lose anyone again."

"So what," Abe said, walking to the window and resting his hand on Artie's shoulder. "What are you saying?"

Artie turned to him, his face wet and flush, and bit his cheek. "I think we should end this, while we still can."

"So you don't want to lose anyone else, but you're willing to lose me? Is that what you're saying?"

"No. I can't risk losing you, that's why I have to leave. I have to make a decision for myself, I can't let the world fuck it up for me."

"Artie, that's not how the world works. You can't just run away from it."

But there was nothing Abe could say to make Artie waver. He'd made his resolutions for 1997 two weeks late, and for a few short years, he stuck by them.

12

2022

AS HE PORED over the manuscript that morning—he always read the previous day's work before starting anew—he felt a genuine warmth for the story that hadn't yet struck him throughout the process. Those first days of writing had indeed been a breeze in terms of word count, but now that those words had begun taking a discernible shape, he was starting to see it as something with true potential. He didn't even want to outline the story because every day spent writing had been so fruitful—the story came out with such force and abundance that he thought trying to rein it in with strict parameters so early in the process would prevent all the best, most surprising ideas from reaching the page.

But today was different. Thousands of words came out in a single sitting, and his hands only stopped typing to grab a drink from the mug on his desk. Then he decided Peter could have sex. The only problem was he didn't know how he should go about it. His fingers wrote out a terrible placeholder sentence.

PETER AND COLLIN HAVE SEX. [SEX SCENE TK.]

He winced at the line, as if it had burst off the screen and started prodding his side. Technically "Peter and Collin have sex" was all the scene needed. *It's economical*, he thought. *No, it's embarrassing.* If this were to be a real queer novel, it needed to have real queer sex. A line like this was the equivalent of a camera panning into the shadows after a kiss, ashamed of everything it left unsaid. But as he watched the cursor blink beside the sentence, it begged him to offer more detail, like where they put their hands, who got undressed first, how their bodies ended up, and what they said throughout. *Not now*, he finally decided, realizing that sex with Carson could be exactly what he needed. Not only because he wanted to—and, god, he suddenly wanted to—but also because it was research.

The knock at the door was so startling that Artie nearly fell over while pouring another cup of coffee. Dennis hadn't buzzed anyone up, Carson wouldn't be over in advance of movie night for hours, and no one had called or messaged him all morning. He placed his mug on the island, grabbed his crutches, and hopped to the front door, taking a moment to acknowledge his agility and feeling certain that he couldn't have completed this task faster months ago, before the fall.

"Surprise!" Halle screamed when the door was opened. She dropped her bags at her side, reached through the crutches, and squeezed him tight. "Sorry for not calling before, I just felt like popping in straight from the airport would be a fun surprise."

He was tearing up before she pulled herself away from him. "Hal! Oh my god! I've never been happier to see someone! I'd offer to grab your bags, but as you can see, I'm badly injured," he said with a smirk, gesturing for her to come in. She threw her overnight bag on the bench to her left without looking, and he was warmed by her familiarity with the place. *She remembered,* he thought. "How long are you here? Did you come with Nolan?"

"Just a couple nights, we'll head back for Thanksgiving. Nolan had to come for work, so I thought I'd tag along before I was officially too pregnant to fly."

"Well, I'm glad you could make it. How's the West Coast?"

"Exhausting," Halle said, flopping onto the couch and pulling off her purse. She cradled her bump in a thoughtless way Artie found beautiful, a connection whose emotional power he could only imagine, one he would never be able to experience himself.

"Where are you staying? The guest room is made up if you need it."

"Nolan's boss put us up in a hotel in Midtown, near the office."

"Well, that's nice. A shame you're not staying longer, though. Would have given me a reason to cook a big meal."

"What will you do instead?"

"You know that center I joined?"

"GALS?"

"Exactly. They're having a Thanksgiving lunch, so I'll be going to that, and then one of the members, or one of my new friends, I should say, is having a few of us over for dessert and drinks and all that."

"Aww, your new friends, how sweet. I'm so glad you're meeting people."

"Have you made friends yet?"

"No," Halle said, breaking eye contact with Artie and letting out a quiet sigh. "But I think it'll be easier when the baby's here."

"I think you're probably right. Just three more months?"

"Almost exactly."

"I can't believe it."

As if a switch in her had been flipped, Halle stood up and put her hands on her hips. "If you're free, maybe the two of us could get a bite?"

"I was about to suggest the same thing, actually. That sounds great."

"Great."

"We can go to Il Passatore."

"I was hoping you'd say that. There's no good Italian near us, it's pure misery. But I should run to the hotel and drop off my things. Want to meet for lunch?"

"How's one o'clock?"

"Perfect," she said, already halfway to the front door.

"You sure I can't get you anything? A coffee?"

"I've already had my one cup of the day."

"Oh, right, the banned foods."

"Do you know how much I miss soft cheeses?"

"I don't know how you're alive," Artie said, opening the door for her. "Well, see you over there."

They hugged, and after pulling apart, Artie let his hand hover in front of her stomach. "Do you mind?"

"Feel away. The bump's all yours." He pressed his hand against Halle's belly and showed his surprise at its tightness with the bulge of his eyes. "Thought it would be squishier, right?"

"I did," Artie said, his hand still lingering. "You know I've never felt a pregnant person's belly before?"

"Really?"

The force of Artie's shaking head brought tears out of their wells, and Halle leaned in for another hug.

"I'm so happy for you," Artie said. "It's really a miracle, isn't it?"

"Me being pregnant? It was more of an accident, really, but we can talk about that over lunch," she said, zipping her coat back up.

Artie laughed and wiped his eyes with his sweater. "Sorry about the waterworks. One?"

"One it is," she said, hugging him once more. It wasn't until she'd pushed the down button at the elevator that she turned and shouted, "Love you dearly!"

"Love you dearly," he shouted right back, closing the door behind him as softly as he could.

··•●•··

HALLE WAS SITTING on a bench outside the restaurant, mindlessly flipping through her phone, when Artie approached.

"Hungry?" he asked.

"Starving. I missed this place so much."

"Did you walk?" Artie asked, noticing a slight sheen of sweat on Halle's brow.

"I did. Nine thousand steps so far today. That's more than I've walked in a day since the move."

She stood and opened the door for Artie, placing her hand on the small of his back as he made it inside, an action that made him swell with pride. He hoped the host would assume they were related, that he was a real uncle and not just a glorified neighbor whose love and generosity Halle had been forced by a guilty parent to accept.

Knowing they had such little time, Artie worried Halle would want to rush things, but she seemed to be in no hurry from the moment they sat, insisting they order one course at a time, from her nonalcoholic cocktail to several appetizers and finally a plate of pasta. She finished every plate, which made Artie as proud as if he'd cooked the meal himself, and was a font of fun conversation. She told stories about new neighbors as if Artie knew them already, treating him like someone she chatted with daily, who already knew every necessary bit of context. He followed only 30 percent of what she was saying but cherished every word as though it were a poem written just for him. She seemed so happy, he thought, feeling happier for it.

But then, just as a small sliver of olive oil cake was placed between them, her stories stopped, as if someone had pulled the emergency brake on her voice. Her features softened, and her posture drooped.

"What?" Artie said. "Is that not what you wanted? Should we have gotten the chocolate?"

"No, no," Halle said. "I just, I need to tell you something."

"Feels like you've told me everything in the last hour and a half." Halle didn't laugh, which made Artie's own smile all but disappear. "Is something the matter? Are you feeling OK?"

"I thought this would be easier if I built up to it a little and, I don't know, got some momentum? But it didn't work. I have to tell you something and it's not easy for me, but no one else will do it, and I guess there's a chance no one should, and maybe I'm fucking up by saying anything at all, but I think you deserve to know, and I think my mom is wrong for not telling you at all, even though she meant well. I think. No, I know she did, but this sucks. I wish she wouldn't have told *me*, but I guess I always knew."

"Hal, Hal, slow down," Artie said, reaching across the table to grab her hands as they twisted a napkin into a sort of dirty white rope. "Are you OK? Is someone sick?"

Halle let out a heavy sigh. "No, it's not that. Everyone's healthy as far as I know, I just . . ." she said, pulling her hands out from under Artie's. "Remember that night I came by your apartment? After your birthday?"

"Yes, of course." Artie felt his heart racing but tried his best not to show it.

"I wanted to tell you then, I promise. But I couldn't."

"Tell me what?" He took a deep breath and held it.

"A few years ago, on my birthday, my mom told me something about Abraham."

"What did she say?"

She offered him a pitiful smile, the sort of smile that looks like the end of something. "That he's not my real dad."

"No, that's wrong. What are you talking about?"

"Apparently my mom and Danny got together long before Abraham died, and I guess, uh, he never found out."

"Huh," Artie said. It's all he could muster. Of course Vanessa was fucking Danny before Abe died, he thought. She knew their marriage was over just as well as he did, and when she found out about him, why wouldn't she try to meet someone else? Like so many terribly obvious terrible things, Artie had willed himself not to see it. And now, confronted with a truth he'd subconsciously hid from for so long, he was angrier at himself than Vanessa.

"I'm so sorry. I wanted to tell you then immediately, but she told me not to. She was worried about hurting you."

"She said that?"

"Mom cared about you. She still does."

Artie shook his head quickly, forcing his own feelings of misery out of the front of his mind, at least temporarily. This wasn't about him; it was about Halle. "How did you feel when you found out?"

Halle gave a flash of a smile, then returned to a somber stare. "To be frank, I barely remembered Abraham, even then, so I guess I was a little relieved to know I didn't have to worry about missing out on him anymore. I don't mean that cruelly, it's just that it was exciting to stop mourning my father and get to know him instead."

"And did your relationship actually change?"

"Almost immediately. Night became day. I used to hate him so much for no reason. He was always good to me. I just didn't let myself realize it until Mom told me about Abe."

"Then it was the right thing for your mom to do."

Halle reached across the table, pulled Artie's hand from his water glass, and held it tightly. "I don't mean to be repetitive, but I can't help myself: I'm so sorry I didn't tell you earlier, like right when I knew."

"This never should have been your burden to bear. Don't ever apologize for that."

Halle grabbed a spoon and cut off a bite of cake. She chewed it slowly. "How are you?"

"Don't worry about me."

"Too late."

Artie shut his eyes, both to stop the tears from falling and to imagine Abe's face instead of looking at Halle's. It should have been obvious; Halle was right. Maybe he knew all along and chose to ignore it. Halle looked like the child of Vanessa and Danny. Not Vanessa and Abe. Years of resentment crashed down on Artie, and he felt like the ceiling of his apartment had collapsed. "Damn him," he said, almost ducking to avoid the rubble of his memories.

"Damn who?"

"I wish you could have known Abe," Artie said. "Even if he wasn't your father, I wish you could have really known him. You two would have gotten along. Maybe even better than you and I have."

"That's impossible."

"Eh, that was the thing about Abe. He could surprise you. He could make the impossible . . . quite possible. Even if you hated him at first, or thought you did, he found a way in. You know the only reason I became a writer is because of him?"

"You've told me."

"Of course I have."

Halle's phone began to buzz, and Artie saw her eyes dart to and away from the screen.

"You can check it. I don't mind."

"It's just Nolan. He's probably just asking if I told you. He's been almost as anxious about this as I've been. God, Artie, I should have told you so much sooner. This was so unfair of me."

"Halle, I won't say this again: Do not apologize. You did nothing wrong. And you have so many things that *deserve* your attention right now. So many things to prepare for. So much life. My foot will heal soon, and then it's back to normal for old Artie. You're going to have a baby. A new home. A new life. And I'm going to be fine. Same as I ever was. So text Nolan back. Tell him you told me and that I'm fine." He paused and leaned across the table for dramatic effect. "Because I am."

"Please don't pretend you're going to have an easy time with this, Artie. Not to me."

"Fine," Artie said, his muscles stiffening. "I'm not. But the fact remains that it's not your burden."

"Then whose burden is it?"

"You know what, Halle? That's a great question, and I'm glad you asked it. It's mine. And that's OK."

"I just don't want you to hate Abraham because of me."

Artie finally unhooked his hand from Halle's and playfully smoothed out the napkin on his lap. "I hate Abraham for all kinds of reasons, and none of them have anything to do with you. But the love's always been stronger . . . That's what I'm saying about him, he was magic in a way. A terrible asshole on one day, the kindest person you've ever met the next. Cold and hostile, warm and comfortable. Smartest man in the city, a student of law and history and literature, but couldn't find his way around a post office or a grocery store. When I lost my best friends in the whole world, he saved my life. And whether he was your dad or not, you saved it all over again. I'd never get to have you in my life without him in mine. So no, don't apologize. And pick up your phone or Nolan's going to send the cops to my apartment."

Halle laughed through her tears and followed his orders. When the bill came, he put his card down and shut down all of Halle's offers to pay. They hugged on the corner outside, Halle resting her head on Artie's shoulder, perhaps for as long as she'd ever hugged him in the past. "Well," she said as she pushed herself away from him, tears welling in her eyelids, "I should probably get going."

"Give Nolan my best."

"I will."

"And what should you not do?"

"Worry about you."

"Exactly. Because if you worry about me, I'll have to worry about you."

"Fine. It's a deal."

"Good."

She hugged him once more, briefly this time, and wiped her eyes.

"Love you dearly," she said.

"Love you dearly."

As she walked away from him for the second time in the

span of a few hours, Artie looked up at the intersection—8th
Street and 5th Avenue—then pulled his phone from his pocket.

Forgive the late text and random request,
but would you want to meet up for a drink
this afternoon before movie night? I could
use the company.

Hello! That sounds nice. Where and when?

Julius'? Now-ish? I'm leaving Il Passatore
now and about to roll over.

Oh! That's right around the corner from me,
literally my block. Let's walk together. I'll
meet you on the corner in five.

They were just north of Washington Square Park, in a part
of the Village that Artie felt always seemed to be half retirees
and half NYU students. Of course, he knew there were people
who must fall somewhere in the middle, people who didn't fit
that vision he had of the place; New York is too dense and diverse of a place to treat neighborhoods in such rigid terms. Yet
from the moment he moved to New York City, every time he
walked up 5th Avenue as the arch slowly disappeared behind
him, he felt like the only person around who was stuck in the
middle of their life. Everyone seemed to be either older or younger than him, and if he saw a contemporary, someone he recognized as a peer, they would share a knowing glance, widened

eyes that seemed to say, *Aren't you jealous?* Jealous of the ones getting high in the park who still had time to decide who they wanted to be, and of the ones reading library books on the benches who were comfortable living out the results of those choices. As he scooted around the corner now, his hands growing sweaty on the handles, a man not too much older than him, holding an elegant mahogany cane with a sparkling gold handle, nodded in his direction. He finally belonged.

Artie had only been waiting outside for a minute when Carson burst out of his apartment building, scanning the street like he was looking for a family member at a hectic arrivals gate.

"Hey," he said, finally finding Artie leaning against the facade of the building. "You got here quick."

"Something about this street makes me speed up," Artie said.

"Is everything OK?"

"Want to start walking and rolling first?"

So they did, and as Artie recounted his lunch with Halle, he never once looked at Carson. His face turned from the sidewalk to the street, to tourists taking photos of the glowing arch from much too far away, to the pathetic-looking dogs being dragged by their owners more concerned with their phones than with Fido, to the empty storefronts as well as the lively ones. When he was finished speaking, which he did without Carson ever interrupting, not even with a one-word question for the sake of active listening, he stopped half a block from Julius', turned to look his friend in the eye, finally, and said, "Can I bum a cigarette?"

Carson didn't laugh or smile; he just grabbed a pack of Marlboro Lights from his pocket. "How'd you know? I've never smoked in front of you."

"Your first time at GALS. You smelled like someone who'd just bathed in artificial scents, like a man who really wanted to keep it secret. After that it was more subtle, but sometimes you slipped. Plus, there was that time I saw the outline of a pack in your pocket."

Carson smiled. "Interesting."

"Why's that?"

"I only put them in my back pocket."

Artie blushed.

"I was a big smoker in my twenties. Quit in my thirties. Then a while back I read an interview with some actress who said she smokes one cigarette a week. Said she had a drawer in her living room where she kept a single pack and a single lighter. When I read that, I thought, *What a great idea.* So I copied her; Roger even joined in. Then he died, and once a week became once a day. Then a whole pack a day. And now I'm back down to, well, still too many, but I'm trying." He removed two and handed one to Artie. They sat down on an empty bench nearby.

"So how do you feel?" Carson asked finally.

"About Halle? I'm not sure yet," Artie said, taking a long, elegant drag and blowing it out of the side of his mouth, toward Carson's right ear. "But about this cigarette? I think it's just fantastic."

"When was your last one?"

"Not since before he died."

"You really cut it all out, didn't you?"

"I did. But it wasn't just because of him. I mean, it was all because of him, but I also lost other people," he said, his voice trembling as if uncertain where the words would take it. "Who didn't, I know. Everyone did. But they were my closest friends."

"Let me guess. There were three of them?"

Artie nodded. "And after Abe, I just threw in the towel."

Carson put his hand on Artie's cast and rubbed it softly as they finished their cigarettes. "So you're getting this off soon?"

"Monday. I wonder how I'll feel when it's gone. Another loss."

"But you get your leg back, don't you? Doesn't that count as a gain?"

Artie scratched his eye and tried to hide his smile. "So I break even."

"Think about the last couple of months. You might be net positive."

"I might be," Artie said, letting Carson see his smile. "I might be."

·· • ● •• ·

AFTER FINISHING THEIR blisteringly cold vodka martinis, they hailed a cab to movie night, at Jim's apartment this time, a dim and cramped but wholly charming two-bedroom on the Upper West Side. "The boys are here," he shouted after swinging the door wide open. "And it looks like they just screwed." Jim invited them in and asked Carson to remove his shoes. Artie's, he said, could stay on. The one exception to the rule.

"Go on into the kitchen and fix yourselves a drink. We're just gossiping in the living room. Bathroom's down the hall, if you need it." Jim's home was warm and old and friendly, the kind of place that screamed, *I'll be dying here*, which really meant rent control.

"Jim," Artie shouted from the kitchen as he watched Carson pour them both glasses of red wine from a half-empty bottle on the counter. "How much is your rent?"

"Five hundred forty-five dollars," he squealed, delighted by the question he must have hoped would be asked. "Now ask how much the twenty-five-year-old down the hall pays for the same layout."

Artie mouthed a number at Carson, who gestured for him to raise it. "Twenty-nine hundred," Artie yelled.

"Three! Thousand! American! Dollars!"

Artie heard a loud slap and pictured Jim striking his knee in a fit of laughter.

"I'm not leaving this place unless it's in a body bag."

They entered the living room, where the five other guests sat in the assortment of plush chairs and love seats surrounding a massive wooden coffee table topped with several stacks of art books and surrounded by walls of small, dark oil paintings, all of which seemed to be of a similar style.

"What's the movie tonight?" Artie said, waving at the crew of friendly, wrinkled faces.

"It *was* going to be *Moonlight*," Gregory said. "But Jim broke his damn TV. Maybe that's why we never do these over here."

"I didn't break my damn TV, I broke my damn TV stick," Jim said, holding up two pieces of a once functioning Roku stick. "Yanked at it too hard when I was moving it from the bedroom TV. I'm not paying for two."

"So I have to look at all your faces instead of Mahershala Ali's?"

"What a shame," Gregory said, clutching his glass of wine like he was afraid it would be stolen. "Now we'll have to keep each other company."

Jim watched Artie after he sat down on the chair closest to the worthless television, noticing his eyes dart from still life to still life hanging on the walls. "Who painted these?" Artie asked. "They're kind of spectacular."

"Who do you think, you dumb queen?"

Artie's eyes widened. "I had no idea you were an artist, Jim. I thought you worked for the MTA."

"You don't know shit," Jim said with a Cheshire grin. "Painted every single one of these over the past, oh, fifty years. Fifty-five, maybe."

"Well, I love them."

"Thank you."

"And thank you for keeping us around the past few movie nights. I know it's a pretty exclusive little club, and I was happy to keep getting invites."

"It's less about it being exclusive than it's about no one being able to stand it but us," Ellis said. "Plenty of people have come once and never again, but it's open to all who ask to be invited."

"Has Annabelle ever come? Anyone but the old cis men?"

"She was invited but never showed. Jazmine makes appearances at Ellis's sometimes, but I suppose this is for the grumpy old queens more than anything."

"Well, I'm happy to be here, as a burgeoning grumpy old queen myself."

"Me too," Carson said.

"Oh please," Ellis said. "I have magazines in my apartment older than the two of you."

"Ellis is a hoarder," Gregory said in his charming falsetto, getting a giggle out of Artie. "I'm not joking," he added gravely.

"No need to be cruel," Ellis said. "Where do you two live, again?"

"We're both in the Village. I'm near Washington Square Park and Artie's near Jackson Square," Carson said.

"See? Downtown is for the young."

"Did you all go there back in the day?"

"The things we did down there before the plague. Not just the men but all the dancing. Were you here for the Holy Spirit?"

"Sure," Artie said with a laugh. "A friend and I were regulars, though he was always a little more fun than me. I really was just there to dance."

"Maybe I knew him," Jim said, a wistful glint in his eye. Knowing Adam, he probably did.

"How long have all of you been friends? I can't believe I've never asked before."

"I've known Gregory since the eighties, the rest of us met at GALS."

"Did you always like it, or was there a bit of a learning curve? GALS, I mean. Everyone seems so comfortable there now."

"Takes a while to swallow your pride, so to speak," Ellis said, shaking his glass of seltzer on ice in his hand. "I didn't really start to have a nice time until I'd been going for a year.

Almost quit, but there came a point where it was either that or be alone all day. Glad I went, or I never would have met these fools."

Gregory stood, his outfit of bright, clashing patterns finally on full display for the room, and asked if anyone wanted another drink.

"Seltzer for me," Ellis said.

"Sober?" Artie asked, slightly concerned that he was prodding.

"Twenty-seven years," Ellis said, sounding quite proud.

"Congratulations."

Ellis shrugged. "Always feels funny to be congratulated for *not* doing something. Anyway, I thought we were replacing movie night with an airing of grievances. Who's got something to complain about?"

"Unfortunately you two missed a long rant about Ali."

"The coordinator?" Carson asked.

"Meanest lesbian I've ever met, and I knew Fran Lebowitz."

"Ali's not a lesbian, they're queer. And you didn't know Fran Lebowitz," Jim yelled. "You just took an elevator with her once."

"And in that amount of time she called me an asshole!"

"Because she caught you trying to close the door on her!"

Artie howled. "You tried to shut an elevator door on Fran Lebowitz?"

"It was the thirty-fifth floor! Would you want to ride an old elevator for thirty-five floors with that woman?"

"I always get the feeling they don't like me," Artie said.

"Fran Lebowitz? She didn't like anyone."

"No, Ali," Artie said, shaking his head with a laugh.

"Oh, don't worry about Ali. They don't like anyone," said Jim. "And if *we* can't stand them, I can't imagine how much the *staff* hates them. What did you think of them when you were the center's oldest volunteer?"

Artie let out a mocking laugh. "They were very curt, I guess. Seemed to not want me around. I thought it was just because of my age at first, but there's something about their demeanor that makes all that negativity seem personal. And by the way, I wasn't the oldest volunteer."

"Really? Name an older one."

Artie licked his lips and thought for a moment. "I'll have to get back to you. For now I need to use your restroom." Artie hopped onto his scooter, then rolled toward the hallway. He noticed the paintings filled every wall in the home, not just the living room, and when he finished in the bathroom, he lingered in the darkened hallway, examining each small framed piece with a curatorial eye. The paintings on one side of the hall were portraits, all of men in varying degrees of undress. Those on the other side were still lifes in the style of seventeenth-century Dutch and Spanish masters, but with food from New York City establishments. There was a table covered in Nathan's hot dogs. A box of Entenmann's donuts on a crystal platter. A tuna melt. An egg cream. Chinese takeout boxes. Hal's seltzer. Scores of paintings filled nearly every square inch of Jim's walls, and he felt compelled to give each one its fair share of attention. When Jim approached him, a few minutes into the endeavor, he had made it beyond the New York City food period and into the more traditional works featuring cheese and fruits and vegetables.

"I had to figure out stuff like apples and plums before I could master a soft pretzel," Jim said.

Artie smiled. "These are all so much fun, Jim. Really gorgeous. I could stand here for hours."

"Thanks. Another reason I can never leave this apartment. I'd never be able to afford a place with this much wall space. Furniture I can take or leave, but this stuff? I don't know what I'd do if I couldn't look at it."

"Are all the portraits of people you knew?"

"Yeah," he said after a brief hesitation. "I started painting all my friends when they got sick." He walked past Artie and pointed at the portrait of a regal-looking young white man in nothing but briefs sitting, legs crossed, on a stool. His skin was covered in lesions, but his face seemed stern and dignified, impervious to sickness. "That's Billy Woodson. First friend of mine who died of it. January 1983. After I did his, word started getting around. I painted anyone who asked, knew most of them already, had been intimate with some. You know how it was back then."

"Did you let them pick how they wanted to be depicted?"

"Always. Sometimes they asked for suggestions, but deep down they knew how they wanted to be seen. A lot just wanted their faces, as you can see. Beautiful faces, all of them. Some wanted to be naked. Some wanted to look sick, some wanted to look healthy. But by the time they got around to posing, they couldn't hide it, you know. They looked it. Couldn't walk down the street anymore without getting yelled or spit at."

"I remember."

Jim pointed at the portrait to the right of Billy's. "Freddie Powers, artist." He pointed to the right. "Jason Graham, lawyer. Patrick Taylor, actor. Martin Pelagry, lover *and* actor. Tim Murphy, lover and photographer. Stephen Davies, dancer. Thomas Green, bartender. Felix Torres, Tony Award–nominated actor who refused all my advances. Freddie Cox, writer. Mario Aguilar, lover and dancer. Willie Fraser, lover." He sighed. "It's nice to see them every day. It's what they wanted, too. I told them, 'You know I'm doing this partly for me, don't you?' I said I wanted to look at them every day, and that they could pick how they wanted me to see them forever."

"That's amazing."

"A friend of mine who owns a gallery wanted to display them for Pride one year some time ago, but I told her they weren't to leave this wall until I was dead. So maybe one day they'll be in a place where more people can see them, but for now I want them for myself. Maybe that's awful."

"I don't think so."

"I forgot what it's like to meet people your age."

Artie laughed. "What do you mean, my age? You're acting like I'm a millennial."

"No, I'm serious," Jim said, the faces around him seeming to ease in closer to listen. "When did you move here?"

"To New York? 1986."

"You just missed it."

Artie filled the silence by scratching his knee resting on his scooter. "I always thought I got here right in the middle of it."

"It makes me sad, knowing people only a few years younger

have no idea what it was like before everyone started dying. I say this without rose-colored glasses, too, believe me, it wasn't nirvana. But it was something else."

Artie nodded. "I don't like thinking about it, to be honest. The way it could have been for me, for everyone."

"I think that's healthy, but sometimes you can't help it, can you? Thinking about who you would have met, lovers you could have had, lovers you *couldn't* have had. Just, people you could have known."

"Exactly," Artie said, wiping a tear from his right eye.

"The people up on those walls, I know all their names. And if I type them into Google, which I do sometimes, nothing. *That's a different Mario Aguilar. That's a different Thomas Green.* Or maybe it says no results at all."

Artie looked up at all the faces after trying to ignore their lines of sight. He invited them in, finally. Allowed them to be seen and to see him right back.

"To people your age," Jim said, "being gay, queer, whatever you want to call our kind of difference these days, it was built on tragedy. On death. Their lives were defined by the plague. Do you feel that way?"

Artie nodded. "I always have."

"So was ours. So was everyone's. But people my age had the luxury of the rearview mirror. Tragedy was there, it was just a little further behind. You know what I mean? HIV wasn't the first tragedy to befall us," he said, almost laughing. "Sometimes I think it's easy to forget that."

"I think that might be true."

"It also might be a bunch of drunken bullshit. But it sounded nice, didn't it?"

Artie laughed louder this time, and Jim joined in. "So," he said. "When did you start on the food?"

"You know the sort of nice part? Food came when fewer people were dying. The food's hope, in a way. I said, I still need things to paint, so I just painted what was around."

"Do you have more fun doing the modern food or the classic still lifes?"

"I love the classic stuff. The pears and the peaches and the wheels of cheese."

"I like the moldy ones. The fuzz on the cheese and the wrinkled peels. All those blisters and bruises."

Jim smiled and grabbed Artie's shoulder. He leaned into Artie's ear and said conspiratorially and in a near whisper, "Old fruits are so much more interesting, don't you think?"

"Yeah," Artie said. "I think that's right."

Pulling back from his friend, Jim returned to his normal-speaking voice. "I never see you at the GALS events, just meals at the center. Why is that?"

"All the walking," Artie said, only half lying. While it was true that he didn't love the idea of walking through museums and gardens and other spaces in New York City with a GALS-sanctioned tour guide for physical reasons, he also didn't expect to find any of the events all that stimulating. After learning about the activities at one of his first GALS dinners, he imagined a group of catatonic people thirty years older than himself being wheeled around the Museum of Modern Art by mute nurses dressed in overstarched white uniforms. At dinner they were a homogenous bunch of elders sitting down and chatting, their real ages masked by food and conversation. Out in the world they were aged up by their surroundings, pathetic creatures offered extra assistance by people who could see nothing but fear when looking in their direction. *God*, he imagined those young people thinking. *I hope I don't end up like them.*

"Well, we're doing one at the Dahesh Museum next week. If you like these, you'll like their current exhibition. Why don't you come?"

Artie scratched his neck, feeling a pang of guilt for avoiding the full extent of what GALS had to offer for so long, and decided that he wouldn't just go halfway. A smile washed across his face. "Sure. Sounds nice."

"Great," Jim said, a lilt in his voice.

The two of them returned to the living room and found the conversation had moved into politics. All of them were complaining about the mayor, relaying recent headlines they'd seen and exchanging exasperated reactions to each one, as if they didn't already know the stories. Jim put out a few bags of chips and pretzels that he'd forgotten to open earlier, and they were eaten by the time everyone decided to leave, after they talked about movies they'd seen and friends they once had and people they once loved. Artie and Carson were the last to walk out and lingered in the hall as they said an extended goodbye to Jim through the open door.

"Thank you again for having us," Artie said. "I didn't realize how much I've been needing these boys' nights."

"Whatever it was, it certainly wasn't a 'boys' night,' but of course."

"I'll be at the next one with bells on."

"So will I," Carson said. Once they were both turned toward the elevator, the slam of the door was followed by two pronounced sounds of locking mechanisms. The night was officially over, save for the journey home.

"That was fun, wasn't it?" Carson said as they emerged from Jim's apartment building onto 91st Street.

"It was," Artie said. "I like them all a lot. I had no idea Jim was such a wonderful artist."

"I didn't know he was an artist at all. I just thought he was an asshole. And he isn't!"

Artie laughed. "I never thought of it like this until now, but GALS is sort of like an office. I've only known them in a specific, single context for weeks, and now, being outside of it all, I know them in a completely different way."

"GALS is a job. Making friends at our age, hell, meeting people at all? That's work. It doesn't happen the way it did when we were kids. When we were in our twenties and thirties. Nothing's organic, you have to put in the effort."

"I'm still impressed you were able to do it so quickly. To go through what you did and find everyone at GALS. To find me," Artie said. They walked half a block before he continued. "Everything just takes longer for me. It always has. I wish I didn't feel so comfortable in my own head. It's not that fun of a place."

"I've never felt too happy in mine," Carson said. "Maybe that's the difference. I've always needed an external distraction."

The comment gave Artie a prickly feeling, and he considered asking if he was nothing but a distraction, but then Carson kept talking.

"I don't mean that in a dismissive way at all, I'm just incapable of being alone. I've been told that my whole life—by my parents, by my friends, by my lovers, by my therapist. They always say it with such disdain, too." He lowered his voice to a new register and imitated them. "*You're incapable of being alone.* So what? I seek people out. Always have. They're not always people I'd like to have around forever, but I'd rather have a dud than silence."

"Does that mean I'm not a dud?"

"That's exactly what it means. So what happened?"

"What do you mean?"

"You say you hardly socialized since Abe died, but you don't act like someone who's been that reclusive. I have now been to a few parties with you and have witnessed nothing but normal to better-than-average party behavior. What's the deal?"

Artie stopped walking and brought the wheels of his scooter to a halt while he touched his eye in a manner Carson couldn't decide was scratching or wiping a tear. "They were— God, it would feel reductive to call them my entire life. They were my twenties and thirties. They were my New York family turned my only family. I wrote a fucking book about them, and then they died. Then Abe died, and all I had left was Halle."

"You had yourself, too."

"It took me a very long time to realize that. I think I was so used to losing people that it only seemed logical to take myself out of the picture, too."

"Hence the ghostwriting. You could be all sorts of other people. Anyone but yourself."

Artie squinted and apprehensively tapped the scooter's right handle with his thumb. "It's a little on the nose, isn't it?"

"Maybe, but it makes you make sense to me."

"Halle was all I had left of them. Not just Abe, but the others. Watching her grow up made their deaths feel . . . not justified, obviously, but it made it hurt less. I know that sounds disgustingly selfish."

"It does and it doesn't. But you know what they say, funerals are for the living."

Artie laughed. "You know the silliest part? I told myself I'd never go to another funeral again. And I haven't. Not since Abe. I've been to enough funerals to last a hundred lives—I'm sure you have, too. And here I am making friends with people who could die any minute. Yourself included, no offense."

"None taken. Everyone could die at any minute."

"I'm aware. But you know what I mean. We're all in hospice."

Carson stayed silent.

"When did you move here again?"

"'92."

"What if we'd met then? What if we'd met in the last twenty years?" Artie asked, looking beyond Carson at the city, the country, the whole world that surrounded him. "I fucked up, didn't I?"

"You didn't fuck up."

They stood still and stared directly into each other's eyes as a muffled siren moved north until the sound finally dissipated.

"You would have liked them, you know," Artie said.

"Your friends?"

"Yeah. I think you really would have loved them."

Carson nodded. "You know why you've been feeling so nuts lately?" he asked, a wave of wisdom glossing over his face suggesting he had an answer.

"Because I broke my foot? Because the closest thing I'll ever have to a daughter moved across the country? Because I'm making friends? Because I'm officially old? Take your pick."

"When's the last time you had a new feeling?"

Artie's eyes widened, and he looked up to search the hazy black above him for the answer.

"That's what getting older is," Carson said, figuring it out as he went along. "That's all it's ever been for as long as you've been getting older. From the time you were a minute old. New feelings piled on new feelings. You've gone out of your way to avoid them so that you can avoid the feelings you hate. The feelings that wrecked you. You chose no feelings over new ones. Because new ones are a risk."

"Thank you, Doctor. I think you're probably right."

"I've been known to be right from time to time."

"I think I'm ready to ask you," Artie said.

"Ask me what?"

"What you thought about *Four Squares*."

"Oh," Carson said, scratching around his Adam's apple like Vito Corleone. "I don't read much fiction, and don't think I know how to say the right things about it, so take everything I want to say with a grain of salt."

"I'll take it with a whole chunk, and there's no wrong thing to say."

Carson held his breath, then exhaled with a confusing reluctance. "Well," he said, dragging his thoughts out to the point that Artie almost broke, "I thought it was amazing. I felt like I knew all of them, and it made me cry."

"What part made you cry?"

"The end. When they realize they're never more at home than they are with each other. Not when they're dancing or in bed with some new lover or whatever it may be, it's just when the four of them are all together. That's what the book's about, right? The pleasure of finding your people?"

Artie offered Carson a half smile. "It's about whatever you think it's about."

"Don't give me that author shit, Arthur. What do you think it's about?"

Artie shrugged. "It's about that."

"I thought so," Carson said with a satisfied nod, and the two continued their southward march.

··•●•··

ARTIE CONSIDERED ASKING Carson up when they approached the door to his building, and Carson considered asking for an invitation, but instead they ended their night with a long hug. "Thank you for the company. I don't usually drink that much. Or smoke that much. I feel like I'm thirty again."

"Ditto," Carson said.

"Walking home?"

"May as well go all the way, right?"

Artie laughed as Ronald, one of the night doormen, pulled

on the handle. "Good night, Ronald," Artie said. "Good night, Carson."

"Good night, Mr. Anderson," they both said at once.

Once upstairs, Artie shut his apartment door behind him and leaned against it with all his weight to sigh with a purpose, as if he were exhaling an entire life's worth of breath. As he inhaled a new one, he felt a rustling against the door. Turning to put his ear against the cold, painted metal, he could hear it, too. Nothing was visible through the peephole but the wall across from him, but the noise continued, so he opened it up and turned his head from left to right and then, finally, down.

"Hello, Walter," he said as the cat wrapped its shiny gray body against the rough, fading purple of Artie's cast. "Where've you been?"

13

2004

FROM THE MOMENT he first saw him at the end of the bar, Artie knew Abe would ruin his life. Even after Way and then Adam and Kim were gone, and then Abe, in his own way, when Artie claimed to believe no relationship could ever last after being forged in the shadow of such extreme tragedy, when his life was in utter shambles, he expected a third act. Abe was like a comet that circled Artie's life in an erratic, unpredictable orbit. Even when he wasn't glowing directly overhead, he was out there, somewhere, floating through the unknown with no order to his journey beyond the simple fact that Artie was somehow the unwitting celestial body in its center.

For the first few months after the funerals and the subsequent breakup, Artie simply avoided everything. He stopped visiting Julius' because the memory of his friends made the mere sight of its flimsy corner door physically painful, and if he happened to see Abe on the street, he'd turn the other way or duck into a store. In time the sightings stopped entirely, and he assumed Abe had either fully committed to Vanessa's apartment on the Upper West Side or found someone. Maybe even both. A part of Artie wanted that for him, too. More pessimistic than ever, he imagined Abe's happiness as a satisfactory replacement for his own. That would do, he thought, burying himself in a bigger workload than ever before and churning out copy more quickly than his agent could ever expect or even want. At such a breakneck pace, the ghostwriting job made him feel like a man on the run, hiding out in someone else's life for a few months before the heat was turned off and he had to find another one in which to squat. They weren't all bestsellers, but no one in the industry would ever fault him for a memoir's failure. Artie was reliable, quick, and easy to work with.

By the summer of 2004, he had worked up the kind of momentum that made his career feel invincible. With over twenty books under his belt, writing now felt like the only functioning part of his life, the cantilever upon which every broken part of him rested. He was happy, but only by default. Still, his long-term lack of active unhappiness led him to consider ending a seven-year drought and start seeing people again. He never lost his interest in sex, but all the fears surrounding it had only intensified. For as long as he'd been fucking, he'd been afraid of it, and even when he allowed himself to be thrilled and consumed by a new body, the dopamine rush was inevitably followed by a crippling fear. He couldn't bear to lose anything else—not another man, not another reliable hookup, not a friend, and certainly not his health. When he wasn't writing, he was going for walks, cooking, exercising at home, reading, watching movies at the theaters within walking distance. He filled every minute of his day with an activity so that there would be no time for another man, another friend. He thought that if he kept to himself, people would keep away. Which was why, because he never expected any kind of company, the buzzer was so startling.

It was so sudden. Tinny and small and casual. The voice bubbling out from the panel on Artie's wall was scratchy and competing with street noise in the distance, but its speaker was obvious from the first word. "Artie?" he said. "It's Abe."

Artie dropped the pen in his hand; then, shaken by the noise it made hitting the wood floor, reached down to grab it before responding. He pressed the talk button and inhaled. "Hi." Release. Listen.

"I'm glad you never got rid of this place." Release. Talk. Release. Listen.

"Can I come up?" Release. Buzz.

Artie looked around at his apartment, suddenly fearful that it was too messy for his first guest in years, but it wasn't. As usual, everything was in order. He saw it now as the respectable, perhaps even enviable home of a working writer. He was less confident about his face, however, and he studied his week of stubble and shaggy hair with a hint of concern. Would he still be desirable with his paleness and newfound grays? He shook his head to force out the onslaught of insecurities. He placed his hand on his chest upon hearing the knock at the door and noted the perfectly normal beating of his heart and general feeling of calm. He'd made a whole life for himself, and he was content in it.

The first thing Abe said was "I'm sorry." Artie hadn't even finished pulling the door open and there it was, an apology. He wasn't even sure what Abe was apologizing for, but like most apologies, he appreciated hearing it.

"Hi," Artie said in reply, an octave higher than he expected to. They shared a timid, squeezeless embrace in the doorway before Artie invited him in. "This is a surprise."

"I said I'm sorry," Abe repeated.

"I heard you the first time, and I'm sorry, too."

They let their apologies speak for everything an apology could, and moved to the living room, where they sat beside each other on the couch, intimate but awkward, both of them looking forward with their backs straight and fearful of the cushion behind them.

"So what brings you back here," Artie said, masking his discomfort with a dissonant playfulness. "I thought I heard you and Vanessa finally got married."

"You heard that?"

"It was in the paper. Nice photo, by the way. You and Vanessa make a very handsome couple, like the concept of repression sprouted two pairs of legs."

"I deserved that," Abe said.

"That's why I said it."

"Well, there's no sense boring you with the details, but that's over. Also, the *Times* announcement was her parents' idea."

"Sure. Nice ring," Artie said, still looking at the small blank television across the room.

"We're still married, but we've decided to end it," Abe said, twisting the band with his right fingers. "That's not quite right, actually. She did. There's another guy. His name is Danny."

"And you thought, *Artie's probably free. Artie will help me pick up the pieces. Artie knows what it's like to be cheated on. Artie certainly has nothing going on*," Artie said, whimpering, finally turning to face the man beside him and taking in all the ways it had grown older while trapped in an unhappy marriage of his own making. There were more grays and more wrinkles, but a clear polish of pride. He had the face of someone who was content to look in the mirror and see the number time had done on him. Yes, Abe was still the best-looking person Artie knew. And when he spoke, even after all those years of silence, it was the voice Artie most wanted to hear.

"No," Abe said, meeting his gaze. "I came here because I was thinking about you. And I was thinking about you because I'm always thinking about you. I never stopped thinking about you. I used to think I could, but I couldn't. I can't. And I don't want to. Ever."

"Well, now that you're here, what are you thinking?"

Neither of them could decide on an answer, so they kissed.

·•◉•·

ABE WAITED UNTIL after both of them had come to bring up Halle. "I have a daughter," he said, his left leg wrapped around Artie's right, both of their bodies covered in sweat and drowned in light from the scorching summer sun. "And I want you to meet her. I just need some time."

Artie wanted to be mad—mad at himself for not knowing,

mad at Abe for not telling him before they had sex. But the thought of a child, even if she wasn't his, wasn't something he could bring himself to direct even the slightest bit of anger toward. Abe had never mentioned wanting children—nor had Artie—but now that there was one, even if she was only his and that wretched Vanessa's, how could he resent her?

"What's her name?" Artie said, his eyes on the ceiling and hands on Abe's thigh.

"Halle. She's amazing."

Artie bounced up without warning and climbed on top of Abe, pressing both hands against his chest. "I just got to a point in my life where things are good. Where I was only thinking about you *some* of the time," he said, taking a few deep breaths and pressing harder into Abe's body, locking him onto the bed. "If we do this, we do this. There's no more leaving. Not again."

Abe nodded and grabbed Artie's wrist. "No more leaving."

"We're going to be happy," Artie said, nearly convincing himself that was indeed something he could demand. "And we're not going to fuck with someone else's life. Especially not a kid's."

"We will. And we won't."

·· •◉•·

FOUR MONTHS OF happiness was all they got. Four months of evenings together—dinner and drinks and movies and walks around the Village. Four months of sex, every night they were together. Four months of Abe gently laying the groundwork with Halle, Vanessa, and Danny for their eventual combining of lives. Four months of Saturday night movies on HBO and ordering in. Four months of Artie assembling a new vision for his future, bit by bit, as he let himself decide a future was possible.

Then, one Sunday morning, when he finally grew worried by how late Abe was sleeping in, Artie touched his partner's body and found it limp. After panicking, he listened for a breath, then called 911 and kept listening. He tried CPR but later learned he hadn't compressed Abe's chest hard enough, so nothing he did made a difference. By the time the ambulance arrived, he'd pulled all the sheets off Abe's naked body. He felt a sliver of life in him—there must have been a little, or the paramedics wouldn't have promised to do all they could as long as he would just get out of the way. "Move," one of them finally yelled. So he did. He stood in his bedroom and watched through the door as they tried to make Abe's heart start back up, and then he called Vanessa.

···•●•··

SUNDAY MORNINGS HAD been a miserable time for Vanessa since Abe left. She hadn't yet worked up the nerve to get Danny to move in, on the advice of the lawyer her parents paid for, and hadn't the slightest clue how to keep Halle entertained without their nanny, Pauline, around. When the phone rang, she was sitting in the armchair in her office reading the newspaper and drinking coffee, turning up the volume on her stereo to drown out whatever nonsense Halle was watching on the Disney Channel in the other room. Maybe she'd ask Pauline to start working six days a week, she thought after hearing the second ring. A home and a child were too much to take care of when she was completely alone, and she knew Danny wouldn't be much help even when he finally got the go-ahead to move in.

"Hello," she said once the receiver was to her ear. The breathing on the other end was loud and annoying, so she adjusted her tone accordingly and repeated her greeting. "I'm going to hang up if you don't say something in two seconds. One . . ."

"Is this Vanessa?" a quivering voice on the other end said.

"Yes. And who is this?"

"This is Artie, Abe's—"

"I know who you are. What do you want?"

"The paramedics are here. I think he had, I don't know, I think he had a heart attack. A stroke. He's unconscious. The paramedics are here."

"You said that already. Can I talk to him?"

"He's unconscious."

"Of course. Where are they taking him?"

As she listened to him ask the EMTs, she scoffed into the phone, unable to imagine not asking the question immediately.

"They're taking him to Lenox Hill."

"Good," she said. "I'll be there soon."

After hanging up, she reopened the newspaper and let her eyes pan over a story about the war in Iraq, only no words made their way in. She tossed the newspaper on the floor and turned off her stereo, allowing the piercing screams of precocious children to flow into her office. She would have to tell Halle, but first she'd have to decide what to tell her.

Her anger—with Abe, with herself, with Danny, with the world—prevented her from being even remotely optimistic with regards to her husband's health. She knew he would be dead before she arrived at the hospital, so there was no need to rush and scare the poor girl. She recalled the plan she and Danny had made some weeks earlier. Halle would be told the truth about her father in blunt terms, with the hopes that the lack of a biological connection would render her uninterested in continuing a relationship after the divorce was finalized. Abe was never more than her mother's dear friend, and marrying him had been a mistake because she really loved Danny, Halle's real father. She worried about those kinds of nuanced adult emotions and scenarios confusing her daughter, but the thought of ripping Abe out of both their lives like a rainbow Band-Aid would make it easier to move forward, and for Halle to forge a relationship with the man who actually helped create her. But now what? It was one thing to explain an unhappy marriage and sexual affairs to a child, but to throw death in at the same time? She couldn't, not right then.

"Halle," she said, after flipping off the TV. "Can I talk to you for a second?" Halle was lying on her stomach on the floor, her head propped in the palms of her hands—the precise TV-watching position that made her mother furious. Despite the black screen, Halle didn't flinch. "And can you sit up straight and look at your mother, please?"

She did as she was told with the aggrieved pace of a teenager, despite being only six years old.

"Halle, I have to tell you something very important. Your father was just taken to the hospital."

Halle's eyes narrowed, and the muscles in her tiny face twitched as she tried to figure out what that could possibly mean. "Is Daddy sick?"

"I think so," Vanessa said, sitting down on the floor in front of Halle and placing her hands on her knees. "But we need to go to the hospital to find out. We need to talk to the doctor and see what they say."

"Is he going to die?"

Vanessa sucked in her lips and took a breath. "I don't know, sweetheart. That's why we need to go and see him."

"Is this because of the divorce?" Halle said.

"What? Of course not. People don't get sick because of divorce. Divorce can be a good thing, just like I told you."

"You said I'd get to see him again."

"You will, sweetheart, we're going to go see him now."

"OK," Halle said, standing up slowly and walking toward her bedroom.

"Now, go put on your shoes. Do you need me to help?"

Halle shook her head and disappeared on the other side of the door, leaving Vanessa alone on the floor. While she waited for Halle, she dialed Danny, who answered after a single ring.

"I think Abe had a heart attack," she said.

Danny sighed directly into the phone. "Jesus Christ. Is he going to be OK?"

"I have no idea, but Halle and I are going to the hospital now."

"Do you need me to come? Do you want me to?"

"I don't think that's a good idea now, I think it would just . . . complicate things. But I want you to know."

"OK. OK. How are you feeling?"

Vanessa didn't respond because she didn't know the answer. "I'll call you when I know more," she eventually said, hanging up the phone to see Halle waiting patiently in the doorway.

"I'm ready," she said.

"That's good," Vanessa said, hoping she could hide the fact that she wasn't ready at all.

· · ● ● ● · ·

THOUGH SHE'D NEVER seen his photo, Vanessa recognized him immediately. Her jaw was tight, and she thumbed her wedding ring in a manner Artie couldn't decide was aggressive or nervous or both. "So you're him," she said. "You're the one he always wanted."

"I'm Artie," he said. "And you're Vanessa." He pretended not to notice Halle hiding behind her mother, a courtesy both she and her mother silently respected.

"So what did he say?"

"What do you mean?"

"Before the ambulance came. What did he say?"

"He wasn't conscious. When I found him, I mean. He didn't say anything."

"How long had he been out when you found him?"

"I'm not sure. Could have been minutes, could have been more. He wasn't cold, there was still a warmth to him."

"That's good. That's something. Maybe he'll be fine."

"He will be. They said they're doing everything they can."

"I want to talk to a doctor. Where's a doctor?"

"He said he would check in when there's an update," Artie said, and they both sat down, an empty chair between them, as Halle slinked over to a vending machine down the hall.

"I knew we'd have to meet eventually," she said when the sounds of the hospital, other emergencies, other traumas, became too much to bear.

"I know it's complicated for everyone."

"Some of us more than others."

"How is Halle?"

Vanessa shut her eyes and pretended not to hear the question, and they sat beside each other—one of them looking forward, the other inward—for half an hour, when a voice interrupted both their despondent trances.

"Mr. Anderson, hi," a handsome man in a white coat said, ignoring Vanessa. Artie flinched and looked up at the doctor as Vanessa stood, towering over them both.

"Well, I don't know what you've been told," the doctor said. "And if you'd rather do this without your daughter, maybe—"

"I've been told nothing, and I won't be hiding anything from her," Vanessa said, grabbing Halle's hand.

The doctor gave Halle a painful smile, which said everything Vanessa and Artie needed to know. "Well, ma'am, after resuscitating your husband in the emergency room, I'm sorry to say his heart gave up. He had a massive cardiac arrest, and once we were able to get inside, there was nothing we could do." He grabbed her hand and apologized once more.

"So that's it," Vanessa said. "No surgery? No transplant? No nothing? He's just gone?"

"We tried all the options available to us, but with an attack that massive, it wasn't possible. I don't think we would have been able to do more even if he'd made it here sooner."

"Can we see him?"

"Yes, follow me please if you'd like. And Mr. Anderson, if you—"

Vanessa snapped, "Not him. Just Abraham's family."

· · • ● • · ·

ARTIE SAT DOWN. Alone again.

When the lawyer told Vanessa Abe had changed his will two months before and left the apartment to Artie, she asked him to repeat himself. An hour later, she offered to buy the apartment from Artie, and when he rejected her generous offer, she hung up the phone without a goodbye and flew into a rage. Not because she was in love with the space—they'd always lived in her apartment uptown—but because she didn't want her life to intersect with that of this peculiar man who had infatuated Abe in a way that she never wanted, or perhaps would never be able, to understand.

As time went on, though, Vanessa began to reconsider. Perhaps it was because she felt guilty for not inviting him to the funeral. Perhaps it was because she felt sorry for his loneliness. Perhaps it was because she wanted Halle to have a little piece of Abe in her life, even if he wasn't her father. But five months after Abe's death, she gave Artie a call.

"I'd like you to meet Halle," she said, as if there had only ever been warmth between them. "Properly."

"I appreciate that," Artie said.

"245 West 74th. 8A. Come Sunday for dinner. Six."

So he did. And he did the following Sunday. And every Sunday he was asked to return.

14

2022

THE FIRST AND only person Artie sent a photo of his newly bare foot to was Halle. For the better part of two months he had tried not to think about what lay underneath his cast, imagining something mangled and horrific that would repulse him. Even when it stopped hurting, when the healing stage was at full steam, he didn't want to consider what his foot had become. Living without knowing what this piece of him looked like anymore seemed entirely feasible, if not reasonable. Examining it then, as the doctor was off doing lord knew what in another part of the office, he was surprised by its normalcy. His left foot looked the same as it did when he'd last seen it: pale and old and covered in wisps of hair. What a relief.

LOOK WHO'S FINALLY FREE. (My foot.)

He added the image and tapped SEND, only slightly worried that she was around people who might be confused by the sight of an old man's foot suddenly appearing on her phone. Surely she would know how to explain it, he thought, although what she would call him by was uncertain, now that their relationship was newly undefined. But by sending a photo of his foot, ready to walk down the road to recovery's home stretch, he was asserting his place in her life. Yes, he decided while listening to the hum of fluorescent lights above him, sending the photo was the right thing to do.

When the doctor walked in, he was still beaming at his foot.

"Sorry about that," she said, shutting the door behind her softly with that casually formal doctorly manner. Dr. Sanchez was tall, well over six feet, which Artie now decided was reassuring because tall people, with their bigger limbs and feet, would somehow take matters of the feet more seriously. The theory didn't make sense, but that didn't stop him from deciding it was true just then. "X-rays look great. The bone healed just like we wanted it to."

"I think I wanted it a little more than you did," Artie said with a sigh to match. "So I can ditch the scooter and the crutches? Just walk on this boot you have for me?"

"Don't get ahead of yourself. Walk on the boot while your body gets used to the pressure, but don't toss anything out just yet. If you're in pain when you walk, get back to rolling. But try and walk as much as you can without them—I mean it. You won't heal properly unless you start putting those muscle systems to work again with assistance-free walking. Be sure to listen to your body, but don't baby it. It's capable of more than you think."

"Sounds good."

"No running, though. Not for a few more months at least."

"I've never been a runner. No time to take anything in. I prefer a walker's pace."

"Great. Is there anything else you need at the moment? Any questions about the recovery?"

"No questions. Just relieved you didn't find a tumor or something in the X-rays."

Dr. Sanchez smiled and said, drolly, "I don't see a lot of foot cancer."

"Perk of the job, I guess. Not a lot of, you know, 'I'm afraid I have some bad news' chats when you're focused on feet," Artie said, immediately regretting it. "Anyway, thanks for everything."

Dr. Sanchez wished Artie well and stepped back into the hall. At the front desk he was given a sheet of foot exercises and a list of over-the-counter scar medications and sent on his merry way. Out on the sidewalk, holding both handles in one hand and looking south, he considered walking the thirty or so blocks home, but after a few blocks realized the scooter was considerably more awkward to carry than to use, so he walked carefully down the steps of the 42nd Street stop, hopped onto the just-arrived train, gladly taking a seat offered to him by a man who didn't appear to be much younger than he. When he reached 23rd Street, he checked his watch and bolted up. "You can have it back," he said to the young man while fumbling awkwardly for the door before it closed. On the platform, he took a moment to regain composure as the train continued its journey south and then shifted his weight to his still healing foot. There was a tingle, but no pain. Another step, and again, no pain, but a subtle difference to the gait he once knew. Huh, he thought. Another new feeling.

He hadn't been to lunch at GALS since before Thanksgiving and felt a sudden craving for the comfort of its cafeteria-style food and camaraderie. But when he stepped into the dining hall, he noticed that something was off. There were plenty of people, not a surprise for a Monday, but very little chatter.

"Hello, Artie," Ali said, startling him while he stared at the morose-looking members at their tables from the doorway.

"Oh, hello," Artie said. "You scared me. How was your holiday? Still eating turkey sandwiches?"

"Well, I'm a vegan, so we didn't do a bird. And I hate tofurkey. But yeah, I had plenty of leftover sides."

"Did I miss something earlier? Why does everyone look so upset in there?"

"So you didn't hear, then," Ali said.

"I guess not. Did something happen to one of the members?"

"Annabelle. She died."

Artie gasped and covered his mouth. "Oh god, when?"

"In her sleep, late Thursday or early Friday. Her staff told us this morning, and you just missed the announcement. We're sending out an email later, too, with some memorial information."

GALS included a list of members who had died in their quarterly newsletter and honored all of them at the end of every year, but it didn't surprise Artie that Annabelle was being given special treatment. She was the most significant donor of all the

299

members, and had been a part of NYC society, not to mention its gay life, since well before the center was founded.

"I just saw her, too. She seemed perfectly healthy."

"Maybe she was," Ali said.

Without asking for permission, Artie fell into Ali and gripped them in a tight hug, sobbing into their shoulder with a ferocity and suddenness that made them gasp. They buckled under Artie's weight at first, then stood firmly, rubbing his back as he cried it all out.

"I'm sorry," Artie finally said when he rose up from Ali's shoulders. "I know you hate hugs, it's just—"

"Don't apologize," Ali said. "It's never easy."

"Why did I think it would get easier? After all this time, all these people." Artie wiped his nose with his sleeve, a pathetic, vulnerable gesture he didn't even try to hide. But before he could politely exit and leave Ali to themself, they put a hand on his shoulder. "Call me crazy, but I thought the vegan comment would do it. I know that's all she told you about me."

"Do what?"

"Do you really not remember, or have you just been pretending?"

Artie gave Ali a look that expressed as much confusion as it did mortification.

"So you *don't*. Better than the alternative, I guess."

"I guess I don't. How would we have met before?"

"I'm only about ten years younger than you, and we never officially met, but—" Ali said right as it hit him.

"Oh my god," Artie said gravely. "You and Kim."

Ali nodded.

"How did I not put that together? I'm such an old fool."

"I don't think we spoke at the funeral, but I still thought you'd recognize me. For a while I thought you did and that you just didn't want to acknowledge me. That it made you too, I don't know, uncomfortable. Guilty."

"Guilty?"

"God, I'm sorry, I'm not saying you should feel guilty," Ali said with palpable regret, their stern facade all but disappeared for the first time since he'd been coming to GALS. "I just, I never told you, how could I have, that, and this is absolutely crazy and sad, but . . ."

"What?"

"I talked to Kimberly on the phone the day before. Or the day of. And the whole conversation was about you."

"The last conversation you ever had with Kim was about me?"

"She was so goddamned mad at you," Ali said with a wistful laugh.

"Because we were going to be late?"

"Because she wanted as much time with you as possible before she—we—left."

Artie narrowed his eyes. "What do you mean, 'left'? Where was she going?"

"She'd accepted an apprenticeship in California. Just a year, working with some big photographer. We were planning on going out there together."

"And I chose Abe over her."

"In retrospect she was being a little unreasonable, but at the time, whew. It was the first time I'd seen her that angry. I can still hear her voice. I remember one line verbatim."

"What was it?"

Ali shut their eyes and shook their head. "You don't want to know."

"Yes. I do."

"She said, 'Sometimes I think he's the most selfish and insufferable faggot I've ever met.'"

Artie was unmoved. "Yeah, well. She wasn't wrong."

"I was so mad at you, and I didn't even *know* you. I was so convinced her death was your fault—entirely your fault—that I wanted to confront you at the funeral. I actually planned to! Scripted it all out in my head. I wanted to humiliate you in front of a crowd. I wanted to make you feel as awful as I felt. And then I saw you there, as miserable as I was, probably more, and it all just melted away. Then I finally decided to read your book. I read it a few times in those first few years after, actually. It kept Kimberly alive in a way."

A tear fell down Artie's cheek, and his eyelids began to twitch. "I'm glad it was able to do that for you. I read it for the first time in decades not too long ago, actually. Surprisingly wasn't that bad."

"No, it was great."

Artie smiled and looked down at his feet, as incapable of accepting a compliment as ever. "I'm sorry you never got the chance to move away with her."

"I'm sorry she never got the chance to hate Los Angeles."

Artie laughed and looked back up at them with a warmer gaze, the kind you reserve for friends. "So you still gave it a shot?"

"Just for a year. Wasn't for me," Ali said, biting their lip. "As

I've gotten older, I've realized that's what so much of life is. Just endlessly figuring out what is and isn't for you. I wasn't prepared for all the changing."

"I know exactly what you mean. Sometimes I wonder what they would all be doing now. Where all those little forks in the road would have taken them."

"Kim and Adam?"

"All of them," Artie said. Then, after a pause, "Can I give you another hug?"

"No." The two of them stood there awkwardly until, finally, Ali reneged. "OK, fine. But make this one quick." So he did.

"I'm sorry I didn't put the pieces together. It's just, how do I put this, I see them everywhere, but it's hard for me to think about them. So sometimes I just try to ignore their presence. I don't know how it is for you."

Ali nodded. "Yeah. It's not easy. It never was. Anyway, I just wanted to tell you. I needed to get that off my chest. I've needed to for a long time, actually. Now I'm upset with myself for waiting so long."

They left him in the doorway without a hug or a goodbye, but also without malice. Like so many people he was meeting these days, he had an urge to learn something from their behavior, that economy of conversation that revealed what needed to be said in a manner that lacked judgment and subtext. Ali wasn't curt or cruel or passive-aggressive; they'd just told Artie how they'd felt and for how long, and they'd left him to sit with their reveal, to do with it as he pleased, for their part was now over. *This is yours now, too*, Ali seemed to be saying.

He waved to his friends with a pained smile and nod, to let them know he knew, as he picked up his food from the buffet. By the time he was seated at a table, the mourning had entered a lighter stage, with people telling their favorite stories about Annabelle's antics. Some he'd heard before, most were brand-new, and they all made him laugh. He laughed like he knew her better than he did, and took pleasure in knowing he could still learn more about her even in death. When his phone buzzed, a text from Carson, he shoved it back into his pocket without responding. At two, Ali and the other staffers didn't tell the members, as they normally did, that it was time to leave the cafeteria so it could be cleaned up. They were allowed to stay as long as they liked, and as the stories wound down at around 2:45, so did the laughter, and the pure sadness of Annabelle's death, the realization that she would never be sitting among them again, hit them all at once. She'd even be missing the New Year's Eve party, her favorite GALS event of the year. If only she'd made it a few weeks longer, they all thought together. And there it came, roaring back. An experience they would never grow numb to, even decades after it became a central fact of their lives: the realization that their friend was gone, and they remained.

· · ● · ·

ARTIE WAS MORE productive than ever in those first weeks without his cast, and found the cane to be so delightful as a prop for his daily walks that he considered using it even after being told he was fully healed. He kept going to the center but turned down all of Carson's invitations to dinner and drinks with only the two of them. Dates, Artie assured him, would only get in the way of the writing. So for a month, he suffered the same daily, irritatingly adorable text.

> Finished yet? :)

And for a month, he wrote back the same daily, irritatingly coy response.

> You'll be the first to know.

But on New Year's Eve, the final Saturday of December, Carson followed up with another question.

> Since Jim and Ellis canceled movie night
> because of NYE, will I see you at GALS
> tonight to watch the ball drop?

> Not big on New Year's celebrations, but I'll
> see you all at dinner on Monday. Give everyone
> my best.

He hoped the borderline curtness of his message would shut Carson up, but when it did—Carson didn't even start typing another—he didn't feel a bit of relief. He hadn't celebrated the new year in over twenty years, and unable to bring up the story on his own, he wanted Carson—specifically Carson—to ask why. But there was no response, so Artie put his phone back on the desk and returned to his laptop. The first draft of his manuscript had been nearly finished for weeks, having turned from a story that grew longer and longer with every passing day to a collection of 92,000 words, give or take a couple hundred that Artie couldn't quite figure out. He chopped a sentence here and wrote another one there. He pasted long-lost paragraphs back in, only to cut them for the third time. He struck adjectives and added new ones, changed names and descriptors and feelings and dialogue until approaching some level of satisfaction with their humanity. He'd read chapters and think, *Is this believable? Are these people real?* And then he'd read them again and, like magic, feel totally satisfied with every line. Writing only ends when you stop writing, but without other plans, he had nothing to do instead.

The book was maudlin and only occasionally funny, but ended with what Artie hoped would be interpreted as a moment of hopeful profundity. That's all anyone ever really cares about anyway, he thought, whether or not the story moves them in the end. Whether or not a story sticks its landing. That's all *he* cared about anyway. While reading through the manuscript for the hundredth time, he wondered if anyone would ever care about a sequel to a long-out-of-print novel, only to remember that he hadn't written it for anyone but himself and the four people in his life who were, at one time, all that mattered.

He had been so lucky to find them, but isn't that the way it is for everyone? That he had anyone at all once he moved to New York was a kind of miracle. Before Kim and Way and Adam, there were other combinations, those early years of twos and threes and sixes and eights. The final four might have stuck, but the others were just as important, because the others had carried him part of the way. A troubling thought came to him then, one he'd had before and always shut out: What if it had ended differently? What if they'd simply drifted apart? What if their friendship had been blessed with banality? It was possible, Artie wondered then. Most things were. Kim and Ali could have moved away and chosen California's eternal sunshine over this godforsaken city. Adam could have met someone else and fallen in love. Or maybe could have moved upstate to his parents' house permanently and opened a bar in the Hudson Valley, a dream he'd mentioned only once, but in a wistful tone Artie had never forgotten. They all could have, simply, gotten older.

By ten p.m. there was nothing left to add, and there was nothing left to change. He scrolled back to the top of the manuscript and rubbed his keyboard with his hands, letting their sharp edges scratch the tips of his fingers. He couldn't send it to Nikki without a title, but he hadn't come close to making a decision about one in all the time he'd been writing the first draft. He turned to his friends for inspiration, swiveling his chair to face the photos on his bedroom wall. There they were, trapped in time forever, looking at his work approvingly from above. He shook his head and returned to the screen. No, this wouldn't be coming from them. Hadn't they given him enough? He thought of his new friends, the ones whose photos didn't yet grace his walls but who would certainly find their place among the other frames if things kept moving in the direction they had been since his injury. They had inspired every page. Surely he could distill what they'd done for him in a pair of well-chosen words. He typed them in an instant and laughed to himself at how obvious it was. *Of course that's what it's called,* he thought. *I bet they're going to love it.* He turned around and stared at Walter, curled up in the center of his bed.

"Hey," he said, causing the cat's head to raise. "Will you be OK without me for a few hours?"

Walter's head sank back into his body. He'd already fallen back to sleep.

··•●•··

THE C TRAIN arrived as he stepped onto the platform, which Artie took as a sign that he'd made the right decision. Though there were plenty of seats open, he stood right in the center of the train, clutching the pole with all his strength, daring the train to screech to a halt in an attempt to send him tumbling to the floor. At 23rd Street, still upright, he stepped out, zipping his coat all the way up as the cold air hit him on the stairwell.

The elevator up was empty—he was, of course, hours late—but the noise of the event began seeping through the car doors a few floors below the center. Once they opened, he was inundated by sound and color. Rainbow lights spun around the room among the twinkling whites jutting off the disco balls, at least one of which was hanging from every ten square feet of ceiling. There must have been a hundred people inside the event space, enough that bodies were pouring out of the double doors and into the main hallway. As Artie stared into the crowd, a volunteer at the front desk he recognized from orientation a few months prior waved him down. The young man looked miserable, as if he'd rather be anywhere—literally anywhere—else, but Artie could not bring himself to feel any pity for him. He knew whatever party he planned on attending would still be waiting for him when GALS shut its doors for the night. "Excuse me, you have to check in here before heading in. Name, please?"

"Oh," Artie said. "I didn't know there would be a list."

"The party's full, sorry. If you didn't sign up online, I can't let you in," the young man said, lifelessly, as if the power he had in that moment could not have meant less to him.

"That's fine," a voice behind him said. "He can come in."

Artie turned and saw Ali, offering him a half smile. They had never looked more casual and were holding a silver cup of punch that matched their sequined suit.

"Thank you," Artie said. "Sort of a spur-of-the-moment thing."

"I figured," they said, surprising him with a side hug.

Artie looked them up and down and clicked his tongue. "Fabulous suit. New?"

"Hell no," Ali said, shaking their head with a laugh. "I've had it for years, but I only wear it to watch the ball drop."

"Well, it's nice on you."

"Thank you for saying that," Ali said before taking a sip of their punch. "OK, I should do another lap and make sure no one's snuck in a flask like last year. Happy 2023."

Artie waved them goodbye, put his coat in the orientation room turned coat closet, and pushed his way into the cafeteria. Ellis was in the center of a bobbing crowd of bodies, testing the limits of his artificial hip while dancing to Bronski Beat. As he shook his head back and forth, he saw Artie through a hole in the crowd and yelped.

"Who let this young man in here?" he screamed. "Go back

to the bathhouse where you belong!" He summoned Artie toward them with a wave of his hand, and they all danced together, surrounded by some faces Artie recognized and plenty he didn't. There was no view of the ocean, just a sliver of Hudson could be seen through the buildings, but Artie saw more hope and possibility in the room filled with his peers than he ever could have in an empty horizon. Sometimes the key to understanding life wasn't a ham-fisted metaphor, he thought as the song wound down. Sometimes life made perfect sense simply by living it.

Once he was out of breath, Artie joined Jim, Gregory, Jazmine, and Helen at a table at the edge of the building, near the south windows. As they talked and laughed, Artie noticed a cartoon film rip reel stuck to a pane of glass beside him and realized it was the one he'd hung on the first and only day of his tenure as a volunteer. He almost brought it to their attention but kept the moment to himself. After all, he thought, Jim was still talking, and he hated being interrupted.

"I was hoping you'd come," Carson whispered, startling Artie as Jim droned on.

"Oh, hi," Artie said, looking for an empty space near the window where they could both talk with a bit more privacy. Jim smiled as he watched them creep off, still in the middle of a story he'd told at least ten New Year's Eves before.

"What made you decide to swing by?"

Artie smiled—he couldn't help it. "I finished," he said.

"Have you told anyone else?"

"Not even my agent."

"Are you happy with it?"

He didn't have to think about it, and he didn't have to couch it with any qualifiers. He just said yes.

"Congratulations," Carson said. "So does that mean you finally gave it a title?"

"It does."

"*Four Squares 2? Four Squared? Five Squares? Four Squares: Electric Boogaloo?* I could keep going."

"I'm sure you could. You'd be a great copywriter."

"No, seriously, what's it called? I can tell you know."

Artie laughed and patted Carson on the stomach. "*Old Fruits.*"

"*Old Fruits?*"

Artie nodded and kept his eyes ahead, totally content. "*Old Fruits.*"

"I love it."

"You know what? I do, too."

When it was 11:58, Ali turned off the music and turned up the volume on the television, where the ball was glistening in the center of the frame.

"Look at all those idiots," Jazmine said as the camera panned the crowds of people cheering in Times Square. "You couldn't pay me to be there right now."

"You couldn't pay me to be there any day of the year," Ellis said.

Then, with mere seconds to spare, Jim held up his can of seltzer in the center of the table, urging the others to do the same. When all the punch and sparkling water were floating together, he revealed a flask from his coat pocket and poured a splash of clear liquid into nearly every willing cup before making a simple toast. "To Annabelle," he said. They all raised their drinks high, repeated his words, and went bottoms up. When Jim looked up from his glass, he saw Ali, arms crossed, beside him. "Oh, come on, Annabelle would have said toasting with just water was bad luck."

Before they could offer him a retort, the countdown started. And when it was officially 2023, Artie leaned to his right, his weight split evenly between Carson and his right foot.

···•··

IT WAS THE first morning since the injury that Artie woke up entirely without pain. In its place wasn't pleasure, exactly, but a kind of preparedness. The clock on his nightstand read 7:29, and he flipped the switch so that it wouldn't buzz a minute later. He moved slowly and stealthily, trying not to stir Carson, then stopped to stare at the silhouette of his body under the blanket, the way its mountains and valleys rose and fell in the dim light sneaking in from the edges of his blinds.

He walked to the living room, instinctively putting most of the pressure on his left leg, then remembered to walk as he once did, with the weight evenly distributed on both halves of his stride. That his gait felt normal wasn't a miracle, it was a basic act of healing, but it felt like an impossible thing for his body to achieve. When he sat down at his desk, still free from pain, he looked down at his foot and wiggled it, a sort of thank-you for getting him from one room to another without making him so much as wince.

At the top of his email inbox was a message from Vanessa sent just hours before. 3:05 a.m. Just after midnight her time.

His breathing became shallow, and he circled the cursor over the message, which didn't have a subject, with trepidation before working up the courage to click.

He removed his glasses and took in the email's length before reading, and was relieved to see a small rectangular blur of gray as opposed to a long one that required scrolling. He returned his glasses to his face and checked over his right shoulder for the coast to be clear before reading it. Something about the timing made the message feel especially private, like it was to be read in confidence, like, maybe, it shouldn't have been sent at all.

So he took a deep breath, held it, and read.

Arthur,

Forgive the late email. Actually, forgive the email entirely. I cannot remember the last email I wrote you, but it must have been years ago. Something trivial, no doubt. Something involving dinner. Maybe a recipe. I think I once sent you a link to one for soup. Pardon the prelude, I'm writing this quickly and I'd only like to write it once, so I won't be reading it before hitting send.

Halle called me last week. She told me what she told you, which means she told you what I didn't. I'd like to say I knew this moment would come eventually, the time when I finally came clean. I'd like to say I knew it since I first invited you to meet Halle all those years ago. But it was never my intention to let you know. I'm telling you this not because I'm angry with Halle for what she revealed,

but because I'm grateful. She only did what she knew
I never would, or could. Not because I despise you, not
because I wanted to keep you in the dark, but because
I thought a connection to Abraham, even one that wasn't
based on the truth, was the only gift I could give you that
would mean something. I considered myself in the unique
position of being able to do good with a lie, however
wrong that sounds written out, and I must say I felt proud
of it for so long. I thought myself quite charitable each
time you came over, and each time you made us a meal.
For so many years of Sundays I felt a private pride
knowing I was filling a hole Abe left behind. I'd have to tell
Halle eventually, of course. That was always in the cards.
But Danny didn't mind. You know him, he never minds
anything. Maybe that's why we're still together. Maybe
that's why Abraham and I could never work.

I never blamed you for anything. I know I've told you that
before, many times, but it's worth repeating, especially
now that you know the truth about Halle's father.
Abraham knew, and stayed with me, faithfully and without
complaint, until I decided I couldn't bear the facade any
longer. His death complicated everything, but as we both
know well, so did his life. I used to regret allowing myself
to fall in love with someone so brilliantly, breathtakingly
selfish. Not anymore. I can chart the origin of my life's joy,
scant as it may be, to the day I met Abraham Ford. Am
I wrong to assume the same is true for you?

FOUR SQUARES

I'm not writing this to apologize, because I'm not sure whether I'm sorry. I just feel you, like everyone, are owed the truth. That it took me this long to recognize is simply how this fact of my life has happened, neither good nor bad. It just is. Perhaps you disagree, which is your right.

I hope, Artie, that you will visit me and Danny one day. No Halle required. I would love to show you the life we're building for ourselves here, just as I'd love for you to share the one you're building in New York. Halle's love for you will never falter, that is one of the only things of which I'm certain. The two of us? That will take work. But it's work I'm willing to do. Finally.

It's strange to be in a new place for the first time in so long. It's hard to make friends and routines, and to merely feel comfortable in a place that's not yet yours. Maybe that's why I'm emailing you now while drinking champagne alone in the darkness of our new home, where the only thing I can see out the window are trees. Maybe I miss seeing all the light at night, knowing the ball is dropping just a few blocks away. Maybe this email is mostly about me. I can admit that. But please know, Artie, that it's partly about you. And I hope that's enough.

With love,
Vanessa

He fell into his chair and ran a hand through his hair, then read the email again. She was never one to open her heart, let alone tip it over and allow its contents to pour freely, but here was proof that she was capable. And if she was, then, maybe, so was he.

Artie opened a new email message and addressed it to Nikki, then added Halle's name below it.

SUBJECT: New Manuscript

Nikki,

I know you're OOO for the next week or so, but it's time for me to send this. I hope you don't mind that I've CC'd Halle Ford, my favorite reader.

Happy New Year,
Artie

He attached the latest draft of *Old Fruits* and hit SEND.

In the bathroom he brushed his teeth as quietly as he could, dressed, and gave Carson's sleeping body one final glance before departing. Walter had taken Artie's spot in bed the moment it was empty and was curled up with his forehead against Carson's back. Before walking out the door, Artie took a moment to look at the framed photo Gina had taken nearly seven decades before, just above the hooks for his keys. Her home. Abe's home. His home. The home of people before and after them all, hanging exactly where she would have wanted it. On the sidewalk he waved hello to Dennis, wished him a happy new year, and began walking toward 13th Street, which he took all the way to Broadway. He considered going into the Strand for some relief from the cold, but instead continued walking down toward SoHo, snaking through the oblivious crowds filling Broadway and Prince as he made his way onto Delancey, which inched upward until he was on the Williamsburg Bridge. In under half an hour he was walking through Brooklyn, unburdened by the pressure to turn around. He walked for miles and miles, through neighborhoods he knew and neighborhoods he'd never visited before. He walked until his legs started hurting, then he walked some more. And when, hours later, Carson asked where he'd gone, Artie didn't even know where to begin.

ACKNOWLEDGMENTS

This book would not exist without Yancey and Will. Thank you for reminding me how important it is to keep queer stories alive, and for allowing me the honor of your friendship. Other people and institutions I'd like to thank here are:

The SAGE Center, whose essential work I discovered both far too late and at just the right time. There would be no GALS without SAGE.

The Center for Fiction for providing a quiet, welcoming place to write.

Gaby Mongelli, for giving me the chance to publish this story, and helping me mold it into one I'm so proud to tell.

Kate McKean, for her faith, her wisdom, and her newsletter.

Ryan Reft, for uncovering a treasure trove of papers and letters without which I would have been totally incapable of completing this novel. To sit in the Library of Congress and sift through the countless personal documents of queer writers—their tragedies and triumphs, their pride and their pettiness, their joy and their languor—gave me a creative jolt and profound understanding of the time. It was a gift I will never forget. I'm indebted to librarians everywhere for reminding me that our histories are right there, waiting patiently to be asked for.

Everyone at Putnam/Penguin Random House who had a hand in this novel, especially Sally Kim, Kristen Bianco, Brennin Cummings, Shina Patel, Ashley McClay, Ashley Di Dio, Tarini Sipahimalani, Andrea St. Aubin, Mary Beth Constant, Alison Cnockaert, Vi-An Nguyen, Sara Wood, Meg Drislane, and Erica Ferguson.

Hannah and Seth Anderson, for choosing a perfect name for their first child and so generously allowing me to borrow it.

All the queer people in my life who have made me smarter, happier, and more hopeful. How lucky I am to have met you all.

My family—the Fingers, the Welshes, and the Fjelstads—for being a constant source of love and support.

Josh, for telling me the novel needed more Walter the cat, and for wanting to become an old fruit right alongside me.

Julius', for the martinis.

Every queer writer whose work has enriched my life. Without your stories I would have none of my own.